THE JERICHO FLOWER

A HACKSHAW MYSTERY

THE JERICHO FLOWER

A Hackshaw Mystery

Stephen F. Wilcox

Mystery and Suspense Press
San Jose New York Lincoln Shanghai

The Jericho Flower
A Hackshaw Mystery

Mystery and Suspense Press
an imprint of iUniverse, Inc.

For information address:
iUniverse, Inc.
5220 S. 16th St., Suite 200
Lincoln, NE 68512
www.iuniverse.com

ISBN: 0-595-21509-2

Printed in the United States of America

For Pauline and Bennett, for overlooking my crimes and misdemeanors.

Contents

CHAPTER 1

A little knowledge is a dangerous thing.

Wiser words were never uttered, but don't ask me who uttered them; my mind doesn't retain such things. What my mind does seem to retain is a cornucopia of minutiae, arcanum, and general detritus, a by–product of my years writing a breezy news column for a small upstate New York weekly called the *Triton Advertiser*.

My name is Hackshaw, by the way. My column is called Ramblings, as in a running commentary of who's who and what's what in our circulation area, interwoven with presumably interesting factoids aimed at giving our readers something to chew on every Thursday morning along with their wheat toast and bran flakes.

Nothing actionable, as the lawyers say; just simple name–dropping and did–you–know items with no greater ambition than to end up magnetically affixed to somebody's refrigerator.

Trivia is what it amounts to.

Take the Jericho flower as an example. Hardly a flower at all, really, but an ugly brown clump of deadish leaves and roots that when immersed in a cup of water will suddenly and miraculously resurrect itself into a vibrant green plant. I'm told that pairs of gypsy girls with larcenous hearts sometimes sell the flowers door–to–door as a means of beguiling their way into a gullible mark's home, at which point one of the little charmers keeps the unsuspecting homeowner occupied while the other steals through the house searching for cash and totable valuables.

Now, I'll bet you didn't know a thing about Jericho flowers and gypsy girls up till now, and I didn't either before all this trouble began. But that's my point.

The problem is, people think an expert is anyone who knows slightly more about a subject than they do. More wise words. Just don't ask me who, et cetera.

Anyway…

❦ ❦ ❦

It happened in January, that bitterest of winter months, when holiday expectations have expired and all that remains is to count the frost–bit weeks until the Easter thaw. Naturally it was a Monday, ten o'clock in the morning, which means I normally would've been slaving at my desk at the *Advertiser's* spartan office in Chilton Center, or at least been on my way. But on that particular morning I detoured from my crib in Kirkville to the Philby Brothers' ad hoc automotive garage just north of town at the behest of the eldest brother, Dwight.

It was a converted cow barn really, with the stanchions removed and a grease pit added. There were three brothers; Dwight Eisenhower Philby, George Patton Philby, and Omar Bradley Philby. Their father was one of those congenital hardright conservatives whose flat feet and farm duties had kept him out of double–u double–u two, but hadn't diminished his enthusiasm for the sacrifices of others. His sons, to their comparative credit, had no particular politics at all short of a nativist distrust for all things outside their ken, which covers most of the known universe.

Be that as it may, the brothers have a reputation for dependable mechanical tinkering at reasonable prices, which is why I use Dwight whenever my vintage Jeep Cherokee goes on the fritz. There are those who say the Philbys can afford to keep their prices low because most of the replacement parts they use come to them by way of what is known as the five–finger discount. I don't know if this is true or not, but my sense of fair play combined with the lowly state of my personal finances have convinced me that the boys deserve the benefit of the doubt.

But I wasn't there for Jeep repairs that morning. The truth is, I didn't know why I was there, except that Dwight had suggested over the phone that he might have something of interest for me.

In my capacity as editor–in–chief and featured columnist for the *Advertiser*? I had asked him.

No, in your capacity as a scrounger of second–hand junk imbued with niche marketability, Dwight had replied. Or words to that effect.

A moment's exposition here.

I don't know about where you come from, but here in the tri–town area—Kirkville and the abutting townships of Chilton and Port Erie—small–town jobs pay small–town wages. To be sure, those willing to make the daily twenty–mile commute to Rochester can find ample compensation at places like Eastman Kodak and Xerox and Baush & Lomb and dozens of mid–size firms. But that's the city and its close–by suburbs. Out here in the hinterlands, many of us make do by moonlighting; the apple farmer who drives school bus, the waitress who hawks Avon products, the school teacher who doubles as a real estate agent.

So be apprised: If you want to work only one job and still make a decent living in a small town, go into insurance or plumbing. Or open a liquor store that has rear parking and a discreet back entrance.

Whatever you do, don't go into newspapering. Not if you like to eat.

In my case, when I'm not rushed off my feet putting the news together I pick up a shekel or two renovating old houses, mostly Victorians. And since restoring such elaborate beauties usually requires quite a bit of searching around for missing pieces—authentic glass doorknobs, for example, or period light fixtures—I've acquired a knack and a reputation as a discriminating scavenger; someone who can sometimes find treasure in other folk's discards, and turn a small profit in the process.

Thus, Dwight Philby's Monday morning summons.

The cow barn–cum–garage was so chilly we could see our breath, which in Dwight's case was blue.

"Cold enough out there to freeze a quart a Mexican piss, Hackshaw." He was wearing coveralls that looked like ticking from a seedy motel mattress and a greasy Mopar baseball cap, the better to disguise a rampant case of male–pattern baldness. I sported a wool watch cap and a navy pea jacket over chinos and Dexter boots, and still I was shivering.

"I'm late for work," I said through clenched teeth, "so if we could skip the weather report..."

"No problem." I followed his lead to the back of the barn, toward a large, old Mercury sedan that had seen better days even before its entire front end had been crumpled like an accordion. Dwight came to a stop alongside it and jerked his thumb. "So, you know the guy who killed himself going off Black Creek Bluff early yesterday mornin'?"

"No."

"Well, this is the car he did it in."

I held my temper, but barely. It's getting so there's no such thing as conversation anymore, just competing monologues. "Did what in?"

"Huh?"

"You asked me did I know about some guy who died going off Black Creek Bluff yesterday, Dwight, and I said `no'. As in I don't know who or what you're referring to."

"You didn't hear about that? Jesus, Hack, where you been?"

"Out of town." Out of country, in fact. Jackie Plummer had spirited me off to Toronto for a weekend of wining, dining, sightseeing and the zillionth performance of The Phantom of the Opera, courtesy of a prize she'd won for her pottery in a competition arranged by the Greater Rochester Artisans Guild. The only cost to me (other than bar tabs, halvsies on breakfasts, and two hours of Lloyd Webber melodies) had been a promise to Jackie that I wouldn't tell anyone she'd "kept" me in a luxury suite at the Toronto Four Seasons for three days and two nights. For an independent woman, she's sometimes awfully sensitive about what other people think, particulary when the principal other person is her sixteen–year–old daughter Krista, who's already on the pill herself. Talk about closing the barn door after the cows have run off.

"Okay," said Dwight. "So you prob'ly don't know we had a snow squall come along early Sunday mornin', after a thaw Saturday afternoon and a hard freeze Saturday night."

"I wasn't aware of that, no." Toronto, situated due northwest across Lake Ontario, often has the same weather we do but, Mark Twain not withstanding, Torontonians have managed to do something about it. In addition to a clean and efficient subway system, the city's downtown is intraconnected with underground walkways and shopping concourses. Despite our hectic itinerary, Jackie and I had hardly stuck our heads out into the biting Canadian air the whole time we were there.

Dwight again gestured toward the wreck. "What they think happened is, this guy was from out of town, didn't know how tricky that curve over on Park Road can get when it's slick out. Plus he didn't take into account how all that nice fresh snow on the road was only coverin' up solid ice underneath, like sprinklin' sugar on a glazed doughnut." He momentarily confused himself with the bad analogy, but persevered. "Anyhow, the guy comes haulin' ass down the hill, don't start easin' off the gas till he's almost to the curve and by that time it's too late. He skids straight through the curve and over the bluff into Black Creek."

"He didn't drown?" I asked. "There's only five feet of water along there."

"And three of it's ice this time a year. Guy put his gourd right through the windshield, I heard."

I glanced at the sedan's windshield, which was no longer there, and winced. "No seatbelt, I take it."

Dwight snorted. "Don't get me started on those things. You were outa town, I guess you didn't hear what happened to Judd Ames."

"Judd Ames?" I frowned. Then, "Oh, the produce man at the IGA?"

"Right. Cruises around in that cherry Charger—which I don't guess he'll be doin' any more seein' that he smashed it up and broke his back Saturday afternoon."

"My God, what happened?"

"Well," he smirked. "The way I got it, the whole problem was Judd forgot to fasten his seat belt."

"Yeah, but what happened?"

"I told you, he forgot to fasten his seat belt."

Some days you need the patience of Job. "We seem to be confusing cause and effect here. What I'm asking is, what caused the accident in the first place?"

"That's what I'm saying, Hack. It's that dumbass state seat belt law did Judd in. He remembered he forgot to fasten it while he was drivin' along on Mumford Road, out there near the Town Line turn-off?"

"Yeah?"

"So he reaches around, tryin' to get the damn thing hooked up—he's got a gut on him for a vegetable guy—and, anyways, he drifts across the center line and clips a Snap–on Tool truck coming the other way and bounces off and ends up nose to nuts with a Douglas fir. Crippled himself permanent, they say, and smashed that mint old Charger of his all to hell."

"That's terrible."

"Yeah, you can't hardly find replacement parts for a sixty–eight Dodge hemi anymore."

"I meant Judd, Dwight, not some stupid hot rod."

He took offense at my tone. "Shit, takin' a primo set of wheels like that out in the middle of winter? The son of a bitch shoulda known better. Always did drive like a Chinaman."

I decided to get off the subject, both for the obvious reason and because talk of dying, or almost, in bizarre circumstances always makes me cringe. I'm not sure why—maybe it's just that I've written so many tragi–comic human interest items myself over the years—but one of my pet phobias is that I'll expire in some ludicrously colorful way that reduces my death to a two–inch wire service filler with a provocative headline like "Man in chicken suit killed crossing the road" or "Wordsmith chokes to death on alphabet soup." You know what I mean; something the rest of us can't help but chuckle about over our morning coffee.

So I said, "What's poor Judd Ames's misery have to do with a totaled Mercury? For that matter, what's this totaled clunker got to do with me?"

"Confucius say follow me," Judd said, chuckling at his alleged witticism.

I followed him anyway, around the wreck of a car and into the wreck of an office. There was the obligatory cheesecake calendar on the wall, some breathtakingly endowed girl apparently ecstatic about an impending gynecological exam, and the obligatory male mayhem everywhere else I looked. Piles of invoices, stacks of cartons, piles of stacks and stacks begetting piles. And on the rough cement floor a space heater, glowing red, in case the piles of papers and stacks of cardboard and mounds of oily rags weren't capable of spontaneous combustion.

"You can't possibly be insured," I muttered, shaking my head at the inflammatory mess. But Dwight, who was busy clearing a patch on one of the desks, misheard the remark.

"No, the guy wasn't insured, I guess," he said, still rearranging. "That's how come the fuzz called me to yank that big Merc outa the creek. Sheriff's Department knows I'll waive a tow fee if they give me salvage rights."

"I didn't say...never mind."

By then, Dwight had finished his housekeeping and was lifting a small wooden box from the floor and placing it on the desktop. It was maple, well scarred, about the size of a shoebox, and relatively heavy judging by the way he handled it. When the box was in place, he bent down again and came up with a cloth bag with a drawstring, which he also set on the desk.

"Found this stuff in the trunk, Hack. I got no use for it myself, so I thought maybe you'd make a deal on it."

At Dwight's urging, I flipped back the lid on the box. Inside, neatly arranged into their proper compartments, were an old hand printing press and a versatile set of type blocks—numbers and letters, upper and lower case, in two different fonts. Tucked into a sleeve on the lid was a sheaf of blanks; plain white reinforced paper rectangles used for printing business cards, which was about all a portable press such as this was used for.

I said, "Huh. Interesting."

"Yeah? How interesting you figure, in dollars?"

In lieu of an answer, I picked up the cloth sack, worked open its drawstring, and extracted the contents. It was the approximate size and shape of one of those gizmos store clerks use to run a charge card over a three–ply sales slip, only slightly thicker and with an electrical cord dangling from it. Also included in the sack was a handful of clear plastic strips.

Dwight said, "I think that's for sealing plastic over licenses and IDs and shit—whaddya call it?"

"A laminator," I said as I set it next to the press. I looked from one to the other and frowned. "Hmmm."

"What? These're worth somethin', right?"

"You find anything else in the trunk?"

"Nah, nothin' you'd be interested in, Hack. Just a clipboard, a pair of overalls in real good shape, a white hardhat. Stuff I can use around the garage."

"Hmmm."

"What?"

I stared at the little printing press for another moment, then held up a few of the blanks. "Offhand I'd say your Mr. Mercury was a flim–flam man, Dwight."

"Huh?"

"A con artist. Grifter, swindler, mountebank—take your pick."

"Yeah?" He ogled the press. "How d'ya figure?"

"An educated guess," I told him with a world–weary insouciance that would come to haunt me. "They use the press to knock off phony business cards for all occasions and the laminator to dress up doctored drivers licenses and other ID, like you said. I expect the clipboard and overalls and so on are handy for getting in and out of places easily. Nobody challenges you if you look official."

"Man." Dwight shook his head at the wonder of it all and fixed me with a one–eyed squint. "So how come you know about stuff like that, Hack?"

"Well—" I opened my mouth, then snapped it shut.

Because I realized I couldn't explain how I knew about a con man's tools of the trade, any more than I could account for knowing that Warren Harding's middle name was Gamaliel or that the capital of Namibia is called Windhoek, at least until the next revolution. It was simply one of those slivers of near–worthless knowledge an inquisitive newsman accumulates over the years.

Anyway, I was still late and still freezing.

"Never mind how I know," I said. "I'll give you ten bucks for the printing press."

"Make it twenty."

"Ten."

"Aw, c'mon. I got a lot invested in this stuff."

Next he'd be claiming sentimental value. "You found it lying in the trunk of a car, Dwight, which you hauled in here for the price of a tow. Ten."

"How 'bout the laminator?"

"Not interested."

"I'll let you have both pieces for twenty."

I sighed. "Fifteen."

He did the eye thing again. "Cash or check?"

CHAPTER 2

And that's all there was to it. That single morning visit to the Philby brothers' drafty garage comprised the sum total of my knowledge of or interest in the mysterious stranger who had driven his Mercury off Black Creek Bluff.

But try telling that to the law.

The next two days passed much the same as any other forty–eight hour stretch of time in our neck of the woods, which is to say uneventfully. Then it got interesting, beginning with our antediluvian receptionist, Mrs. Hobarth, who materialized like a harbinger of doom in the doorway of the *Advertiser's* little newsroom Wednesday morning. That she'd bothered to shuffle the thirty feet from her desk in front was enough by itself to raise alarm bells, she being retired civil service; the saccharine 700 Club smile appliqued to her kisser was downright unnerving.

You'd think someone who had the advantage of being born again could've gotten it right the second time, but no such luck. Compared to our Mrs. H., Cotton Mather was the life of the party. As best I could construe her theosophy, she believed man was put on this earth to suffer and die and it was her job to see that he did. Naturally, she was a widow, her husband long–since having decided a fatal aneurysm was the lesser of two evils.

It goes without saying she hates me.

After an excruciating interval in which her skeletal remains simply stood motionless in the doorway, she intoned in her best Old Testament voice, "Your time has finally come, Hackshaw."

Lesser men would've fainted dead away.

"Shouldn't you be toting a scythe?" I asked.

She pretended to understand the crack and to dismiss it all with the same prunish pucker. Meanwhile, an all–too familiar grumble from somewhere offstage—the hallway behind her—said, "You mind, lady? I haven't got all day here."

That explained the shadow Mrs. H. appeared to be standing in. It also explained her glee, still in evidence even as she was being none–too–gently nudged aside by the possessor of the gravelly voice: Mel Stoneman.

Stoneman is the sheriff's chief (re: only) criminal investigator for the southwest sector of Monroe County and, for reasons too ancient and convoluted to go into, a nemesis of mine. Suffice to say he doesn't casually drop by the paper to swap gossip or invite me to lunch. No. When the Melster comes calling, it can only mean yours truly is in, as the Brits say, a spot of bother.

Mrs. Hobarth knew this as well as I did, thus the skull–splitting grin and reluctance to withdraw to her crummy kneehole desk out in the anteroom.

"Thank you very much, Mrs. H.," I said pleasantly, knowing it would ruin the mood for her. "I think I can handle things from here."

She opened her mouth to protest, then slammed it shut and, reluctant as an Aztec virgin, retreated back up the corridor.

Stoneman, meanwhile, just stood there with his brogans planted and his paws plunged into the pockets of his ever–present trench coat, his buffalo–chip brown eyes studying me like I was some microscopic bacterium floating in a petri dish. As if he could read me like a book. As if he'd ever actually read a book.

I took his glare for as long as I could, which was about a second and a half, and said, "Okay, what d'ya want? I haven't got all day either."

He laid on a couple more beats of silence, just to prove he was on top of things, before stepping up to the front of my desk. "Edgar `Slow Eddie' Williamson."

"Who?"

"`Who?'" He snickered as only a two–hundred–twenty pounder with a badge can snicker. "Your buddy the con man, that's who. Make that the late, unlamented con man."

The question caught me off guard, so I answered honestly, for all the good it did me. "Oh, you mean the guy who skidded off Black Creek Bluff over the weekend?"

"Go ahead, play dumb."

"I wouldn't think of infringing on your franchise. At any rate, I don't know where you got this `con man buddy' crap, but I wouldn't know your Slow Eddie Williamson if you wheeled him in here on a gurney."

"Oh, yeah?" Not one of your snappier rejoinders, but the sneer was first–rate. "That's not what Derek Drummond says. He says you bragged to one of the Philby boys all about this Williamson character being a flim–flam man."

"Drummond? The funeral director at Woodson's?"

"You know any other Derek Drummonds around here?"

It was the `Derek' part that threw me. I suppose I assumed professional ghouls got by with just a surname, like Dracula or Torquemada. "I haven't spoken to Drummond in months, so don't ask me where he's getting his information."

"Uh–huh." Stoneman dug deep into the trench coat's baggy pocket and produced a small red notepad and flipped it open; the gospel according to Mel. "You deny telling Dwight Philby that you knew the deceased—Edgar Williamson—and that he was a con man?"

"Yes and no." Before his head could explode, I added, "Yes, I deny telling Dwight that I knew the deceased. And no, I don't deny speculating that the deceased was a con man of some sort."

"Of some sort. Okay, wiseass. If you didn't know Williamson, how'd you know he was a con—"

"Deductive reasoning. You've probably heard of it."

"You're this close to a ride down to the substation, Hackshaw."

A fate worth avoiding at almost any cost, particularly on a Wednesday, with a paper to get out the next morning and the rest of the staff—all three of them—out doing God knows what.

I sighed. "What happened is, Dwight showed me some things he found in the guy's trunk and it just looked to me like the sort of stuff a con man might keep handy."

"Like what sort of stuff?"

I started to answer, then hesitated. "I don't know—just stuff. Anyway, the guy's dead, so what difference does it make?"

"Because I wanna know, that's why, and you've got no reason not to tell me, unless you've got something to hide."

Which I did, in a way. I'd sold the portable press to my brother–in–law, Ron Barrence, who's a printer by trade. He had the thing over in his office at the print shop adjoining the *Advertiser* newsroom, displayed with some other mechanical knickknacks he's collected over the years. It would break his heart to have to hand it over to Stoneman as evidence or whatever, almost as much as it would break my heart to have to refund Ron's thirty–five dollars. Especially since I'd already wagered it on what I was sure at the time was an unbeatable pair of aces.

"A laminator," I said finally, reasoning that a half truth was like half a loaf. "I bought it off Dwight. You know, one of those little machines for putting plastic over IDs and—"

"I know what a laminator is, Hackshaw. What I don't know is how you could've figured out a guy was a professional con man because he had a laminating machine in his car."

"That's not all there was," I protested, and proceeded to tell him about the overalls, the clipboard, and the hardhat Dwight had found. When I finished, he regarded me with total disdain.

"Well. If you ain't the little detective—a regular Hercules Perot."

"Gee, I always wondered what the aitch stood for in H. Ross—"

"Not that Perot, moron. Didn't you ever watch any Agatha Christie movies, for chrissake?"

You see what I was dealing with?

"Here's a novel idea, Stoneman. Why don't you tell me what's going on, so at least one of us will know what we're talking about."

He leaned forward, laying his thick hands two feet apart on the top of my littered desk and bringing his canine incisors within twelve inches of my nose. "Your pal Slow Eddie didn't croak from putting his coconut through the windshield of his Mercury, Hackshaw. Because he was already dead from carbon monoxide poisoning before the car went over the bluff. Before he even got behind the wheel, the M.E. says—long before."

I tried to gulp, but couldn't come up with the spit. "You mean he was—"

"Murdered." Stoneman assaulted my already addled senses with another hot blast of spearmint breath. "The car skidded through the Park Road curve, or was pushed or driven through it more likely, sometime before dawn on Sunday. But Williamson kicked off a lot earlier, like Saturday afternoon or early evening."

"Damn." I muttered the oath less in disbelief than in bitterness. I'd had a run of bad luck lately, vis a vis dead bodies. Not as bad as the victims, admittedly, but still, the last thing I needed was another stiff complicating my otherwise bucolic...

"So where were you those hours?"

Stoneman's growl yanked me out of my self–pitying reverie. "Where was I—when?"

"What were we just talking about? Where the hell were you from approximately noon on Saturday to, say, seven o'clock Sunday morning?"

I brightened, thinking I'd spotted a silver lining.

"I was out of town the whole time," I said. "In Toronto with a, uh, friend."

He put pen to pad. "Her name."

Then I remembered something else, and my silver lining evaporated; merely a trick of the light shining off all that gray cloudiness.

"I can't—that's none of your business."

"Hah! Shacking up with somebody's wife again, huh?" His smirk should've come in a plain brown wrapper. "All right, just give me the name of your hotel so I can call and verify you were really—"

"I'm afraid I can't tell you that, either. See, we were registered in the lady's name."

"Bull–*shit*." His cataclysmic eruption nearly dislodged one of the drop–in ceiling tiles. "What kinda bill of goods are you trying to peddle? One minute you claim you have to protect this broad's reputation, the next you say you two lovebirds checked into a hotel using her name."

The worst part is I was telling the absolute truth. The reservation was in Jackie Plummer's name because it was Jackie who had won the pottery contest. Of course, I couldn't explain all that to Stoneman without tipping him off to who I was with, and I couldn't do that because I'd promised Jackie I wouldn't. Little wonder why chivalry died out.

"Look," I said. "If you don't want to believe me, go talk to Dwight. He'll verify that what I've told you is the truth; I don't know this Williamson character from Adam."

"Oh, yeah?" Stoneman interjected, proving he was repetitive as well as unimaginative. Still, I don't mind admitting I was somewhat spooked by the cocksure gleam in his eye. Like most fools, Stoneman considers himself foolproof, but I'm under no such delusions myself.

I've been tripped up too often by numbskulls with no more going for them than a position of authority and dumb luck. And when his hairy paw once again dug deep into the pocket of the trench coat, I knew it was about to happen again.

"You bet your ass I'll be talking to Philby," the sheriff's bully was saying as he brought his clenched hand out of the pocket. "But right now I'm talking to you, Hackshaw, and I don't like what I'm hearing. You say you got no connection to the murder victim, let me hear you explain these."

"These" turned out to be a trio of clippings from the *Advertiser*, specifically my last three Ramblings columns. Stoneman ceremoniously spread them out on the desk like Tarot cards, as if their import sealed my fate. Which, as it turned out, they more or less did.

I frowned. "So?"

"So guess where I found `em."

"Don't tell me."

Stoneman's smirk turned joyous. "In the wallet of a certain unlamented con man."

That was the second time he'd used unlamented, which meant he'd only recently discovered the word and was trying to commit it to memory. I, for my part, was busy memorizing the handful of names, highlighted in yellow marker, that jumped up at me from the columns.

"Arlene Grebwicz, The Pedersens, Jeff Klekzo, Mary Margaret Hoos..." I began to read, then glanced up. I was about to ask Stoneman what possible interest Williamson could've had in the people who's names littered my columns, and why these particular people, when I spotted the common thread.

Mrs. Grebwicz, who'd called up the *Advertiser* all excited about winning the bingo super jackpot at St. Paul's a couple of weeks past. The Pedersens, Linda and Dave, who managed to get their picture taken with Tom Jones while on a Christmas junket to Las Vegas. Jeff Klekzo, a Port Erie dentist and self–styled gentleman sportsman, who'd bought himself a half–share in a two–year–old filly named Toothsome Girl. And my personal favorite, Mary Margaret Hoos, whose claim to immortality was a recent Lotto win that had netted her $34,536 per annum for the next twenty years and a unanimous vote from the junior class at Chil–Kirk High as the person they'd most like to have speak at their Career Day festivities.

Gamblers one and all, and long–odds players at that.

"A suckers list," I mumbled, scanning again. "He must've been lining up marks."

"An idiot could see that, Hackshaw." And obviously had. "Lining up marks for what? That's the question."

"Well, what do these folks have to say?"

He snatched the columns out from under my tapping finger. "Haven't interviewed any of `em yet. There hasn't been time—I only got the toxicology findings from the medical examiner an hour ago. Up until then, it was just an accidental death. Now it's murder."

So was the glare he was giving me. "Look, I was only guessing with all that stuff I told Dwight. If you haven't checked this Williamson out with anyone yet, how do you know he really was a con man?"

"Because his parole officer in Ni—" He broke off in mid–syllable. "I'm here to ask questions, not to answer them."

"You're here to harass an innocent taxpayer, is what it amounts to. You come hotfooting over the minute you think you can make a connection between me and a dead man."

"I don't *think* I can make a connection." He waved the crumpled columns. "I'm holding the connection right here in my hand. Not to mention how you shot off your mouth to Dwight Philby, or how you refuse to explain where you were last Saturday."

"That's all perfectly innocent—"

"Innocent is the one thing you ain't, Hackshaw. Now, I'm not saying you gassed this guy—yet. But you and Williamson were in cahoots on something, I'd bet my pension on it. And you can bet, once I get a line on where this clown was hanging out and who with—"

Stoneman was brought up short by the clop–clop of galoshes on linoleum. The boots belonged to our student intern, Alan Harvey, who strolled into the newsroom swinging the Minolta by its strap and humming something Sondheimish from Streisand's second Broadway album.

"Top of the morning, Hackshaw." Alan glanced appraisingly at the hulking Stoneman, then tucked the camera under the arm of his greatcoat like a clutch purse. "And this must be the famous police investigator Mrs. Hobarth was just telling me about. Should I leave and come back, or is the interrogation over with?"

"Actually, I think he was just about to break out the rubber hose."

"Ooh, I'd hate to miss that."

"Christ." The epithet oozed from Stoneman's twisted lips. He'd been studying Alan with the same critical intensity a cobra gives a mongoose and, predictably, he didn't like what he saw—the matching stickpin earrings, the fussily casual pageboy do and paisley silk scarf tossed devil–may–care over one shoulder, the elastic hand–on–hip bearing that screamed *GQ* and gay simultaneously. Stoneman turned toward me and rolled his eyes while, behind his back, Alan made the same gesture.

My personal take on homosexuality is best summed up by "to each his own"—literally in this case—but some men seem to suspect it may be a contagious condition. This explains why Stoneman visibly flinched when Alan began slowly unbuttoning his coat. I barely resisted the urge to hum the theme from that old Noxzema shave cream ad.

Stoneman pulled his ratty trench coat tighter around his convex midsection and growled, "Laugh all you want, but this time I'm gonna laugh last, Hackshaw. Put that in your two–bit rag."

Then, with one last paranoid glance at Alan, he huffed out of the office with as much energy and bluster as he had huffed in.

"Have a nice day," I hollered to his retreating footfalls.

Alan, sighing with the world–weary weight of his twenty years, said, "I know what he has against me, Hackshaw. But why does he hate you so much?"

If I'd had the time, I could've told him about the occasional piece I'd written on the shortcomings of the sheriff's department in general and one of its chief investigators in particular. I might also have mentioned a case or two where my own admittedly lucky maneuverings had outwitted both killer and cops, for which the latter seemed to hold the longest grudge. Or, in a more philosophical vein, how bullies naturally gravitate toward jobs that give them power over us mere mortals.

Instead, I said simply, "He thinks I'm not afraid of him." And then, before my young apprentice could ask the obvious follow–up, I yanked a half–completed item on the Chil–Kirk school board out of my typewriter, rolled in a fresh sheet of three–ply copy paper, and began hammering away at my serendipitous scoop for the next day's edition:

Kirkville—Sunday morning's accidental death of a man whose car skidded off Black Creek Bluff was anything but an accident, investigators now claim. The victim, an alleged professional con man named Edgar `Slow Eddie' Williamson, is believed to have died of carbon monoxide poisoning hours before his car nose dived into the frozen creek…

CHAPTER 3

"The usual, Hack?"

I nodded, then canted my head toward the solitary figure holding down the short end of the ell–shaped bar. "And freshen up whatever the good doctor's having."

Buddy McCabe's brow folded into deep brown furrows. "A double Dewar's? On your tab?"

"Yes, on my tab." I flashed him a perfunctory scowl and continued on down the bar and took a stool kitty–corner to the only other patron in the taproom, a common circumstance at that hour of a mid–week afternoon.

"To hear some people talk," I said, loud enough for it to carry back to the beer taps, "you'd think I never bought anybody a round before."

"I don't want to appear ungrateful, Hackshaw, so I'll reserve comment." Doc's wry smile hung just above his glass like a quarter moon over an amber pond, the fissures and craters of his wizened face lending further credence to the lunar analogy. Close by on the bar were a pack of Winstons, a well–worn Zippo lighter and an ashtray containing more dead butts than a proctologist's waiting room. He took a sip and a drag, then pushed a hank of limp gray hair back off his high forehead. "Haven't seen much of you lately. That sister of yours keeping you on a short leash, is she?"

"She likes to think so."

He wasn't far off the mark. Duty and deadline fever had kept me pinned behind my desk until well after one o'clock, when I was finally able to hand off layout chores to Ruth, who squawked predictably until I told her about the Williamson developments and the exclusive I'd just finished writing and how I needed to verify a few points to be on the safe side. Then I beat it out the door before she could ask me why I couldn't verify them just as well over the phone.

My first inclination had been to head straight to the Philby brothers' garage to give Dwight a good grilling, but Stoneman was likely to be of the same mind and I didn't want to risk crossing his path again so soon. Anyway, Dwight didn't figure to have any of the information I was looking for. But I knew who might, and I also knew where I was liable to find him on a cold Wednesday afternoon. Or any other Wednesday afternoon, for that matter.

In addition to being Kirkville's only resident general practitioner, Doc Gordon was also the town's coroner, whose main job was to show up at fatal accidents and declare the victims officially dead. On his day off his routine was to settle in at Norb's Nook and indulge straight scotch and Winstons, a pattern he'd developed in the dozen years since his wife, Tildy, had passed on from lymphatic cancer. A tragic figure, some folks called him, but I preferred to think of the doc as a man who'd survived the worst blow fate could lay on him and had been thumbing his nose ever since.

Buddy McCabe arrived with a draft Twelve Horse for me, a half–filled tumbler of undiluted Dewar's for Doc and an attitude.

"I hope you're sitting on your wallet, Doc," he said, grinning like a two–hundred sixty pound black cheshire cat.

"Shouldn't you be rinsing glasses or watering the whiskey or something," I suggested. Just then a pair of suited salesman types wandered in tentatively and claimed a pair of stools at the other end of the bar. Buddy tossed a cheerful profanity at me before heading their way.

Doc, meanwhile, was watching me with jaundiced expectation. "All right, I have to ask. Just what is this drink going to cost me, Hackshaw?"

I thought about pasting on a wounded look, but medical men are immune to that sort of thing, having learned to ignore it in their patients. So I laid my cards on the table, right next to my reporter's notepad. "Tell me what you know about Edgar Williamson—the guy who took a header off Black Creek Bluff the other morning. Also what you know about carbon monoxide poisoning."

He tapped out a fresh cigarette, plugged it into the corner of his lip and lit up, never losing eye contact or the pessimist's grin. "I'd heard you'd sworn off messing around in murder investigations after that fiasco over in Port Erie last summer."

"So, you already know that Williamson was murdered?"

"I'm the one who alerted the medical examiner's office to the possibility in the first place. And you still haven't explained what you're doing messing around—"

"I'm not `messing around' in the investigation. I'm a newsman, remember? All I'm doing is covering a story." I'm not sure which of us I was trying to convince, but at least one of us wasn't having any.

"If I were you, Hackshaw, I'd stick to chasing skirts and inside straights and leave killers to Mel Stoneman. It'd be safer all around."

"Especially for the killers."

"I'll concede the point. Still, he's the one with the badge and the major medical plan."

"And I'm the one with an eight o'clock deadline. Now, are you gonna save me some time, Doc, or do I have to dogsled back to the office and spend the rest of the day playing phone tag with the county?"

"Well, I wouldn't want that on my conscience, would I." He primed the pump with a swallow of scotch. "The sheriff's people rang me out of bed about seven Sunday morning, said they had a single–car fatal on Park Road and could I please hurry over and pronounce the deceased deceased so they could get the body, the car wreck and their own freezing hind ends out of there. Unfortunately, as soon as I got to the scene I could tell it wasn't going to be that easy to clear."

"Why not?"

He frowned. "The blood wasn't right."

I frowned back. "What d'ya mean, `the blood wasn't right'?"

"There wasn't enough of it, for one thing, and what there was was a bright cherry red." He pulled in a lungful of nicotine. "When the car skidded over the bluff and crashed grill–first into the ice below, the driver's head punched a ragged hole through the windshield. Ferocious impact. The poor fellow's neck was severed halfway through, his face lacerated to the bone in a dozen places."

I covered a grimace with a sip of ale. "And?"

"Normally there would've been blood splattered all over, but there wasn't. Oh, there was a pretty big pool of the stuff welled up along the crease of the dash, but that had more or less drained out of the body, as opposed to gushing out—you see what I mean? The blood in a living person is under pressure, which means that when massive trauma occurs, it's like turning on a garden hose."

"I get the picture. If he'd been alive on impact—"

"Major gusher. Then, when you factor in the distinctive bright red coloration of what blood was evident, well, the first thing that came to mind was possible carbon monoxide poisoning. It's a common indicator."

Not to me, it wasn't. "Can you spell it out, Doc?"

"You know about carbon monoxide, right? An odorless gas that results from the incomplete burning of carbon fuels, like natural gas or gasoline?"

"So far, so good."

"Well, what happens is, the carbon monoxide atoms replace oxygen atoms in the red blood cells and make it harder for the remaining cells to release their oxygen to the body—and turns the blood crimson in the bargain. If you happen to breathe in too much it leads to unconsciousness, then respiratory failure and finally death by internal suffocation. You remember back around Christmas, that family on the south side in Rochester? Four people killed in their sleep when their furnace went kaflooy during the night and pumped the house full of the stuff."

I nodded as if I recalled the incident, but the truth is I only read tragic news stories when I've written them myself, and only then to check my facts.

"I guess there's no way that Edgar Williamson could've been just an accident, too," I said. "Like that he might've pulled to the side of the road late Saturday night, tired or drunk, and fallen asleep with the car running. A faulty exhaust pipe—"

"That's the first thought that occurred to me out at the scene, particularly after I noticed the victim was a heavy smoker." Doc laid his own burning cigarette on the rim of the overflowing ashtray and held up his palm. "See the yellow nicotine discoloration here between my first and second finger? This Williamson's left hand showed the same sort of staining."

"Which means?"

"A heavy smoker has less resistance to c.m. poisoning, because his smoking has already caused as much as six percent of his red blood cells to become saturated with carbon monoxide. So your scenario was worth consideration, but only until I factored in everything else, such as the signs of lividity and rigor in the body. Not forgetting the key question; how a dead man in a parked car managed to drive himself off an embankment."

"So there's no question that he was already dead."

"None. I called the county serologist last night, just to see if my surmise about the carbon monoxide poisoning had been verified. It has been, as you've apparently already heard, and the autopsy confirmed the man had been dead for up to twelve hours before the car wreck."

"Damn." I'd been half hoping Stoneman had gotten his facts screwed up, as usual, or had at least been guilty of gilding the lily in order to sweat me. While I pondered the implications, Doc retrieved his Winston and worked on perfecting his smoke rings. One of the sales reps at the far end of the bar gave him an annoyed glance and tried out a dry cough, but Doc wised him up with a pretty good glare of his own.

The taproom's official no–smoking section consisted of a single table tucked in next to the back door. Not exactly letter of the law, but I suppose Norb figured anyone who'd risk the food had no business worrying about second–hand smoke. Normally I wasn't one to complain about the arrangement. After all, I enjoy a good briar myself when I'm relaxing at home. But Doc's carbon monoxide news flash was enough to make a Carolina tobacco farmer think twice.

"Tell me something," I said. "Knowing what you know, I mean, what cigarettes and booze can do—"

"Physician heal thyself, that what you mean?" He squinted at me through the nicotine fog. "Let me tell you something, Hackshaw. I'm sixty–three, my mother's eighty–five. She's over at the Chilton Manor nursing home, got the constitution of a horse, probably got another fifteen years in her. The problem is, most of the time she doesn't know me from Adam—can't even figure out who her grandkids and great grandkids are any more. It just doesn't seem like a hell of a lot to aspire to, if you ask me." He picked up the tumbler of scotch and emptied it in three breathless swallows, then nodded toward the critic down the bar. "You ever notice, it's always the assholes who want to live forever."

* * *

Curiosity is what it came down to.

I was reasonably confident, despite Stoneman's bluster, that he'd never prove a connection between me and Slow Eddie Williamson, because there wasn't one. Still, it wouldn't be prudent to stand around doing nothing while Stoneman was out feverishly attempting to frame me. Besides, I wanted to know myself just what Williamson had been up to on my turf, especially since he was apparently using the information in my columns to do whatever it was he was doing.

Which is why, despite the hour and the pile of deadline–day chores that awaited me at the *Advertiser* office, I took a minor detour on the drive back. Jeff Klekzo, the dentist–cum–race horse owner, practiced out of a cookie–cutter professional building on Port Erie's south side. As it turned out, I had to wait fifteen minutes for him to get his fingers out of some poor woman's mouth and all I learned for my time and trouble was that Klekzo had never heard of Edgar Williamson.

"No, I haven't been approached lately by anyone touting get–rich schemes," he told me, as he peeled off a pair of throw–away plastic gloves. "Certainly not in the week since your column mentioned my buying into Toothsome Girl, Hackshaw. I owe you for that, by the way—the ladies have really sat up and taken notice." He did a hubba–hubba move with his bushy eyebrows. "Babes and horses, y'know what I mean? Attracts 'em like flies to sugar."

Klekzo was a once–happily married man who had divorced his wife a few years back in a fit of male menopause and who, ever since, had been trying to define male–female relationships according to what he read in the Penthouse Forum. That helped to explain the racehorse gambit, not to mention the red Porsche he drove, the tanning salon bake job and the bad toupee. And yes, I realize `bad toupee' is redundant, but in Klekzo's case the curly brown furball atop his head was so blatant it should've come with flip–down earmuffs and a sun visor.

"No solicitations at all?" I pressed. "Condo time shares? Ostrich farming? `You may already have won'—things like that?"

"Nothing. And even if I had, I'd have referred them to my investment adviser to handle." He chuckled. "Ostrich farming. What kind of fool do you take me for, Hackshaw?"

No kind of fool at all, I assured him, doing my damnedest not to glance up at the fright wig.

When I got back to the office, Mrs. Hobarth was at her reception desk, running her nose slowly down a page of copy. She peered up at the sound of my boots stamping off on the mat and greeted me with, "About time you showed up. You don't pay me to do this sort of work, you know."

True. Alan Harvey, our volunteer student intern, is the one we don't pay to do that sort of work. If Mrs. H. had been somehow coerced into proofing duties, it could only mean Alan was tied up over at the college and Liz Fleegle was still struggling to complete her puff piece on the Chilton Winter Ball, leaving Ruth short–handed on our busiest day of the week. In other words, I was in for martyred looks and a violin solo the moment I entered the newsroom.

"It's good therapy for your astigmatism," I told Mrs. H. as I headed toward the back.

"Wait a minute, Hackshaw. Long as you're here, you might's well answer a question." She tapped a finger on the copy paper lying before her. "If this doomed sinner's dead, does that mean I should still run his classified ad? Or should we pull it?"

"Huh?" I came around behind the desk and followed her pointing digit to the piece I'd written on the late Edgar `Slow Eddie' Williamson. "What are you talking about?"

"Him." She tapped the article again. "I'm pretty sure this is the young hustler who came in at the first of the month and placed a classified to run for four weeks. Tall, well dressed, talked real slow, but soothing–like, if you know what I mean. Only he said his name was Smith."

I exhaled heavily. "Well then, for pity's sake, what makes you think it's the same guy?" My copy didn't give a physical description of the dead man, mainly because Stoneman hadn't given me one.

"I knew right off he was some kind of crook—I know a phony when I see one." This from a woman who sends monthly `love offerings' to every TV evangelist who comes down the pike. "Besides, the car's the same. I used to own a Mercury sedan just like that, the exact same model and year, only mine was robin's egg blue and this one was maroon with that real dark tinted glass all around."

I blinked down at her. "You're sure that's what your Mr. Smith drove?"

She indicated the big plate glass window that fronted the reception area. "He parked it right by the door there in the fire zone when he came by to place his ad. I told him that was illegal, but he didn't pay me any mind—"

"The ad," I said. "What was it for?"

"Hmm? Oh, a house. He had a house he was trying to rent out, someplace over in Kirkville, I think."

CHAPTER 4

❀

It's not as if I had anything better to do.

Thursdays are always slow down at the office, what with the latest edition of the *Advertiser* just then hitting people's porches. And I was between rehab jobs at the moment, as is the norm in the nadir of an upstate winter. So there was really no good reason not to check out the curious advertisement Mrs. H. had told me about.

Not if you don't count common sense, there wasn't.

I had her dig out a copy of the ad for me and I read it through once or twice and stuck it in my pocket. That was Wednesday. The rest of that afternoon and deep into the evening, I was too busy putting the paper to bed to even think about it. But the next morning, over my coffee and Cheerios, that old bugaboo, curiosity, revisited.

Taken on its own, the content of the classified was innocent enough:

> *Kirkville Area: Small single–fam., clean 3 bdrm.,*
> *country kitchen w/appl.; pets OK.*
> *$450+ security, util. 274–8530.*

Cheap, even for Kirkville, but otherwise unexceptional.

My first move was to call the number. As I expected, repeated rings produced no answer. My second move was to call a woman I know at Rochester Telephone, an old flame, to ask what she had on the listing. After a few minutes of nostalgic small–talk and vague promises to get together for coffee and presumably harmless flirtation some day soon—it seems hubby was a three–leagues bowler—she came up with the name Edwin Smith and an address on Bing Road, a decidedly rural byway on Kirkville's northern extremity.

Edwin, I noted—which was close enough to Edgar to minimize the likelihood of coincidence—and Smith, every cheater's favorite pseudonym.

The house was only about a three–mile drive from my own place on the north side of the village. A basic rectangle of a ranch, prefab construction, low–pitched gable roof, yellow vinyl siding, set well back from the road on a large lot that sloped away toward dormant fields and woods. The closest neighboring houses were both on the other side of the road, a hundred yards down in either direction.

The driveway, presumably gravel, was hidden beneath several inches of fresh overnight snow. As I drove in, I congratulated myself for having had the foresight to switch the Jeep over to four–wheel drive before leaving my carriage house apartment. A few minutes later I was cursing myself for not having the foresight to wear something warmer.

There were no footprints other than my own in the new powder and no signs of habitation coming from the house. The windows were dark in the morning overcast; there was no response at the front door other than the hollow sound of the bell echoing within. I trudged around to the side door, stomping the snow off my Dexters onto the small wind–swept wooden stoop. Three hard raps, a pause, and three more, to no effect. I pulled the collar of my pea jacket higher and plodded down into the snow again, out behind the house, where I first tried to boost myself up for a look through one of the first–floor windows—a tad too high—and then knelt for a peek through an undersized basement window. A bare, unfinished basement, from what I could see.

I was making my way back to the Jeep, about to give up, when I noticed the fake terra–cotta flowerpot and saucer tucked into the corner of the side door's stoop, empty but for the potting soil. Now why, other than sheer laziness, does someone leave a pot of frozen dirt sitting out all winter?

The pot was plastic, and light enough in spite of the soil. I lifted it up and placed it to one side. The saucer contained no secrets. But then I flipped it over and—eureka; a tarnished brass key. Sophisticated security by local standards. Twenty years ago, even ten, most of Kirkville left it's doors unlocked day and night. But times had changed, even in the bucolic backwaters of small town America.

It just doesn't pay to trust anyone these days, I reminded myself with a twinge of regret, as I slipped the key in the lock and stole into the strange house.

A tight vestibule—mud room in contemporary parlance—led directly into an eat–in kitchen. Cheap wood cabinetry ran for ten feet along either side of the room, the floor in between covered in green–and–gold patterned vinyl sheet goods. Green, too, were the Formica countertops. The refrigerator was brown, the electric range white, the dishwasher nonexistent. A typical scheme for a rental property.

After calling out a cautionary "Hello," I stamped my boots on the vestibule's rag rug, took a swipe at the snow soaking into the knees of my jeans, and began my tour.

At the opposite end of the kitchen work area was a dining nook, maybe nine by ten, with a bow window that overlooked the deep backyard and the woodsy farmlands beyond. A pair of beat–up lawn chairs and square folding table were the only furnishings in the nook. Resting on the table were a black rotary telephone, a slim directory for the tri–town calling area and a tin ashtray, empty. I picked up the phone, listened to the dial tone, and replaced the handset. A quick skim through the phone directory provided nothing; no marked pages or highlighted names.

I moved on, into the carpeted living room, past the front door and down a short corridor leading to three progressively smaller bedrooms and a cramped bathroom that smelled faintly of mildew and PineSol.

As it turned out, the nook's chairs and table were the only furnishings in the whole place. The dry, musty air was well above freezing but still cold enough that I could see my breath. The surfaces in every room except the kitchen had an undisturbed film of dust.

The place fit to a T the description given in the ad Williamson had placed in the *Advertiser*. It was equally obvious that neither he nor anyone else had been living there in recent weeks. Even more curious, I thought as I made my way back toward the kitchen, was that a stranger—a reputed con man—should be placing ads to rent out a remote house that he almost certainly didn't own…

"All right, freeze, dipshit!"

I froze, everything stock–still but my fluttering heart.

"Heh, heh."

The nasty little laugh was familiar enough for me to risk turning my head ninety degrees. There, filling up the vestibule with his bulk, in a slight crouch and aiming a mini–cannon at me, was Investigator Stoneman.

"Caught you red handed this time, Hackshaw."

"Oh, for…"

"Hey! I told you to freeze—"

"Dipshit. I heard you the first time." I continued moving anyway, over to one of the lawn chairs, where I took the load off my quavering knees. "For God's sake, Stoneman, you could give a person a coronary."

He tucked the gun away inside his voluminous trench coat, apparently deciding not to shoot me for sitting down. Even more unsettling than the gun was his grim smile."My, oh my," he said as he stepped into the kitchen proper. "This doesn't look good for you, Hackshaw. I've got you dead–bang for breaking and entering, and that's just for starters."

"In the first place, I didn't `break' anything. I let myself in with the key I found out on the stoop."

"Which legal–wise amounts to the same thing. Unless you had the Koon's permission to enter—and you didn't."

"The Koons? You mean Marion and, whatshisname, her husband?"

"Bud. They own this place. And since you obviously didn't know that, you've just admitted entering illegally."

"Oh, come on. That's a technicality."

"Yeah? Well, so's this." Whereupon he began reciting my rights under Miranda.

"You're going to arrest me?"

"And people say you ain't perceptive," he said, grinning wider. But it was the long pause afterward that carried the greater import. This was Stoneman's way of saying cooperate or else, with the threat of my arrest constituting the or else part.

I surrendered a sigh. "Look. I found out that a man who may've been Edgar Williamson has been running a classified in the *Advertiser*, offering this house for rent. A man calling himself Edwin Smith. I merely swung by this morning to see if there was such a man, or if Smith and Williamson were in fact one and the same."

"Oh, they were one in the same, all right. The Koons described their tenant to me this morning, the guy they thought was Edwin Smith. Said he moved in the first of January."

"He may've rented the house the first of the month," I said, "but he certainly didn't move in. Take a look for yourself."

Stoneman frowned, ordered me to stay where I was, then took off on his own whirlwind inspection. While he was gone, I examined a few pieces of the unhappy coincidence that had brought us together.

It was apparent that Stoneman already knew about the classified ad before I mentioned it. And I had little doubt who had brought it to his attention; dear Mrs. Hobarth, who had probably phoned the cops the minute she found out about my interest in it. Stoneman had most likely followed–up much the same way I had, tracing the name and address through the phone number in the ad. Only he had taken things one step further, by looking up the ownership of the house at the town clerk's office and then interviewing the Koons before swinging by for a look–see.

He was back, grumbling. "So this house wasn't anything more than a phone drop for Williamson's scams."

"This house *was* one of his scams," I pointed out. "He must've been showing it to prospective tenants the last few weeks, offering a low rent, then collecting security deposits and first–month's from as many suckers as he could, with the understanding they could move in on February 1."

"By which time good old Slow Eddie would be long gone with everybody's dough, leaving the real owners to deal with a bunch of pissed off renters. Slick. But that's the Koons' problem." He fixed me with his favorite interrogatory glare. "Let's get back to your problem, Hackshaw. Namely how deep you were in cahoots with Williamson."

I settled back in the lawn chair and shook my head wearily. "Do you really expect anyone to believe I was involved in some penny–ante scheme to defraud would–be tenants?"

"Penny ante is your middle name. Anyway, who says it's so penny ante? We're talkin' a first–month's rental deposit of four–hundred and fifty bucks, plus a matching security deposit—that's nine hundred bills right there. And if he got, say, five different suckers to plunk down deposits, that's over four grand in pure profit. Even with a two–way split, your end comes out to a nice piece of change."

"My end? *Think*, Stoneman. Assuming I would've been willing to go along in the first place, what possible reason would Williamson have had to split anything with me? Does he—or anybody else—need my permission to place a classified ad? Or to clip a few of my columns?"

"Maybe not, but he might want a little local help to clip a few of your readers."

"That's very witty, but you still have no basis for accusing me of any criminal involvement with Edgar Williamson."

"Oh, yeah? So why did you lie about not knowing the son of a bitch?"

"Lie? How did I lie?"

He splayed his stubby fingers and started ticking off my supposed transgressions. "First, you told Dwight Philby all about the guy bein' a con artist."

"I told you, I made an educated guess."

"You even knew Williamson was driving an uninsured vehicle. Or was that another educated guess?"

"Uninsured—?" Then I remembered the passing remark I'd made, about Dwight's fire–hazard of an office being uninsurable. "That was just a mistake. Dwight misheard me, thought I was referring to the wrecked Mercury, when I—"

"Was Philby mistaken about the printing press, too? Cause that might explain why you didn't mention it to me yesterday when I asked what the hell you found in Williamson's trunk."

I lapsed into a guilty silence, hung by the heels of my own petty avarice.

"Or how you claim you were out of town when Williamson was killed, but you won't—or can't—give me a name that can verify your story. And now I find you sneaking around the dead man's house. What were you up to, Hackshaw? Selling subscriptions to the Trite door–to–door? Or making sure there's nothing to incriminate you further lying around the joint?"

That's when I gave up Jackie Plummer. I know I'd promised discretion when she invited me along on the Toronto trip, but I had a reputation of sorts to protect too, didn't I? Anyway, my situation was starting to look a little more serious than worrying that your sexually active teenage daughter might find out you both had the same nocturnal urges.

So I blabbed about my weekend with Jackie. Then, since I was already in a confessional mode, I explained about selling the portable printing press to my brother–in–law and subsequently squandering the thirty–five dollars he'd paid me for the damn thing. It was a pathetic performance, I have to admit, and Stoneman ate it up with a spoon.

"Well, well, well," he said, smiling down at my abjectness. "And I didn't even need the rubber hose."

Remember what I said earlier about being tripped up by numbskulls with authority and luck on their side? This is what I meant. What stung even worse was, now that he'd gained the advantage, Stoneman decided to turn magnanimous.

"Tell you what, Hackshaw." He was pacing now, hands clasped behind his back. "I'm going to check your alibi with Mrs. Plummer and with the hotel in Toronto and if it turns out you're in the clear for the hours in question—I'm inclined to cut you some slack on the B and E."

That sounded like another way of saying he was going to give me enough rope to hang myself, but I was in no position to nitpick the semantics. "You are?"

"Mmm–hmm. Not that I can't take you in for it later, if need be." Now he stopped pacing and stood facing me, rocking sedately back and forth on the balls of his brogans. "Y'see, I still think you know more about this Williamson than you're owning up to, but petty con games don't interest me right now. I've got bigger fish to fry."

"So, um—" I stood hesitantly. "—I'm free to go?"

"Free as a bird."

Said the cat to the canary.

CHAPTER 5

It was too easy, of course.

That Stoneman was rotten with ulterior motive was a given. What I couldn't figure out was *why* he'd let me off lightly.

But I didn't dwell on it, either. At the time, I was too mortified with my own cowardly collapse to concentrate on anything but slinking out of there. My only excuse is that I'd been in the county lock–up before—just for one night, and nothing bad happened if you don't count bunking above a flatulent drunk. But we've all heard the stories of what *can* happen.

By the time I'd driven halfway back to the village, however, mortification had moved over to make room for anger. And it was the anger, in combination with my continuing curiosity, that compelled me to turn the Jeep around and head straight back to Bing Road.

"Oh, the yellow house?"

"Yes, ma'am."

"Well, I know there was a family living there up to about last fall sometime. Some sort of coloreds," she added, with reproach. "Don't ask me where they came from or where they went."

She was stick thin and determinedly middle–aged with stiff hair and narrow eyes. I had noticed the name on the mailbox as I drove in, but I'd already forgotten it; blocked it out, I suspect. Her own home was set far back from the road, too, more than a stone's throw but still within sight of the Koon rental. I'd already tried the only other house sharing this stretch of Bing Road, a few hundred yards to the east, but there had been no answer to my knock. I was beginning to wish I'd had the same result this time. But since I was already there:

"Then the place has been empty since the fall, as far as you're aware?"

She shivered and hugged her robe tighter at the sound of an icy gust rattling the storm door behind me. We were standing just inside the entry, the front door still swung open on its hinges. It was as far in as her barebones hospitality would allow me, but it was far enough for a full view of the living room and dining room and a glimpse through an open bedroom door. What was a countrified cedar–shingled ranch on the outside had been crammed inside with oversized and overwrought reproduction Regency furniture, a design choice akin to sticking a tiara on Dale Evans.

"Well, I couldn't say it's exactly empty, either. I haven't seen any moving vans come along lately, but there's been some activity over there, off and on, the last few weeks. So I guess it's rented again." Her frown deepened with concentration. "I did see a light in one of the back rooms a few nights when I drove by, and a car in the driveway part of the time. Sometimes there'd be other cars that would stop by, mostly in the early evening, I think. But only the one that stayed around for any length of time."

"The one that you saw regularly," I said, "was it an older Mercury? Big? Maroon?"

She bobbed her head, the hairdo moving in synch like a helmet. "A big, old maroon sedan, anyway. I don't know if it was a Mercury or what."

"But you never met the driver? Or had a chance to see him—" See him what? "—hanging around the place," I finished lamely.

"Nope. They drove by once when I was out getting my mail, but that's as close as I ever got."

"They?"

"Uh–huh. Two of `em. A man driving and a woman in the passenger seat."

I pressed her for a description, but she claimed to have seen no more than a blur of heads going by, with an impression of a youngish blond man and an even younger dark–haired woman.

"What's this all about anyway?"

"The man died the other day. A car wreck," I added hastily, not wanting to draw out my stay. "I'm just following up the story."

"And you're with that weekly paper, you said?"

"*The Triton Advertiser*. Yes, ma'am."

"I don't get it, myself."

An old joke came to mind—*They read it, but they don't get it*—and I couldn't resist mumbling, "Perhaps if you read slower."

Her expression told me she didn't get that, either. "What I'm saying is I don't buy your paper, so I don't really know what sorts of things you're interested in. But I was thinking, maybe you could write up something about all the illegal trucks we get through here."

"Illegal—in what way?" Just being polite.

"There's a load limit on Bing Road, no vehicles over four tons. It's supposed to keep trailer trucks and milk tankers and so on from cutting through on the run between Chilton and Brockport. This is a secondary road, with a one–lane bridge over the creek up there at the west end, and neither one was made to handle heavy loads. It's one of the reasons we bought this place; no close neighbors and no noisy traffic. Nice quiet countryside."

As a townie myself, I've never understood the hermit instinct. As much bother as people can be, the ebb and flow of human activity at least keeps things interesting. I uttered a few sympathetic noises and slowly backed away, my right hand groping blindly for the storm door handle.

"It wakes us up in the middle of the night sometimes," she went on, "like they think they're fooling anybody, running through here so late, revving those big engines, gears clanking and clunking."

I began what I hoped would be my exit line with, "Maybe if you tried calling the proper authorities with your complaint—" But the lady of the house cut me off, on a roll.

"Don't tell me about the proper authorities! I've complained to the sheriff's department until I'm blue in the face and they don't do a blessed thing about it."

While she continued ranting, I took out my pad and jotted a few notes, half to appease her and half because you never know. It didn't sound like much of a story but, spun properly, it did involve possible malfeasance on the part of the county sheriff's department. If Stoneman continued to ride my back, it couldn't hurt to have something to trade: I spike a potentially embarrassing piece on the shortcomings of the sheriff's road patrol in exchange for the sheriff's promise to keep his investigator from harassing me about Edgar Williamson.

Grasping at straws, I know, but what did I have to lose?

In fact, the same could be said for the whole enterprise, polling Williamson's nominal neighbors on the off chance somebody might tell me something useful about the man. Still, I *had* learned something new: that our con artist may've been keeping time with a young brunette. As for the occasional early–evening appearances of other cars at the rental house, I figured that might well be explained by the classified advertisement itself. Most likely Williamson had been showing the property to prospective tenants responding to his ad, which specifically requested calls, and presumably callers, "after 5 P.M." Which left me wondering just what had been keeping Williamson busy each day *before* five o'clock?

So, while I hadn't come up with a lot, I had come up with just enough to encourage me to try one last time, at the only other house within shouting distance of the little yellow rental.

If Bing Road could be called one of Kirkville's secondary arteries, Hemford Road was a mere capillary. That the town crews kept it plowed was a minor miracle. It ran due north off Bing a quarter mile east of the rental house; a narrow, deteriorating track that went nowhere, much like the folks it was named after.

The Hemfords had lived in these parts for so many generations it was rumored their ancestors had stowed away on the Mayflower. So much for head starts. Three and a half centuries later the family still hadn't managed to make a discernible dent in the American Dream, proving that despite the best efforts of government and society at large, some people are poor and ignorant strictly out of merit.

There were only two residences on dead–end Hemford Road, both of them inhabited by Hemfords the last I knew. One was a rusting trailer in the middle of a barren field, seemingly held up by the snowdrifts that surrounded it. I decided to direct what little enthusiasm I had left to the other place, the old Hemford homestead. It was a basic farmhouse, no distinguishing characteristics beyond a full–length front porch that sagged dangerously at one end. There were several outbuildings scattered around the property; like the house, none had seen paint or maintenance of any kind in decades. One section of the main barn had long since collapsed on itself. A fitting metaphor for the current brood of Hemfords, I thought, who had abandoned the grunt and grind of dairy farming for a hand–to–mouth lifestyle that was heavy on seasonal employment, under–the–counter odd jobs and public assistance.

My first knock had barely landed before the door swung inward. Standing there, silent and sullen, was a teenage girl. I think.

"What the fuck are *you* starin' at?"

I was wondering that myself. Her hair was shaved to the skull on the sides, spiky orange tufts on top. From one ear dangled a chrome disk approaching the size of a hubcap, while the other lobe supported what appeared to be a real fishing lure, complete with barbed hook. Her eyes were completely encircled with black mascara, an effect somewhere between the Children of the Damned and Rocky Raccoon. Her ensemble consisted of a baggy black T–shirt with SCORPIONS printed across the front, shredded blue jeans, and bare feet.

I braved a smile. "Is your mom or dad home?"

She muttered something unintelligible, then abruptly turned and disappeared into the gloom of the house, leaving the door wide open and me standing at the threshold. I thought about taking the initiative to enter, but then I remembered dogs. The Hemfords of this world always have dogs on the prowl, usually in packs of three and usually of a breed noted for random violence.

I was about to give up and trudge back to my wheels when an interior screech held me in place.

"*April!* You left the damn door open! Do I have to do everything around—oh! Hackshaw? What're you doin' out there?"

"Freezing my butt off."

"Well, c'mon in."

Delia Hemford, the lady of the house, had calculating green eyes, lemon chiffon hair piled high as cotton candy, and an hourglass figure that had somehow managed to keep most of the sand packed into the upper chamber. She was wearing, along with a come–hither smile, a fuzzy off–white scoop–neck sweater that draped decorously across that miraculous bosom like bunting on a new destroyer. Her long legs were encased in leopardskin leotards. On her feet were a pair of fuzzy hi–heeled mules you could chop ice with.

I followed her churning hips from an ill–lit and threadbare central hallway into a living room packed with too much furniture, every piece of it angled toward a console television set. The set was on, blaring one of those audience–participation talk shows that specialize in exhibitionists and professional victims. Adding to the din was the frantic barking of the inevitable dogs somewhere in the back of the house, the furious click of their claws against linoleum suggesting the kitchen.

Delia settled onto a sofa patterned in earth colors, pulled a remote out from between the cushions and muted the TV. She then screeched again—"*April!*"—over her shoulder and, simultaneous with a string of girlish obscenities from somewhere off–stage, the barking hounds quieted.

Now the only sound, other than the rush of blood in my ears, was a moist gurgle oozing forth from behind the sofa. Presently an infant came crawling into view, one chubby hand batting before it an empty plastic baby bottle.

"Come here, you," Delia said cheerfully, and scooped the little cherub up into her arms. It had on a tiny stained sweatshirt depicting a turtle on steroids, white knee socks and a disposable diaper with little blue cartoon characters; a boy, then. His bare thighs were like ham hocks.

"Uh, congratulations," I said, taking a bentwood rocker and repositioning it to face the sofa. "I didn't realize you were even—"

"Pregnant again?" She grimaced. "Don't even think it. This here is May's kid."

"Ah." I'd forgotten there were twin daughters in the family, and yes, you heard right—April and May. The Hemfords also had a couple of sons; Early, the oldest, and A. C., who was younger. I suppose if A. C. had been twins the other one would be named D. C.

If I hadn't regretted my visit before, I did now. The thought of Delia Hemford as a grandmother was thoroughly depressing. She'd been two years behind me in high school, which meant she was still only in her thirties. She was known as Delia Dunkle back then; also known as the fastest girl in town, and not because she was on the track team.

Don't ask me how I know that.

The baby mewed angrily and nuzzled against the swell of Delia's sweater, his hungry little mouth searching for purchase.

Delia caught me staring and amplified the sulky smile. "He's lookin' for a free lunch. Thinks all women are the same, like his grampa."

"Not very observant, is he?" I managed to pull my eyes away, but not far enough. They locked onto Delia's. She wasn't through playing with me.

"You ever get a craving for mother's milk yourself, Hackshaw?"

"Depends."

"On what?"

"The container."

She let me off the hook with a throaty laugh.

"So, what brings your frozen butt to my door? If you're scroungin' for junk, you come to the right place."

I told her I was there in my other capacity, as scrounger of information for the *Advertiser*. When I finished outlining the Edgar Williamson story, she blinked a couple of times and frowned.

"A con man? Why would you think we'd know anything about somebody like that?"

"Like I said, he was renting the house around the corner. You can probably see the place from here, up along the ridge." I gestured toward the living room's side window, but neither of us bothered to get up for a look. "I was just wondering if you or Earl or any of the kids had come in contact with the guy."

"Birds of a feather, is that what you're tryin' to say?" Before I could assure her that wasn't my intent, Delia hollered for April again and, when the miserable girl appeared, handed off the baby.

"Aw, Maaa—"

"Don't `aw, Ma' me. You take Luke up and get some warmer clothes on `im."

"*I* didn't go out and get myself knocked up, so why'm I always stuck with May's brat?"

"Because she's family and she's out tryin' to make somethin' outa herself, that's why. Now move."

The girl kicked her foot against the side of the sofa petulantly, but eventually took the baby upstairs. As the dust literally settled, I told Delia, "I'm asking all the neighbors if they knew anything about Williamson. No one's singling you out, or accusing you of anything."

She digested that for a moment. "You gotta excuse me, Hackshaw. It's just, it seems like any time somethin' goes wrong in this town or somethin' turns up missing, everybody starts lookin' sideways at us. Just because Early had that trouble that one time."

I tried to decipher which trouble, of the several delinquincies her oldest child had been charged with over the years, she was referring to, but couldn't decide.

"Anyways, I don't know any Williamson or—what else did you say he was callin' himself?"

"Edwin Smith."

"Never heard a him, either." As quickly as it had dissolved, the carnivorous smile returned. "I think I've forgotten my manners completely this morning. Why don't you take that coat off, Hackshaw, and stay awhile. Would you like a Coke or somethin'? I think I got some cold Genny in the fridge—"

"No, thanks, Delia. I guess I should just—"

The dogs started up again, their barks rapturous this time and mixed with the sounds of a door slamming and heavy footsteps moving across the kitchen.

Delia sighed. "Shit."

CHAPTER 6

It was an altogether appropriate introduction for her husband, Earl Hemford, who stomped into the living room still wearing a pair of brown and yellow duck boots, his face red with January cold and perennial bluster.

He greeted me with, "What the fuck're *you* doin' here?"

Like father, like daughter.

"Hackshaw's doin' a newspaper story about some—"

The bastard pointed a finger in his wife's face. "There's only two reasons for you to open your mouth around here and talkin' ain't one of 'em."

Apparently it wasn't the first time he'd used the line; the way Delia rolled her eyes, it was plain she'd heard it before and was resigned to hearing it again. That's the primary reason I didn't jump up and give Hemford a good dressing down. The secondary reason had something to do with his burly build and his intimidating glower.

Not to excuse him, but I also had a notion it wasn't the first time Hemford had come home to find Delia entertaining another man, innocent or not. Imagine yourself a dirt–poor rube married to a Dolly Parton clone; wouldn't you be the least bit defensive?

Anyway, Delia seemed as capable at dishing it out as she was at taking it. She scissored those leopard legs of hers and snapped, "You watch your own mouth, Earl, or you won't need to worry what I'm usin' mine for."

"Oh, yeah? I got some news for you, baby—"

This time I did stand up, buttoning the bottom of my pea jacket to signal my intention. "I don't want to hold you people up. I imagine you'll need to start putting Earl's lunch together, Delia." They both looked at me as if I were nuts. "To answer your question, Earl, I'm trying to get a line on a guy who was renting the Koon place, up on the ridge? A fellow named Edgar Williamson, although he may've been going by Edwin Smith. I understand he was sort of tall, mid-thirtyish, blond haired, decent looking guy."

He stared dully at me for almost the whole spiel, shifting his gray eyes momentarily to his wife while I recounted the physical description of Williamson I'd pieced together from Mrs. Hobarth and the woman up the street.

"Doesn't sound like my type," Hemford said, looking openly at Delia now, challenging her.

"I already told Hackshaw, I don't know anything about the guy."

"Well, I guess that's it then." I sidled past Hemford, aiming for the hallway. "Delia, nice seeing you again. Both of you."

"Don't you be a stranger, Hackshaw."

Hemford followed me to the front door, the floppy duck boots quacking. Just as I reached for the knob, his forearm collided with the back of my neck, pinning my half-turned face against the casing.

"Errgghh," was the best I could manage.

He pressed in close—I could see the pores on the end of his nose and the sheen of sweat where his hair had receded above the temples—and whispered, "Just come by to ask a few questions for the paper, did you, Hackshaw? You sure that's all you come by for? Huh?" He jammed the forearm even tighter. "Think I don't know what an ass chaser you are?"

"Aah-shrruu!" That casing needed a good sanding, which it would've been getting if I hadn't shaved that morning.

His free hand was digging under my jacket. "You're really workin' on a story, you'd be writin' stuff down somewhere, wouldn't ya?" He located the notepad in the hip pocket of my jeans and yanked it out. "We'll see."

The arm came away and he backed off a step, forgetting about me while he flipped through the notepad. It was a perfect opportunity to sucker punch him, but that big a sucker I'm not.

"Before you get excited," I gasped, "I'll tell you right now I didn't take any notes while I was here—"

The eyes flashed up murderously.

"—because Delia didn't have anything to tell me. She didn't know anything about this Williamson guy, so what was there for me to write? For Christ's sake, Earl, this was strictly business. Your daughter was in the house the whole time. Go ask her, if you don't believe me."

"Don't think I won't." He went back to flipping pages, albeit slightly less aggressively. "Wait a minute, what's this shit here about?" He read slowly, "`Bing cedar r.; saw W. with young woman.'"

"That should say a young *brunette* woman," I said quickly. "In her twenties." I explained my earlier visit with the owner of the country ranch up on the main road and the description she'd given me of the woman she'd seen in Williamson's Mercury; I even embellished it a bit just to make certain there was no way Hemford could decide it might've been Delia in a wig.

He was still trying to decipher my handwriting. "So what's this other stuff? `Ill trucks Bing, late night, 4 T lim.'"

I interpreted. "Illegal trucks using Bing Road, often late at night, despite the posted four ton limit. The woman in the rustic ranch house again. She says the noise keeps her awake. You probably don't notice it as much down here below the ridge."

"It's bullshit anyway." He tossed the notepad back to me. "Those assholes always got their noses outa joint about somethin'. What the fuck they think a road is for in the first place?"

"Exactly what I told the lady," I said. "Almost word for word."

His mouth twisted into an approximation of a grin. "Lookit, Hackshaw, I guess maybe I was outa line, okay? I mean, Delia, she takes some lookin' after, if you get my drift."

"No problem, Earl." You stupid son of a bitch.

"It's like, sometimes I just gotta show her who's boss around here. They say a man's home is his castle, right?"

"That's what they say, all right."

"Damn straight."

Maybe it's just that I was getting used to humiliation, or maybe it was so ridiculous this time, it was more funny than infuriating. Whatever, somewhere between the Hemford castle's rickety porch and my correspondingly rickety jeep I started humming, and I couldn't get the stupid tune out my head the rest of the day.

Duke, Duke, Duke...Duke of Earl...

❧ ❧ ❧

"You know how it is with me and the law, Hack. If they don't have nothin' on me, they don't get nothin' outa me."

"Yeah? Well, Stoneman got plenty out of you this time, Dwight, most of it wrong."

"That's what I'm tryin' to explain. He comes in here yesterday breathin' fire, lookin' to hang somethin' on you and threatenin' to tear this place apart until he found somethin' he could run *me* in for. Unless I told him what I knew about you and that con man."

I surveyed the drafty barn. There was no sign of Williamson's wrecked Mercury. An old pickup and two newish sedans filled up the bays, in various stages of dismantlement. Tires and brakes for the cars, it looked like, and an engine rebuild for the truck. True to form. Most of the boys' engine work these days was done on older vehicles, like my Jeep. They lacked the diagnostic equipment, let alone the training, to deal with all the fancy, computerized electronics that came on new cars.

I nodded to George as he rolled out from under one of the sedans, then turned my attention back to his big brother. “So Stoneman had you sweating, huh, Dwight? What’s the story, you got another load of hot tires in back?”

“Nuh–uhh. That was a one–shot deal, man. I don’t buy nothin’ off the back of an out–of–state truck no more.” He gave a wink and a nod. “What it is, Omar’s been doin’ a little herb farming up in the loft there.”

“Herb farm?” I frowned as his meaning came clear. “You’re growing marijuana in here?”

“Omar was. Just three or four plants, is all, under one a those purple lights up in the loft. Personal use only, Hack. You know, for his eyes.”

“Omar’s nearsighted, Dwight.”

“Yeah, well, the weed seems to help.”

It had struck me as a good idea at the time, stopping in at the Philby brothers’ place on my way to the office to vent my spleen at Dwight over the mess he’d gotten me into with his fractured garage gossip. Now I was starting to wish I’d never stopped in at all, but it had been that kind of morning.

“Anyway, Hack, I told Stoneman how it was you figured out the stiff in the Merc was a professional swindler, from the printing press and shit in the trunk. I never told anybody you *knew* the guy.” He shrugged inside the loose coveralls. “I mighta mentioned to a customer or two that you said the guy was a con man—but that’s all.”

“Uh–huh. What about telling Stoneman that I knew about Williamson’s car being uninsured?”

“Well, that just sorta came out, y’know? Stoneman was pokin’ around, see, lookin’ up the ladder to the loft.” My sour expression got his defenses up. “Well, you did know about the insurance, Hack. I heard you say so with my own ears.”

I didn’t even bother this time. “Let’s just forget it, okay, Dwight?” Neither one of us had so many friends we could afford to write one off. To change the subject, I looked around again. "So what'd you do with the Mercury? Strip it clean already?"

"Yeah, it's pretty much just an empty shell now, out in the back lot." He grinned. "Stoneman was pissed, too. He came stormin' back in here no more'n an hour ago, talkin' about impounding the thing. I tell him, `You wanna go through all our used parts bins and figure out what's what, be my guest.' Man, he was pissed."

"Hmm. I don't know what he expected to find, impounding the car at this late date."

"Lookin' for fresh leads, is what he said. Asked me did I come across anything like motel matchbooks or receipts or a room key or somethin' in the car."

Dawn broke; suddenly I knew what Stoneman was up to. Indications were that Williamson had spent at least the last three weeks working the Kirkville–Chilton area. But if he hadn't been living at the Koon rental, where had he been cribbing?

Dwight, I noticed, was wearing a self–satisfied grin.

"What?"

"Like I said, Hack, I don't give the law nothin' if they don't have nothin' on me. And I had Omar move those plants a his over to Ma's basement last night."

I've always believed Mother's Day should be at least a monthly observance, but never mind that.

"You found something in the Mercury? And held it back from Stoneman?"

"I figured I'd teach that bastard what happens when you try to jack up Dwight E. Philby. C'mon, I'll show you."

He headed toward the makeshift office in back and I followed, although not without a certain reluctance. When we arrived, he dropped into a creaky chair behind one of the buried desks and began rummaging through the drawer. When his hand came back out, it was holding one of those little metal key cases, the sort that have a magnetic bottom.

"Found this sucker stuck up under the left rear wheel well, mudded up like a wasp's nest." He slid the top open and shook the contents out onto a pile of invoices.

Two keys. One was apparently an ignition key for a car or truck. The other could've been a house key of some kind, but it was a bit smaller than you'd expect. Dwight immediately confirmed my evaluation of the former.

"This one here's an extra for the Mercury. But this here little number—" He poked the smaller key with a grimy finger. "—well, take a look. See what you think."

I started to reach for it, then pulled back. "What I think is you should get Stoneman back over here right now and hand everything over to him."

"Nuh–uh. It's too late for that, he'd lock up my ass for holdin' back evidence." He tipped back his baseball cap with one hand and used the other to scratch at a patch of exposed scalp. "I figured I'd let you have it, like to make up for the other stuff. Maybe you could get a story out of it for the paper, so long as you keep quiet about how you got the key." He shook his head. "Take it or don't, but I ain't givin' it to the cops. You don't want it, we'll just shitcan it."

Later on, when the trouble grows tenfold, I want you to remember that I *did* try to play by the rules, at least on this one occasion. But that's the thing about fate; you can run, but you can't hide.

So I said, "Maybe it's academic. I mean, we may never even figure out what it's for."

"Yeah?" He nudged the key again. "Take a closer look."

With a sigh, I picked it up.

"Hmm." It was silver and, as I mentioned, undersized for a typical house key. But the telling bit was the word that appeared in raised, stylized letters on the key head.

"Nomad?"

"Know what I think that is, Hack? The name for one a those camper trailers."

It made good sense; so good it made me wonder how Dwight had thought of it. "There's more, right?"

The smirk again. "I stripped a ball hitch off the ass end of the Merc. And there was a working set of jumper wires feedin' down outa the trunk, like for runnin' brake lights on a trailer."

I turned the key over in my palm, half of me still wishing it would disappear, the other half remembering the gloat on Stoneman's ugly mug when he caught me in the rental house.

"I still think you should've turned everything over to the law, Dwight," I said, past tense duly noted. "This thing has turned into a murder investigation, you know."

"Hack, you really think Stoneman gives a shit about some dead outa town swindler? All he cares about is pinnin' somethin' on you, man. Know where he said he was goin' when he left here? Straight over to your girlfriend's house to check out some alibi you—"

"*Damn.*" I'd forgotten all about Jackie. I grabbed the phone on the desk and started dialing.

Right after I slipped the key into my pocket.

CHAPTER 7

She was suspiciously sanguine about it.

By the time I called Jackie, Stoneman had come and gone, as I feared. But Jackie took his incursion in stride, confirming that he had barged into her studio a half hour earlier and confirming also, in her sweetest trill, that she had indeed verified my alibi.

"Krista already figured out I didn't go on a trip–for–two to Toronto on my own, Hackshaw," she told me over the phone, "so my main reason for discretion is invalid anyway. And I explained that to Stoneman, too, along with the rest. He's still a bit dubious, I think, but that's his nature, isn't it?."

I was so taken aback at her reasonableness, I didn't even think to say I–told–you–so about the daughter.

I couldn't figure her out, frankly—until Jackie reminded me not to forget our date that evening. Then it made sense. We'd been invited to Harold Morecock's, to share dinner and conversation with Harold and his new girlfriend. Always intrigued with a visit to the relentlessly eccentric Harold's equally eccentric mansion, Jackie was further enticed by the prospect of meeting Harold's latest enamorata. The last thing she wanted to do was provoke an argument that might cause either of us to cancel the date.

After receiving dispensation from her holiness, I continued on to the *Advertiser* office in Chilton Center to pick up my paycheck and to do a few minor chores at my desk, including check my phone messages. They were surprisingly light for a Thursday, our publication day. Usually you can count on a good handful of irate callers, but my editorial for that week was uncharacteristically tame (more sand, less salt to be employed by the towns' highway departments, a topic suggested to me by the worrisome rust on my Jeep's rocker panels) and the rest of the paper was equally uncontroversial. As a result, I had just three little pink memos tucked under my phone; someone upset I'd misspelled his name in my column (Drago Zastawrny, for pity's sake), someone pleased I'd written up their son's recent army promotion to Specialist Fourth Class, and someone congratulating me for scooping the Rochester daily on the Williamson story.

More surprising than the light number of calls was the fact there were none from any of Williamson's victims, or potential victims. But it was still fairly early—many of our readers were out working during the day and wouldn't see the paper until dinner time—so there was a good chance yet that someone would come forward.

Most surprising of all, Ruth didn't bother me about anything, so pleased was she with "our" scoop. That left me free to do all my desk tidying uninterrupted before skipping out to the bank and the Nook later in the afternoon. I honestly had no intention of doing any more than that, certainly not as far as the Williamson matter was concerned, but the key Dwight had stuck me with was burning a hole in my pocket. So, yes, I stuck my nose in a fraction deeper and made a couple of exploratory calls. Nothing that committed me to anything, I assure you. Just an inquiry into one wholly innocuous question:

If I were a camping trailer, in use in the dead of an upstate winter, where would I be?

❧ ❧ ❧

The key thing about Harold Morecock is not that he's the richest man in Kirkville, or that he lives in the town's only true mansion, a grand Gothic Revival pile called Elmwood Manor. Uh–uh. The main thing you need to keep in mind about Harold is that he's dippier than a roller coaster.

"By the by, any luck yet with Jerry Vale or Al Martino, Hackshaw?"

I finished chewing. "Not so far, but the word is out."

For years now, he'd had me searching high and low for prerecorded tapes of his favorite pop crooners. I had come up with a mint condition *Best of Englebert Humperdink* at a Port Erie garage sale only the previous July and a whole shoebox full of mostly Johns at a South Chilton house sale in October: John Davidson, John Gary, John Denver, Olivia Newton John. What made it a real scavenger hunt is that all the tapes had to be eight–track, a format whose popularity came and went faster than the list of balladeers he had me trying to find. You see, Harold had had an eight–track player retrofitted into his pink Edsel station wagon a while back and has refused to admit either mistake ever since.

And the eight–tracks are merely the tip of the iceberg. Wander the manor's fifteen rooms and spacious grounds and you'll stumble over—literally in some cases—every example of faddish, garish, cheap crappola you can imagine, along with several items that defy imagination; everything from the library's paperback bodice rippers and inflatable sofa to the powder room's musical toilet seat ("Yankee Doodle Dandy"). The front yard was festooned with so many tacky lawn geegaws, passers–by often mistake it for a miniature golf course.

"More cake, Mr. M.?" Edna, the enfeebled housekeeper, served us with the urgency of a postal clerk.

"I think not." Harold patted his flat stomach. "Have to keep trim, you know."

Anyone could keep trim faced with a meal like that. The best that could be said for it was that it made it easier for the women to pretend they never eat anything. The main course had consisted of soggy take–out from a Chinese restaurant in Chilton Center, washed down with Tangy Sangria wine coolers. Dessert came from the bakery section at the Super Duper; some sort of rolled sponge cake with a cream center that had its antecedents in Hostess Twinkies. And, of course, freeze–dried coffee.

Speaking of the women, Harold's date for the evening, Penny, turned out to be a revelation. I suppose I was expecting someone as disposable and glitzy as the decor; someone along the lines of Delia Hemford, leopardskin tights and all. But Penny was about as far removed from Delia as you could get and still be talking about the same species. I'd peg her age at about forty. She had pleasant features, brown hair and matching eyes, a trim figure and a quiet but open personality that contrasted pleasingly with her somewhat husky contralto voice. She seemed not so much innocent as guileless, nodding with interest when Jackie talked about spinning clay for a living and somehow managing to hang on Harold's every word about his "collections" of contemporary kitsch, his grandiose theories on what globalization portended for the Home Shopping Channel, his latest get–richer schemes, his assaults on creative writing, et cetera.

It was Jackie who eventually managed to turn our host's filibuster into something resembling a dialogue.

"Well, Harold," she said, "I must say it's refreshing to know a member of the leisure class who isn't content to merely clip coupons."

"You know me, Jacqueline. Always looking for a project to keep me busy."

"Don't you old–money types usually go in for race horses or yachts to keep busy?" Penny wanted to know.

"Either one would violate my first rule, my dear: Never invest in anything that eats or requires ongoing maintenance." He parked his fork and steepled his fingers. "Besides, I like to be involved creatively. And as Hackshaw will attest, my inclinations run in a more literary vein."

"Mmm." I'd call Harold's self–published novels many things, but literary wasn't one of them. I should know, being the only person besides the author to have actually read all of them.

"Now that I've trained myself on my new computer system and desktop publishing software," he continued, "I was half thinking of giving you and Ruth a run for your money."

"Start your own newspaper?" I could see it now; *The Harold Herald*. The prospective competition so terrified me, I signaled Edna for a second helping of sponge cake. I was about to point out that putting together a newspaper, even a piddling weekly shopper like ours, required certain core abilities, such as an attention span. But Harold, a realist in his own fashion, made the point for me.

"A business–oriented weekly newsletter is what I first had in mind. On reflection, I decided I wasn't interested in anything long–term. But the idea of addressing the business audience, now that's a niche worth exploring. So I've decided to try my hand at writing a business book."

"You mean an *Up the Organization* type thing?"

"Precisely." His round cherub face fairly throbbed with enthusiasm. "I've made a survey of the bestseller lists and I think I have a pretty good handle on the basic formula. First, the book should be fairly thin, a good, fast read. Probably a trade paperback, but priced like a hardcover—everybody writes–off these things on their taxes anyway. Needless to say, it wants to be laden with folksy anecdotes."

"And repetitive."

"Definitely. Make three or four key points early, then keep hammering them home, chapter after chapter."

"There's your title," I said. "*Everything I Know About Business, I Covered In The Foreword.*"

"I was planning something a bit more provocative. What do you think of this: *Alexander the Great's Seven Steps to Market Domination.*"

Jackie said neutrally, "It has a certain ring to it."

I said, "A ring would make it *Alexander Bell's Seven Digits to Market Domination.*"

"This is serious, Hackshaw!" Harold attempted a stern frown. "You know how I value your input, but if you insist on being facetious—"

"Sorry. Must be the wine cooler talking."

Jackie to the rescue. "What about historical analogies, Harold? I imagine you'll need to bone up on Alexander the Great."

"Indeed. I'm making a study of all the great conquerors, along with collecting appropriate anecdotes. Oh, and buzzwords! That's where I thought you might be most helpful, Hackshaw, coining a few memorable catch–phrases. In particular, I need a concept, a single word preferably, to build the book around."

"You mean like `empowerment'? Or `proactive'."

"Or `Total Quality Management', that's a good one."

"But too long, and totally overused. I need something fresh. Something cutting–edge."

I gave it half a second's thought, which qualified me as an expert. "How about enablization."

"Ooh, that's good. Yes, I like the sound of that." His high forehead crinkled. "But what would it mean?"

"The act of enabling. Providing people with the means to...do something."

"Self–actuate," Jackie suggested.

"Oooh."

Harold abruptly excused himself and hurried off to his study to process a few words onto his hard disk, leaving Jackie and me to fill in the void with his date while erstwhile Edna palsied away the dessert dishes.

"I'm sorry, Penny," Jackie said for openers, "but I didn't catch your last name."

I hadn't either, because Harold hadn't thrown it out. Too preoccupied with his boyish enthusiasms to remember his manners, I assumed. Until Penny said, "It's Wise."

I blinked at her.

Jackie hastily covered her mouth with her coffee cup.

I said, "Penny Wise?"

Some of Jackie's coffee came back up. "Excuse me."

Penny smiled indulgently. "That's okay. I'm used to it. It's a stupid name, but at least people remember it."

That broke the ice as far as Penny was concerned and we successfully spanned the next half–minute recalling other silly names. My personal favorite was a girl I'd known in grammar school, Sandy Shore. Jackie came up with a college heartthrob named Beau Hunter, but it turned out that was a nickname, so we disqualified her. Penny topped both of us with her dad's name, Guy, which appeared in the phone book as **Wise, Guy**, attracting no end of late night calls from tittering teenagers inquiring if this was the number for ordering up a Sicilian hit man. And could he bring a pizza with him?

"Maybe the phone foolishness is what influenced me to go into the line of work I'm in," Penny said.

"Which is?"

"Well, these days I'm an independent telemarketing representative. That means I get paid to call target lists of people and give them a spiel about a particular service or product. Right now I'm helping a national hosiery outfit test–market a direct–mail line of run–free pantyhose, and in between I do call–arounds for a local lawn–care outfit, which isn't exactly going too well seeing as how there's two feet of snow on everybody's yards right now."

"It sounds—" Jackie searched for a word. "—challenging."

"What I hate the most is answering machines. It seems like everybody's got them, and you never know if people really aren't home or if they're just sitting there screening everything. And there's no point leaving a message, because nobody calls back a phone solicitor." She shrugged. "The good part is I get to work at home now. No more driving to a phone pen in the city, like with my last job."

"Is that how you and Harold met? He hired your service to promote one of his pet projects?"

"Um, not exactly." She looked around for poor Edna, who had finally disappeared in the direction of the kitchen, her serving cart doubling as a walker. Seeing the coast was clear, Penny nonetheless dropped her voice to a cozy whisper. "Actually, Harold and I became acquainted through a nine–hundred number I used to work for. You know—" Her cheeks reddened, but not much. "—phone sex."

Needless to say Jackie was fascinated, but, frankly, it was already more than I needed to know about Harold. Which was just as well, because he just then came bounding back into the room like an English retriever pup and hustled everyone out of the dining room and into the main parlor.

"Brandies all around and a couple of fine panatelas for the gents, hmm?"

It wasn't quite the Kiplingesque scene it sounded. The brandy turned out to be raspberry and Jackie refused to stay in the room if we lit the cigars. You also need to factor in the surroundings; rich wood–paneled walls defaced with Day–Glo paintings on black velvet, sterile modern Italian furniture in blue leather, brass–and–glass occasional tables everywhere. The parts that didn't belong in a landfill belonged in an airport lounge, not an 1859 Gothic Revival country house. But at least we got to relax around the parlor's giant fireplace, the four of us, and chat comfortably while a Duraglow log flared colorfully in the grate.

"By the by, Hackshaw," the lord of the manor said when he tired of talking about himself. "I meant to compliment you on your exclusive in this morning's edition. Quite a coup for a modest weekly. And it's nice to see you can cover a murder for once without getting stuck in the middle of it."

Jackie snickered. "Au contraire, Harold."

"Don't tell me! Amend that. *Do* tell me, Hackshaw, I insist."

"It's really just a big misunderstanding—"

"It always is with you." Jackie again. My utility as an escort now expired, I was fair game.

And Penny chipped in her two cents. "Who got murdered? And what's it got to do with you, Hackshaw?"

"Absolutely nothing." I started out by explaining the ridiculous set of circumstances that had linked me to Slow Eddie Williamson in the first place and concluded with my exploratory trip out to Bing Road that morning. I included almost everything, but severely edited the badgering I'd received from Stoneman at the Koon house and the near–battering by Earl Hemford. And the camper key.

About halfway through my woeful tale Harold's brow had formed chevrons and now he was muttering. "Hmmm, Edgar Williamson. Williamson, Williamson…"

"You know the name?"

"No, I can't say that I do. But I've been trying to remember *something* ever since I first read your—Ah!" His eyes rounded with recall. "Not Edgar Williamson, but the alias you mentioned—Edwin Smith. I think that was the name of the man who tried to sell Linda Pedersen on some sort of risky investment scheme. A riverboat gambling venture over near Buffalo, of all things."

"The Pedersens," I said, remembering the names highlighted in my columns; Dave and Linda, who met Tom Jones on a Christmas junket to Las Vegas.

"Yes. Dave's agency writes my auto and homeowners insurance," Harold explained. "Anyway he called, oh, it must be two weeks or so ago, to ask my opinion of the offer. Of course, I told him to forget it. In the first place, gambling stocks are all wildly overpriced these days if P/E ratios are to be believed, and in the second place, one should never buy *anything* on the basis of a cold–call solicitation."

"Thanks a lot," Penny said.

"Nothing personal, my dear. I was referencing the securities and futures markets. Successful and forthright brokers don't often simply call out of the blue."

"Hmm," I said. "And did the Pedersen's take your advice, do you know?"

"Yes, as far as I remember, they did."

Jackie, I noticed, was staring critically. "Why are you so interested anyway, Hackshaw? You have a confirmed alibi now, thanks to the exasperating interrogation I suffered from Investigator Stoneman this morning—" You see? I knew I'd pay for that sooner or later. "—so you're off the hook as far as this Williamson man's death is concerned. Aren't you?"

"Absolutely."

"You're not going to do anything stupid, are you?"

"Of course not." She was still lasering me with those deep brown orbs of hers, so I threw in, "Cross my heart and…and so on."

CHAPTER 8

Friday morning blew in gusty and gray, with the kind of stainless steel cold that penetrates your bones the moment you step outside and stays with you all day. The drive up to Hamlin was twenty miles and took me just over half an hour, thanks to icy roads and a mini–traffic jam going through the village of Brockport.

I'd learned from the calls I'd made the previous afternoon that all the private campgrounds and RV parks in the area were sensibly closed for the season. That meant the closest place a camping fanatic could indulge his madness in mid–winter was at Hamlin Beach State Park, tucked away in the far northwest corner of the county along the shore of Lake Ontario.

Now, I know what I told Jackie about staying out of things, but I remembered, too, what Dwight had said about Stoneman being more interested in punishing me than in solving a grifter's murder. Don't worry, I'm not going to make a speech about somebody having to see that justice was done and blah, blah, blah. For all I knew justice already *had* been done as far as our friend Slow Eddie was concerned. It seemed likely that one of his victims—an old couple, a slow–witted rube, a well–meaning housewife; typical dupes one and all—had risen up in righteous indignation and put final punctuation to a life gone selfishly bad. So, no, I wasn't particularly worried about balancing any scales.

But there was something else, beyond justice, beyond even a newsie's curiosity. Call it self–interest. Or self–preservation. Jackie may have gotten me off the hook by verifying our Toronto weekend, but Stoneman still had the hook and he was still out there swinging it blindly. If I wanted to make sure he didn't resink it in me, I reasoned, it was only prudent to make sure there were no more damning coincidences waiting out there with my name on them.

The park entrance was open and unattended, the whole place switching over to the honor system along about Thanksgiving weekend. The lake was as merciless and bleak as a Russian novel, with drifts of snow and pack ice backed up along the shore like icebergs run aground. Snow banks bracketed the well–plowed park roads, rising as high as a two–story building in places. Anything that wasn't white was gray, from the heavy pewter skies to the gunmetal lake surface to the bare silver maples and windswept stone outcroppings that seemed to mark each new bend in the road.

Three things people do for fun that I've never understood are sado–masochism, playing the bagpipes and mountain climbing. Looking at Hamlin Beach State Park in mid–January convinced me to add winter camping to the list, right at the top. I suppose afficionados would cite snowmobiling, cross–country skiing and ice fishing on the feeder ponds and tributaries as the irresistible attractions of the place, but that only proves their insanity as far as I can see.

The campground was carved into a thicket of woods that stood back a good three–quarters of a mile from the lakeshore. There were only three camping trailers in evidence, two of them huddled together near the southern edge of the site, along with a couple of large sedans. The third trailer was on its own, a hundred yards away under the skeletal reach of a tall oak. It was not new but not terribly old, two–tone in color, white on top, tan on the bottom, short and boxy, with the name *Nomad* written large in script across the back end. That was one clue I was looking at the late Edgar Williamson's home away from home; the undisturbed icy drifts of snow that surrounded the camper, along with the general air of desertion it gave off, was another.

I checked the two far trailers again—no activity; probably off ice fishing or snowmobiling or doing God know's what—and decided to fall back on an old maxim favored by newspapermen and con men alike.

Act like you belong.

I pulled the Jeep within twenty feet of the camper and clopped through the low drifts like a farmer negotiating a freshly plowed field. After banging loudly on the door a few times, I rattled the knob—locked—then made a show of digging the key out of my pocket. The lock was stiff but the key did its job and, after a moment's hesitation, I pushed open the door and let myself in to do mine.

The interior was about what you'd expect, only colder; a tightly compartmentalized living space, no more than eight by eighteen feet, with a built-in dinette up front, undersized kitchen appliances in the middle and a fold-down double bed in back next to what could honestly be called a water closet—a tiny shower stall you could wash your feet in while sitting on the toilet. The bed was in the fold-down position, with blankets and pillows askew. The kitchen sink held a few dirty plates and two coffee-stained cups, one with lipstick on the rim. An overflowing ash tray sat on the dinette table amid a scattering of old newspapers, including last week's edition of the *Triton Advertiser* with, I noted, my Ramblings column neatly clipped from page three.

I don't mind admitting it felt eerie, being there in a murdered man's portable crib and seeing evidence of a sort—the missing column—pointing to my own tenuous involvement with a complete stranger. I also don't mind admitting I folded up the altered copy of the *Advertiser* and stuffed it into the pocket of my coat.

My breath formed little storm clouds on the brittle dry air as I moved around, looking in high overhead cabinets and in low storage drawers, discovering dirty clothes under the bed and other small pockets of typical bachelorhood everywhere else. Don't ask me what I expected to find, because I couldn't tell you. The first priority was anything else that might possibly further incriminate me, naturally. Beyond that, a tell–tale matchbook would've been nice; something with a local restaurant's logo on the front and a phone number scribbled inside, the combination of which would turn on a light in my brain and instantly provide me with the name of Slow Eddie's killer, just like on the late show. Call it a bonus for my trouble, a fait accompli I could shove in Stoneman's face and watch as he turned six shades of furious.

What I actually did find was an overflowing junk drawer adjacent to the refrigerator: road maps of upstate New York, western Pennsylvania and southern Ontario, pens, batteries, a pocket comb, a disposable lighter, a bent picture postcard of Niagara Falls with no message or address on it, rubber bands and paper clips, and so on. If I were better at this sleuthing business, it would've occurred to me to check the maps for any pen markings that might indicate Williamson's recent travels or his home base or something. But I'm just not that clever, even at times when I'm not freezing and nervous. The only obvious *ah–ha* in the whole mess was an instruction booklet for the laminator I'd bought off Dwight, which I tucked away in my pocket, figuring it might make it easier for me to sell the stupid thing.

I pushed the drawer back in but it wouldn't close all the way and, when I leaned down to check, I could see why; some of the overflow of junk had gotten between the drawer and the back of the cabinet. I pulled the drawer out again and slipped it off its metal runners and set it on the counter. Then I shoved my arm into the cavity and fished out a Buffalo city map, a plastic windshield scraper, half a pack of gum, a bundle of blank index cards and, the reward for my thoroughness, a photograph.

It had been taken with one of those cameras that leaves the date superimposed in the corner, in this case the fifteenth of November, two months past. Pictured were a man and a woman dressed in long fall coats, standing in front of a stone wall. In the background, partly obscured by the pair and the cloudlike mists, was a glimpse of what had to be Horseshoe Falls, the central attraction on the Canadian side of the Niagara River. The man was tall and blond and handsome, probably mid–thirties, smiling confidently. His arm was draped over the woman's shoulder, a cigarette pinched between his fingers. She was much shorter, younger by perhaps a decade, pretty and dark–haired. Her own smile seemed guarded, sly, as if she feared the camera could look too deep.

At a glance, it might've been a young couple on their honeymoon, but I knew it wasn't. The man, I was certain, was Edgar Williamson. Slow Eddie, gazing directly into the lens with calculating gray eyes, that professional smile seeming to mock me for the predicament he'd put me in.

I slipped the photo into my pocket next to the laminator manual, took one last helpless glance around and, for want of a better idea, made for the door.

Trouble was waiting on the other side.

There were three of them. Standing there in the snow, forming a loose triangle, underdressed in leather car coats and street shoes, apparently immune to the bitter cold. The two on the sides were both very young, short and swarthy, bare–headed, their curly dark hair whipped sideward by the northwesterly wind. Each wore a round gold earring in his left ear, a red bandana around his neck, and a chimpanzee grin. The third one was a few years older, also swarthy, but scowling from under the wide brim of a brown cowboy hat.

"Hey, mister," one of the bookends said, showing a gold tooth. "This your trailer?"

"Well, no, not exactly." I stepped down and pulled the door shut behind me. "It belongs to a friend of mine, actually, who asked me to stop by and—" And what? "—and make sure everything's in order." I fumbled the key from my pocket and held it up as proof of my legitimacy, then turned and locked the door.

When I turned back to the trio, the cowboy in the middle said, "So why your friend don't come check on the place his own self?"

Good question. "Well, you see, he's had a terrible car accident and he's in the hospital. In a coma."

"Coma? Y'mean like he's knocked out?"

"Exactly."

"So how could this friend ask you to check out his place, he's knocked out cold in a hospital?"

I think it was the late Speaker of the House Sam Rayburn who said always tell the truth; that way you don't have to remember what you said the first time. Imagine that from a politician.

"What I meant to say," I tried, "was that he keeps drifting in and out of consciousness."

The cowboy shifted his eyes and muttered something to his companions in a strange language that rang vaguely Middle Eastern or Central European, entirely unintelligible to me in either case. Then the eyes settled back into a steady glare and he said, "Where is bimbo?"

"Uh—excuse me?"

"Bimbo." Demanding this time. "Where is she?"

"Um." I glanced at the other two, hoping for a hint and receiving only simian smiles for my trouble. And then I thought, completely irrationally, maybe they're just lonely guys looking for girls, and maybe my reputation had somehow preceded me to this desolate place. And maybe the cold was numbing my cognitive abilities. "Which bimbo in particular are we talking about, fellas?"

It was the wrong response. I knew this because as soon as the words were out of my mouth, the cowboy spewed more rapid-fire jibberish at the other two, whereupon all three closed in on me like Sitting Bull's boys at Little Big Horn. I managed to squeak out half a protest before iron hands grabbed my arms and the lapels of my coat and I was lifted off the ground and slammed repeatedly against the camper's door—*thump, thump, thump*—the trailer rocking in counterpoint to the back of my bouncing skull, the clear blue sky above beginning to fill with shooting stars…

By the time I regained my full senses, one of them—my sense of smell—was under assault from another sort of mob; a gang of odors that included damp wool, burning incense, stale tobacco, garlic and cooking oils, and stagnant overheated air.

I was lying on my stomach on what proved to be a thick Oriental rug stretched across the floor of a camper similar to but older and larger than Williamson's trailer. As I raised my head for a better look, a boot collided with my ribs, hard enough to divert my attention from my spinning head, and someone flipped me onto my back.

They stared down at me, those same three faces. Stared down with teeth bared, like dogs salivating over their bowls, waiting for their master to bring dinner. One of them, the cowboy, was slapping my wallet against the side of his leg while holding in his other hand the picture I'd liberated from the junk drawer. Silent, eager, but holding back.

Waiting for what?

The answer came when the door opened, letting in a blast of arctic air and a short, very fat man. He had a drooping handlebar mustache, a mottled olive complexion, a bulbous nose, black eyes, and more chins than an M. I. T. engineering class. His camelhair overcoat was unbuttoned, revealing an old–fashioned navy pinstriped suit and a white dress shirt, but no tie. Three fingers of each hand sported heavy gold rings studded with diamonds and colorful gems. His scowl looked as if it had been there since birth.

It came together then; the strange language, the dark features, the earrings and bandanas, the colorful rugs all over the trailer, even the trailer itself.

Gypsies.

The fat man's age—somewhere north of fifty—and the other men's sudden silence marked him as the leader. He set about proving it by barking out a string of orders in that odd tongue of theirs. I was yanked to my feet and thrust onto the foldout sofa, with the two curly–haired smilers planting themselves on either side of me. Meanwhile bossman and the cowboy palavered, their backs turned. When they turned our way again, bossman was holding the photograph. He abruptly shoved it in front of my face and, like some third–world Perry Mason, demanded, "Where's this girl. Bimbo."

"Oh, you mean—Bimbo is the girl's *name*?" Suddenly Penny Wise didn't sound half so foolish. "Gee, I'm awfully sorry, but, like I tried to tell your, uh, associates here, I don't know anything about the young lady in that photo."

I was doing my utmost to appear sincere and cooperative, but he wasn't convinced. He threw up his stubby arms as far as they'd go. "You show up out here in the middle of no place, you go straight for the *gadjo's* caravan like you own it, you got a key for the door—you even got Bimbo's picture in your pocket, huh? You speck me to believe you don't know nothin'? Huh?"

"I know it looks bad, but I can explain." Which I tried to do, but it was hopeless; things hadn't gotten any easier to swallow even with the third retelling.

When my story petered out, bossman wagged his hippo's head side to side. "Toma!" he said, followed by a string of foreign commands. The cowboy said, "Aw, shit, Stavo" and began to talk back in the same lingo. Whatever it was about, this Toma finished it by contemptuously tossing my wallet onto my lap.

The big cheese, Stavo, glowered at one and all, saving the best for me. "Lookit, you—Hackshaw, huh? You a newspaper reporter, you know how to find out things, huh? Well, now you gonna find out somethin' for me."

I said, "Huh?"

"You gonna find some*body* for me, huh? This girl, Bimbo Wanka, she's my daughter, okay?" He jerked a thumb back at Toma. "His wife. Married people, young ones like them, they have problems sometimes, y'know? Is a family thing. You find Bimbo for me, we call it even. Forget about you lyin' to me, tryin' to steal the *gadjo's* caravan, ever'thing."

Mighty big of him. I thought about laughing in his face. I thought about telling him to go to the police, or to hell for all I cared—he could find his own runaways and leave me well out of it. I thought all of that, but I also thought about the odds, and the remoteness of the place, and the carnivorous looks they were all giving me, especially Toma. Mostly I thought about getting out of there the quickest and easiest way possible, not including sudden death.

So I said, "Well, I'd certainly be glad to put out a few feelers, see if I can't get a line on your daughter. Uh, in the event I come up with something, you might want to give me a number or an address where I can reach you—"

"Don't worry. We find you. Remember, Hackshaw, we know you now. Who you are, what you do, where you live." He leaned in close and laid his index finger against his right cheekbone. "You don't do this thing for me, I put a gypsy curse on you," he said solemnly. "I can do it, too, I got the evil eye. You believe me, huh?"

"I believe you." Both his eyes looked pretty damned evil if you ask me. "And I'll do my best to help out, Mr., uh, Stavo, is it?"

He continued to study my face for a moment. Then:

"Nah. You don't believe me. We gonna have to convince you a little bit, huh?" He abruptly straightened and barked uncomprehensible orders to his minions.

The two bookends pinioned my arms and pulled me, protesting pathetically, to my feet. Toma the cowboy was slipping on a pair of leather gloves, a bad sign.

But even worse was his smile.

CHAPTER 9

This time I came to on the front seat of the Jeep, stretched out like the featured guest at an Irish wake. I had to give Toma and the boys their due; they knew how to work someone over without making a Hollywood production out of it. I ached almost everywhere and the back of my neck, where Toma had applied some sort of Mr. Spock squeeze, felt as if it had been massaged with a brick. I was sure much of the skin beneath my clothes would be as black as a blues festival. But I wasn't bloodied, my face was unmarked, and I could move okay, if with a certain arthritic hesitancy.

The Jeep was idling, the heater providing a relatively warm blast of air. Considerate. At least they didn't want to see me freeze to death.

On the other hand, I suddenly realized, leaving an unconscious man lying in a running vehicle with the windows rolled up could just as easily produce disastrous results. What if there had been a leak from the engine compartment or a hole in the exhaust pipe?

I shuddered despite the warmth; the possibilities sounded all too familiar.

The final thing I noticed, before willing myself back together and getting out of there, was that the camping area was now empty. Totally. Gone were not only the pair of trailers and gas guzzlers belonging to Stavo's bunch, but Williamson's little Nomad as well, nothing left but a scrambled cross–hatch of tire tracks in the snow. And gone from my pockets were the trailer key and the photograph.

It occurred to me, as I slowly drove back out the park entrance, that my attempts to cover my own tracks had only landed me in a deeper set of ruts. I'd managed to leap out of the frying pan of the sheriff's chief investigator into the fire of a bunch of bushwhacking gypsies.

"Christ on a crutch."

Enough was enough. Somehow I had to find a way to put this business of dead con men and now runaway gypsy girls behind me once and for all, that much was certain.

But first I needed a better idea of just what I was dealing with.

Professor Blednau was the resident know–it–all at the college over in Chilton Center, a hale–fellow type who was as accomodating as he was knowledgeable. What he couldn't tell you about ancient peoples and cultures hadn't yet been hauled out of a Dead Sea cave. I found him, as expected, in his comfortably shambled office on the second floor of the Humanities building.

"By gypsies, I assume you mean the Rom?"

I responded with an abbreviated shrug, the best I could manage in my current condition.

The professor chuckled like an indulgent uncle. "There are several distinct ethno–specific groups, Hackshaw, who've come to be identified by the generic label `gypsy' by dint of common cultural characteristics, such as nomadism and a tendency to live hand to mouth. Or, as some law enforcement people would say—" He chuckled again, only naughty this time. "—hand in pocket. Anyone's but their own."

"What makes these Rom of yours distinctive?"

"Their language, first off. True gypsies, in both an historic and anthropological sense, speak Romany, at root an Indo–Aryan language that, unfortunately, lacks a written alphabet of any sort. They probably originated in Northern India, but that would've been many, many centuries ago. For reasons unknown, they migrated west and fanned out throughout the Middle East and later Europe. One of the major tribes, the Kalderasha—which means coppersmiths, by the way—are thought to have moved into the United States back around the Civil War."

"If they call themselves the Rom," I interrupted, looking to bring him back on subject, "why does everyone else call them gypsies?"

"It's a corruption of `Egyptian', actually. When the Rom first started showing up in Europe back around the fifteenth century, during the Holy Roman Empire, they attempted to curry the favor of their hosts by claiming to be Christians who'd been persecuted and driven out of Egypt by fanatical Moslems. Oh, they've always been a wickedly clever people, Hackshaw, expert at telling people just what they want to hear."

Gypsies were starting to remind me of third cousins; we don't know much about them, but we know instinctively we'd rather not have them hanging around the house.

"I guess what I'm trying to find out, Professor, is how dangerous these folks are. Like, if push came to shove, would they content themselves with evil curses and controlled beatings, or would they really kill somebody who didn't cooperate with them?"

I had given Blednau a rundown on my run–in with Stavo and company, sparing both of us the specifics of the predicament that had brought me into their orbit in the first place. It helped that the professor was almost totally uninterested in anything that smacked of current events, preferring dead civilizations to dying ones.

"Murder? Oh, no, I wouldn't think so, Hackshaw. Not as a rule, certainly." He kicked back in his squeally swivel chair and patted down a shock of white hair with the flat of his hand. "Don't misunderstand, I'm sure there are individuals, even whole vitsas—tribes—that are capable of such ruthlessness. Just as there are in any community, I hasten to point out. But extreme violence isn't a part of the standard gypsy profile. Larceny and fraud, yes, depending on the clan, and they can be pitiless when it comes to separating the gullible from their money. But murder, that's a different game entirely."

"But murder aside, it's true what people say about them? I mean, the fortune–telling scams, the flim–flams—"

"Well, first we need to differentiate between traditional Rom—those who adhere strictly to the old ways—and acculturated Rom, who've long since exchanged the life of the caravan and store-front fortune telling for mainstream American values. There are some who've even become lawyers and doctors."

"Yeah, well, I don't think these guys were with the AMA. Chiro-practors, possibly.

"I'm only trying to be thorough and fair, Hackshaw. And to help you understand what is an extremely complex and, to our Judeo–Christian eyes, extremely vexing culture." That's when he told me stories of how some Rom train their young girls to be good thieves, using trickery like the Jericho Flower to beguile their victims. And the Jericho Flower gambit was one of their lesser treacheries.

I shook my head. "Imagine, hooking their own daughters into that life. Call it a cultural quirk if you like, Professor, but it still stinks."

"It's reprehensible by our value system, yes, but the Rom don't see it that way. You see, they believe they have Biblical dispensation to steal."

"So why don't they go into televangelism like regular folks?"

"I'm serious, Hackshaw. According to gypsy lore, when Christ was about to be crucified, his Roman executioners had four nails; one for the feet, one each for the hands, and the final one for Jesus's heart. But while the soldiers were driving in the first three nails, a gypsy took pity and stole the last nail. In gratitude, Christ supposedly decreed from the cross that from that day forward, the seventh commandment, Thou Shalt Not Steal, need not apply to the Rom."

"That's ridiculous."

"Nevertheless, you'd be surprised how many of them fervently believe the story and claim it appears in the Bible. And speaking of `good books'." Blednau, chortling softly at his little joke, leaned back toward the reference shelf behind his desk and pulled out a thin volume. "I just happen to have a brief history of the Rom on hand—"

Doesn't everybody?

"—which, as I recall, includes a glossary of Romany words." He flicked through the back pages. "Yes. This might get us somewhere. Now, can you remember any of the words you heard these men speaking?"

One came immediately to mind. "The leader, Stavo, he said `gadjo' when he was referring to the guy who owned the trailer I told you about."

"Ah, yes. Definitely the Rom, then. Gadjo, or gadje in the plural, is the Romany term for any non–Rom. It's a bit of a put–down, not unlike the Japanese `gaijin' to describe foreigners, although I assure you any phonetic similarity is purely coincidental."

"How about `marmay'? Something like that."

"`Marimay', perhaps?"

"Yeah. Marimay. And—" I frowned, trying to reconstruct what I'd heard. "`Mulo'? I remember Stavo and the cowboy, Toma, throwing those two words back and forth. Whatever it meant, Toma didn't want to hear about it, but Stavo seemed to take it pretty seriously."

"That he would, as would any traditional Rom chief." The professor tapped at the book's open page. "Marimay, you see, is an elaborate system of superstitions and corresponding ritual practices, most of them centering around sex or sanitation. It can be something as innocent as washing one's hands in a sink that's supposed to be used exclusively for cleaning pots and pans. If a member of the vitsa fails to follow the rules, he or she can become marimay—unclean—absolution from which can only come after following through on a whole series of additional rituals."

He anticipated my skepticism. "It makes a convoluted sort of sense, Hackshaw, placed in historical context. Such proscriptions as separate sinks probably originated centuries ago, when the Rom would designate various parts of a river for special uses, with drinking water taken from a point farthest upstream, followed by human bathing, then the washing of utensils, the watering of livestock and so on down the line."

The professor's eyebrows arched, like two albino wooly caterpillars on the march. "Another example, which may be more germane to the situation you described: if a Rom woman has sexual relations with a gadjo, she would be considered marimay and an outcast from the tribe."

"Hmm," I said. "But, in that case, why would they want to get the woman back?"

"Well, as I said, there are methods for absolution. Maybe she's worth a lot to the tribe. She may be their best fortune teller, or a master pickpocket. Or it may be tied up somehow in that other word you mentioned, mulo." He went back to the book. "A mulo is a malevolent spirit, usually of someone who died before reaching old age. If one of your gypsies, say the chief you mentioned, Stavo, believes himself to be responsible for bringing a mulo down on the vitsa, well, that would be serious marimay indeed."

I drove back toward Kirkville in a funk, my head congested with disparate facts and intuitions. Mental images of a handsome blond confidence man shacked up with a bewitching girl named Bimbo in a claustrophobic camper in the middle of nowhere; of a similarly isolated rental house, empty but for dust bunnies and a working telephone; of Stavo and Toma, a Mutt–and–Jeff gypsy tag team on a single–minded search for a runaway wife and daughter; of a battered Mercury tipped nose–first off Black Creek Bluff, Slow Eddie Williamson's no longer handsome face punching a ragged hole through the windshield.

The more I learned, it seemed, the less I knew.

The first thing you notice when you walk into the Pedersen's small insurance agency is a largish sign thumbtacked to the paneled back wall right beside the obligatory State Farm calendar: **Honesty Is The Best Policy**.

"Hackshaw! Good to see you, buddy." Dave Pedersen came out from behind one of the two desks—the other was unoccupied—and met me at the squat service counter that served as a room divider. He had ginger–colored hair squared off into a modified crew cut and a more or less permanent sunburn, probably due to all those junkets to Las Vegas. Winter or summer, he always wore white short–sleeved shirts with a clip–on tie and a plastic protector for pens in the breast pocket. "Say, are you feeling okay? You look stiffer than the Tin Man."

To save time, I lied. "I did a triple lutz on a patch of icy sidewalk, is all."

"Not ours?" Visions of lawsuits danced in his head.

"No, not yours."

"Well, I see the old warhorse is still in one piece, anyway," he added, meaning my Jeep, which was parked just outside the full–glass door. The observation was more than simple small talk; I buy my auto insurance through Dave.

"I make no claims today," I told him, "except on a few minutes of your time."

"Glad for the company, been slow as molasses in here. We could run over to the Nook for burgers, Hack, but Linda just stepped out for lunch herself. She shouldn't be gone too long—"

"Another time."

"Sure. You know, I've been meaning to give you a jingle at the paper. I got something might be a cute story. You remember the celebrity squash contest last fall."

"How could I forget it?" The contest was held every year during the Kirkville Octoberfest. And no, it was not a sporting event involving rackets, small balls, et cetera, but a competition among backyard gardeners to see who could grow a squash that most resembled a famous person.

"Well, you remember who took first place, right? Betsy Arnold, with that butternut that looked like Charles Kuralt?"

"I did a feature for the *Advertiser*," I admitted.

"I know. But, remember the deal with Lyle VanEmp? The Michael Jordan eggplant?"

"Oh, yeah." VanEmp had been disqualified when the judges determined that eggplants weren't members of the squash family. "He took it hard, as I recall."

"Get this. Lyle comes in here the other day and shows me the thing. He took it to a taxidermist and had it stuffed, or dehydrated or whatever they do. He even had it mounted on a mahogany base."

"Presentation is everything."

"I guess."

I took out my spiral pad and made a note on the fate of the infamous vegetable. Celebrity eggplants may be corny, but the name of the game at a small–town newspaper is to keep the subscribers happy and reading about themselves and their neighbors. It didn't hurt, either, that Dave's agency was good for a quarter page ad each and every week.

Having done my professional duty, I came to the point of my visit, which was to ask him about the phone solicitation his wife, Linda, had received from a man calling himself Edwin Smith. But Dave couldn't tell me much more than I'd already learned from Harold Morecock. `Smith' had called the house one evening, Dave said, and claimed to represent an investors group that was pooling its capital to buy private shares in a proposed riverboat gambling casino.

"It's a real deal," Dave said. "I read about it a month or two ago, one of the big Atlantic City hotels wanting to put a floating casino up on the Niagara River near Buffalo. They figured they could draw from all over southern Canada, as well as western New York. It's a potential gold mine, if you ask me."

"But you didn't bite."

"Nah, I knew Smith was fishy. For one thing, the state legislature hasn't even approved the deal yet. Smith tells Linda, `Yeah, but this is your chance to get in on the ground floor, before the project goes public and the shares get snapped up.' Claimed he could lock us into a shot at the initial public offering—if and when there is one—for a fifteen–hundred dollar `shareholders deposit.'"

"That's as far as it went?" I asked. "Just the one phone call?"

"He called back a second time, but that was after Linda had talked to me and I'd run it past Harold." He grinned sheepishly. "Hey, I knew it was too good to be true, but why not check it out, right? Anyway, I told the guy to take a hike and that's the last we heard from him."

CHAPTER 10

What I wanted was a long, hot shower and a firm mattress. But I had a newspaper assignment I couldn't get out of at six o'clock—the Lutherans were teasing the Catholics with a fish fry fundraiser—and I knew that if I went back to my place in the meantime and crashed, I'd be down for the rest of the day. The only thing to do was to keep moving.

First stop was the Woodson Funeral Home, which occupies a large 1840 Greek Revival house on Kirkville's main street.

Mel Stoneman had thought he was clever, holding back information on the Williamson investigation. But as usual, he'd let slip more than he realized. I knew, for example, that he had talked to the Woodson's snotty funeral director, Derek Drummond. It was Drummond, remember, who'd put the bug in Stoneman's ear about my alleged friendship with the dead con man, a distortion he'd picked up third-hand from Dwight Philby. The question is why would the sheriff's investigator be talking to a local funeral director in the first place? And the most likely answer is because Williamson's body, either right after the accident or after the autopsy was concluded, had been consigned to the Woodson for final disposition or forwarding or whatever.

The broad central hallway was busy when I got there, women in hats and men in dark suits shuffling in and out of one of the two viewing rooms. No tears evident, so the deceased must've been someone very old or highly irascible, if that's not a redundancy. I nodded to a few familiar faces and otherwise did my best to blend into the somber wallpaper as I worked my way toward the offices in back. Drummond was coming out of his when I got there, dressed to the nines in a charcoal gray Italian suit and a stuffed shirt.

He wrinkled his nose predictably when he saw me, then brightened a few watts. "Hackshaw. You must be here to write up Mr. Klinghoffer."

"You must be kidding." Now I remembered seeing the death notice cross my desk. Klinghoffer had been vice principal at Kirkville Elementary many moons ago when I was a mere tadpole. Kling Kong, we used to call him, for his habit of grabbing his little charges by the collar and shaking the bejesus out of us whenever he was a touch irritable, which was constantly. I made a mental note to stop by the viewing room on my way out, just to make sure the old bastard was really dead. "I came by to verify some information on Edgar Williamson. I understand you'll be shipping the body back to his hometown. Niagara Falls, wasn't it?"

It was a stretch, but not much of one. Niagara Falls kept popping up, it seemed—in the photo of Williamson and Bimbo and the post card I'd found in the junk drawer—and I remembered what Stoneman had almost told me before he decided to clam up, about talking to Williamson's parole officer in *Ni*–something. Since Nigeria and even Nyack were too far away to be practical…

"Yes, Niagara Falls," Drummond said impatiently. "And the body left yesterday, all right? Now, I'm rushed—"

"I won't be a minute. All I need's a name and address for the receiving party."

"You should've gotten all that from the sheriff's department."

"Well, yeah, but you know how reliable those guys are. I just need to double check it."

"Hah!" Drummond's bony countenance fractured into mirth lines. "Mr. Stoneman has cut you out of the loop, hasn't he? I take it you're still a suspect, then?"

"Sorry to disappoint you, but I've been cleared. By the way, thanks very much for the rumor mongering."

"My pleasure. And I'm still not giving you that name and address."

"Come on, Drummond, this is public information we're talking about."

"So go get it from the sheriff's office."

He had me and we both knew it. I sighed. "Okay, what do you want?"

He pretended he had to think about it for a moment. "Let me see—your promise to write and publish obituaries on, let's say, four clients of my choosing. One obit per week for a month."

"One obit, period."

"Three."

"Two."

"Of my choosing?"

I sighed again. "Okay."

I knew damn well what he had in mind. He'd pick his spots carefully and I'd end up doing obits not predicated on the deceased's prominence in the community, but rather because the family of the dearly departed included Drummond's two favorite things; lots of aging members and lots of money to spend on funerals.

"I'll have to duck into the office to look up that information," he said.

"Then by all means, duck yourself."

"By the way, Hackshaw," he said brightly. "You look terrible."

"Don't get your hopes up. It isn't life–threatening."

❦ ❦ ❦

The Koons live in a fairly pricey neo–Victorian in Rolling Meadows Estates, a newer housing tract near Harold Morecock's mansion on the village's southern perimeter. As these things go, it's a handsome development, the builder and architect having taken pains to blend it in with Kirkville's older residential streets, including sidewalks, streetlamps, and inviting front porches on most of the homes.

It's a shame they couldn't have been as discriminating when it came to selling the places.

"Yes?" Marian Koon answered my ring with all the charm of a Korean grocer. She was a tall, sinewy woman, not very old but trying hard. Although I only knew them by reputation, Mrs. Koon and her husband struck me as the types who might actually read Harold's business book, and even attempt to put it into practice. Always busy buying up foreclosed properties or otherwise tweaking their investment portfolio. Always busy trying to maximize their return on everything but life, it seemed.

"I'm Hackshaw," I reminded her. "With the *Triton Advertiser*."

"I know who you are. What is it you want?"

She was standing sentry in the doorway, arms crossed against the icy breeze and me. I was a step lower—in fact as well as in her estimation—shivering on a welcome mat that should've been sued for false advertising.

I said, "A warm place to sit, for starters."

My request stymied her. It was clear she wanted to shut the door in my face. It was equally clear that wouldn't be the proper thing to do, and the Koons were rigidly proper people.

"My husband isn't here right now," she tried.

"Still at the office?" Bud Koon worked for the county, I knew; some sort of administrator.

"No, but rush hour traffic being what it is—"

"I only have a few questions. I'm sure you can handle them just fine." I shivered some more.

"Well—I suppose you'd better come in."

She made me remove my Dexters in the vestibule, then led me down a tiled hallway, past the living room—I had a glimpse of plastic–covered furniture and some quality antique pieces that were probably there for financial rather than aesthetic appreciation—and into an open kitchen–family room combination. What struck me most about the house was the complete absence of any smells; no brewing coffee or stale tobacco, no scent of mildew or Lemon Pledge, no flowering plant fragrances or slow–cooker aromas or odiferous cat box. It wasn't until she directed me onto a rattan sofa that I picked up even the slightest whiff of anything, and that turned out to be emanating from my wet socks.

"Nice place," I said for openers, glancing around. The white–on–white kitchen was flanked by a small informal eating nook and the cozy family room, where we were seated.

"It's bigger than we need," she answered, "but we got a good deal on it."

"Lucky."

She scoffed. "Luck has nothing to do with it. It's all a matter of timing."

There was a television on the breakfast bar, tuned to one of those cable channels that give constant stock market updates in a crawl at the bottom of the screen. The program itself featured two guys in thousand dollar suits and hundred dollar haircuts complaining that the "liberals" in Washington were taxing them into the poorhouse. Marion Koon muted it with a flick of the remote next to her chair, a move that reminded me of Delia Hemford. I doubt either woman would be flattered by the comparison.

"What's this about, Mr. Hackshaw?"

I had a feeling she knew, but I told her anyway. "Your former tenant at your Bing Road property, Edgar Williamson."

"He was Edwin Smith, as far as we ever knew. Bud and I were shocked, just amazed, when the police came by to tell us who he really was." She looked away, miffed at the memory. "It was humiliating, having that big sheriff's investigator come to our door like that, throwing his weight around, questioning us almost as if we were criminals ourselves. I'll tell you what's criminal; to think we pay our hard–earned taxes to pay the salaries of oafs like him."

It was good to know Stoneman wasn't a bull only when he was in my china shop. "I'm sure he wasn't accusing you and your husband of anything."

"He hadn't better! We're always very careful about who we rent to, but these things do happen. Mr. Smith—or Williamson, I suppose—was clean–cut, well–spoken, no pets. He even provided references when we asked."

"Did you check them out? The references?"

"No, we didn't." Her hands flapped. "There didn't seem to be any point at the time. The mere fact he provided them was enough, or so we thought. And when we insisted on first month's rent in advance and a security deposit, he paid in full. In cash."

Con men are nothing if not experts in human nature.

"Would you still have the references on hand?"

"I had them written down, but that policeman took them the other day." Her natural frown found new depths. "Why is any of this important now? I hope you're not thinking of doing any more articles for your paper, Mr. Hackshaw. It's been embarrassing enough as it is."

I let that one go by, mainly because I wasn't sure myself what I had in mind on that score. "I understand he had a woman traveling with him at times. Young, dark, pretty."

"There was no woman living with him at our property, that much I know. In fact, it appears he wasn't even living there himself, so you see, we're hardly connected to this man at all. He rented a house from us, but never actually moved in. There's really nothing more to it than that."

"Except for murder."

It was a bit melodramatic, admittedly, but I was getting sick of hearing Mrs. Koon judge everything I said by its potential to embarrass her and her husband. But that didn't stop her from doing it again.

Very measuredly, she said, "I feel sorry about Mr. Smith's—Mr. *Williamson's* death. I was sorry when I heard he had a fatal accident, and I was just as sorry to hear it may not have been an accident after all. But what I'm saying is I don't see what it has to do with us. All we did was rent a piece of property. Oh!"

The minor exclamation was for a sudden low whirring noise from somewhere beyond the eating nook; an electric garage door opener, as it turned out. Bud Koon appeared momentarily through a side door, tall and slim and brown going prematurely gray, wearing a good old Republican cloth coat and one of those woolly caps that don't even look good on Russians. He removed both and stuck them in a closet by the door before saying anything.

"What are you doing here?"

People are always so glad to see me, have you noticed? I like to think it's the nature of the news business and nothing personal. Denial, they call it.

Anyway, I was about to answer his query in detail, but Marion did the honors instead, scurrying over beside her husband and mumbling into his ear like the defendant at a trial explaining to her attorney some piece of damning evidence. He responded with lots of stern nodding.

"It sounds as if you've had your questions answered, Hackshaw, and we have plans, so—"

"I only have one or two more." I climbed up from the rattan sofa and shoved my hands into my coat pockets. "Did Williamson ever try to entice you folks with one of his get–rich schemes?"

Koon was an even better scoffer than his wife. "Of course not. That's ridiculous."

"Why? Didn't he—as Edwin Smith—claim to be an investment adviser of some sort?"

"He told me he was a financial planner with IDS, but, of course, he wasn't really."

"But you didn't know that at the time."

"It wouldn't have made any difference. We're experienced investors ourselves, Hackshaw. We have a broker at Bache who places trades for us, but we do our own research and analysis." He came as close to a smile as he was ever apt to. "We're a little beyond needing IRA advice from a financial planner."

"So you never discussed any investments."

"We never discussed anything beyond rental terms. Now, I'm going to have to insist you—"

"One more and I'm gone for good. Have you heard from anyone yet who may've been tricked by Williamson into putting a deposit down on your Bing Road place?" The simultaneous glances they gave each other were answer enough for me. "Because I'd like to talk to anyone who's been victimized by—"

"I can't help you. We've heard from a couple of people who claim to have paid down payments to Williamson, and one has threatened to take us to Small Claims Court, even though we're in no way responsible. Our lawyer has advised us not to talk to anyone about the matter."

I gave it up then, as happy to be getting out of there as they were to see me go. They watched in silence as I struggled into my boots in the vestibule. Just before I pulled open the door, Koon held a stiff index finger in front of my face.

"Something I hope you'll keep in mind, Hackshaw," he said. "We're victims in all this, too. Our good name means everything to us and it's already been besmirched. If I read one libelous word about us in that penny saver of yours, I'll sue. I promise you I'm just the man to do it."

He'd get no argument from me on that last part.

CHAPTER 11

If I was a building, they'd tear me down.

That's how I felt, trying to dig myself out of the mattress to get rid of whichever idiot was pounding a tattoo on my front door.

Never mind that it was already after nine and I needed to get up anyway if I was going to drive all the way to Niagara Falls and back. The intruder below didn't know that and was therefore just making a thoughtless nuisance of himself, waking up a person who was almost near death at what was almost the crack of dawn on a Saturday morning.

It's disgusting, the way some people think only of themselves.

The hammering told me it was a man's fist at work rather than the insistent rat–a–tat of female knuckles. This I verified when I shoved open the kitchen window; he was standing on the stoop a story below me, wearing jeans and a ski jacket but hatless. I didn't recognize the little bald spot.

I said, "*What*?"

"It's me, Hackshaw—Web Tice."

I could see that, now that he was staring up at me. Webster Tice owns one of Kirkville's few small manufacturing companies, an outfit called CLF Inc., which stands for Custom Leather something–or–other. They make up leather upholstery, mostly as an independent supplier for one of the big three automakers, as I understand. What I didn't understand was what Tice and his fancy GM four–by–four were doing at my carriage house, this or any other morning.

"I tried calling half a dozen times yesterday, but you weren't here or at your office. You should get an answering machine."

I should get an unlisted phone number. "What d'ya want anyway?"

"Can I come up? I have a job proposal to discuss with you, some renovation work on my house."

"*Your* house?"

"Yes."

That made very little sense to me, but then not much does before I've had my caffeine transfusions. I told him to come on in, it wasn't locked, and while he was clomping up the stairs, I got the coffeemaker loaded. Tice wanted to jabber the moment he came through the door, but I made him wait, quietly, in the living area until I could shower and shave and ease myself into a pair of comfortable corduroys and a bulky sweater. Then I made him wait a little longer, three swallows worth.

I sighed as I lowered the mug from my lips. "Now. Why would you be doing renovation work on your house? It's only, what, five years old?"

"Six. But there are some changes I've been wanting to make, things I'm not satisfied with."

"Such as?"

"Well," Tice put his mug on the wicker table between us and massaged the side of his jaw. He was around forty and medium height, with sandy hair and large light blue eyes that always seemed on the verge of tears. "First I thought I'd like to build a kind of a solarium off the back, something for year–round use. A passive solar thing. And I'm also thinking of adding a lot of new trim in several of the main rooms, maybe crown moldings for the living room and library, some oak paneling and ceiling beams in the dining room. Make the formal rooms a little more...formal."

I blinked. He was hoping to make a silk purse out of a sow's ear, but it was much too late for that. Tice's house, frankly, looks like it had been designed on the back of a cocktail napkin at the country club, which probably isn't far from the truth. Oh, it's huge, and hugely expensive, but it's also graceless and ugly and eclectic in the worst ways; sprawling across the site, one–story at the ends and two–story in the middle, constructed all of dark brown brick with tinted casement windows that screamed suburban professional office building. The clashing rooflines went from gables on two wings to hipped on the two–story section to a shed roof over the attached four car garage. I shuddered to think what the inside was like.

It reminded me in some ways of the ostentatious manor houses that many nouveau riche Brits built for themselves in the nineteenth century; cold, square, brutish expressions of power and wealth in which egos overruled architects.

I said, "I don't think I'm the man for the job. I do Victorian restorations, for the most part—"

"I know, I know. What you did with the main house here is fantastic. I remember when it was a tumbled down rooming house."

He was talking about the picture–perfect Victorian Stick that shared the corner lot with my carriage house. I own both, although the bank would argue otherwise. You might say I got carried away when I restored the place to its original charms. That's the reason I live in the former servant's apartment above the three–bay carriage house and rent out the main house to the Johnsons, a pair of retired teachers: it's the only way I can afford the mortgage payments.

"Tell you what, Hackshaw," Tice said. "Come over, let me walk you through the place. I'll pay you a consultant's fee just to look things over, give me your best advice on what can or can't be done to give the place a boost."

It sounded hopeless, but I liked the part about a consultant's fee. God knows, Webster Tice could afford to throw his money away; he'd already proved that.

"I'm busy today," I said finally. "But maybe tomorrow sometime."

❦ ❦ ❦

I took the old roads west, undulating two–laners that snaked through snowy fields and thick woodlands, in and out of farming hamlets like Clarendon and Erie Canal villages like Middleport and Lockport. Traffic was light and the day was sunny and about as warm as could be expected for January. Still it was a seventy–five mile drive, and one I would've preferred not to make even if I wasn't aching from my soles to my sinuses.

The name and address Drummond the undertaker had supplied belonged to, of all things, a Niagara Falls cop named Elgin Hazard. I called him around five Friday afternoon, right after getting home from the Koon's house. I tried to get him to answer my questions over the phone, but he resisted. If I wanted to talk about Slow Eddie Williamson, Hazard told me, I'd have to do it on his terms and on his turf. I didn't have any leverage, so I agreed to meet in his office at noon, and I was running late.

Armies of giant power line towers and the decaying hulks of rust belt factories surrounded me as I entered the city from the northeast, one eye on the directions I'd been given. The police shared space with other municipal departments in the Niagara Falls Public Safety Building on Hyde Park Boulevard. The building was maybe thirty years old and not aging well, a squat two–story concoction of extruded aluminum and green mirrored glass and, as Tom Wolfe described them in *From Bauhaus to Our House*, "those little beige bricks."

Remind me some time to explain about Walter Gropius and Mies van der Rohe and the sterile International Style they championed; why it's to blame for the uniform blandness of so many of the schools and office highrises and public buildings erected in this country over the past sixty years. It's just one more atrocity to lay on Adolph Hitler, really, for scaring the minimalist crowd out of Europe and onto our shores in the first place, but don't get me started.

A uniform ensconced behind a thick sheet of Plexiglass directed me down a narrow corridor of flush doors. Hazard's was the fourth on the left.

"You Hackshaw?"

He was behind a tiny desk in the tiny office, or maybe everything just looked Lilliputian compared to him. He was big, bigger even than Buddy McCabe, and just as black.

"Me Hackshaw. Sorry I'm a little late."

"I had to be here anyway." He indicated the messy desktop—"Paper work."—and then a molded plastic chair. "Have a seat."

While I settled in, Hazard brooded awhile, studying me. "You don't look especially crafty to me."

"You've been checking up on me."

"A couple of calls. I like to know who I'm dealing with before I start handing out information and quotes."

"Don't believe everything you hear, Sergeant."

"After seventeen years in this place, I don't believe half what I hear from anybody." He followed up with a sardonic smile. "Just so you know, I don't particularly give a shit what happened to Eddie Williamson, long as it didn't happen on my beat. And I sure don't care what gets written up about the case in some small–town weekly two counties east of here, okay?"

"Gotcha." If he wanted to think my interest was purely journalistic, fine with me.

"So ask your questions."

I took out pad and pen. "If you don't have any interest in Williamson, why'd you have his body shipped to you?"

"I did it as a favor for his brother, Pete." He flexed a shoulder. "There was a little red tape, clearances needed from the sheriff's office at your end. I said I'd handle it, is all."

"You're a friend of the family?"

He laughed. "I've arrested the two of `em so many times, it almost seems that way."

His eyes went off me and searched the middle distance for a moment, looking for a starting point.

"I work bunco, okay? Which is one of the only growth industries we got left in this burg. Most police departments don't even bother much anymore with the stuff I'm talking about, the pickpockets and flimflams. It just ain't a cost–effective use of manpower when you got violent crime going up. But around here we got grifters comin' out our ears during the high season and it still pays to try and keep `em under control. Millions of tourists still come to Niagara Falls every year, Hackshaw, and it's getting more so since the Canadians opened that big casino on their side. But we get our share of rubber-neckers, too, lots of `em foreigners who don't speak the language too good or starry–eyed honeymooners or old folks who believe any-thing a good–lookin', smooth–talkin' white boy tells `em. That's where Slow Eddie comes in, and his little brother Pete, too. Until recently, anyway."

I told him I was still trying to figure out where he came in.

"I sent Pete up three years ago on a forged instruments rap, pho-nying personal checks and credit card charges. Eddie was in on it, too, but we couldn't prove it. Anyway, Pete did eighteen months and came back out with a new attitude. He came by to see me, said he was done with Eddie and scamming. He had a legit job already lined up, part of his parole requirement, but he'd been into photography most of his life—used to make up fake licenses and IDs and shit for him and Eddie—and he wanted to take on some freelance work. I've been able to get him some assignments for the department here and with a couple insurance outfits. He does a lot of weddings, too, and he's been doing all right with it. We still get a lot of weddings in this town."

It appeared the hard–bitten cop might have false teeth. "Why'd you decide to help Pete?"

"Because it was better than having him back on my caseload. And because I figured Pete just might have it in him to go straight. Eddie was a different story." He consulted infinity again, then went on. "Pete's three years younger than Eddie, always tried to be like his big brother, right down to the way he walked and dressed. From twenty feet, you couldn't tell one from the other, but close up you could always see the difference. Slow Eddie had a hardness underneath the polish, a cold cynicism that'd seep out through his eyes. Pete never had that."

"Why was he called Slow Eddie?"

"His style, the way he talked when he was working a con. He never went for the mile–a–minute hard sell like most of these punks. Eddie'd play a mark like one of those late–night FM deejays, super cool, laid–back, no pressure. Until it was time for the blow–off, when he'd squeezed all he could outa the sucker and it was time to split."

Hazard told me that the Williamson family, of which Pete and Eddie were the last of the line, had a long tradition as bunco artists; practitioners of so–called short cons using one or two accomplices and with little advance preparation. Playing off the wall, as it was known among grifters. The gold brick game, the smack, the hidden value scam and half a dozen other classic cons designed to separate the greedy and the gullible from their money as quickly and as cleanly as possible.

"The back of the truck game was one Eddie used to work regularly, back before he started shootin' for bigger payoffs," the sergeant told me. "What you do, you show up at some busy spot—noon hour in a business district is always good—and you pop open the back of your truck or the trunk of your car. You start offering passersby your wares—expensive watches, gold jewelry—and the key thing is you're real nervous about it. You wanna make a sale and get outa there and you're willing to take any decent offers, right?" He chuckled, more a mirthless growl. "Only the nervous bit is just for the chumps, so they'll think you're selling hot goods dirt cheap. The truth is that Rolex you're offering up for fifty dollars is a worthless Chinese fake you bought by the gross for a few bucks apiece."

I made some notes because it was expected, then asked what he meant by bigger payoffs.

"Stuff that took a little more planning and research, is all. I'm not talkin' *The Sting* here, but I hear Eddie had pretty much moved on from the slash–and–burn tactics of the street to slightly bigger cons. Set–ups. I couldn't really say what he was into lately. The last time I nailed him on anything was like six, seven years back, workin' the obit con here in Niagara Falls and down in North Tonawanda."

That caught my attention. "How's that one go?" I thought I knew, but it never hurts to ask an expert.

It was beautifully simple, as Hazard described it, provided you weren't burdened with a conscience. You check the obituaries and death notices, then show up on the grieving widow's doorstep in whatever passes as a delivery man's uniform, a wrapped package under one arm and a clipboard (*ah–hah*) under the other. A C.O.D. for John Jones, you say. He's just died, says Mrs. Jones. Sorry to hear that, ma'am, but what should I do with this (fill–in the blank: inscribed Bible, anniversary ring, limited–edition commemorative plate) he special ordered for, let's see here—a Jane Jones. That wouldn't happen to be you, would it, ma'am?

Naturally, poor, vulnerable Mrs. Jones is touched and runs to get her purse. Later, when the `delivery man' is gone and the box is opened, she finds it's stuffed with old newspapers and a rock to give it heft.

"Did he ever work with a woman partner?"

Another lazy shrug. "It wouldn't surpise me. A woman, something young and pretty, comes in real handy for stuff like the old badger game, or the Spanish prisoner, that's a classic."

I knew about the former—boy meets girl, girl suggests they go to her place, boy gets half undressed, raging `husband' bursts in and demands satisfaction, which turns out to be all the cash boy can come up with in a hurry—but before I could ask to be enlightened on the Spanish prisoner, Hazard had a question of his own.

"You have any particular woman in mind, Hackshaw?"

That's when I told him about the gypsies, or what little I knew myself. He listened patiently, his expression moving through various phases of amusement. When I finished, he got up abruptly, told me to wait, and left the office. Maybe five dull minutes later he returned and handed me two sets of mug shots, profile and full–face.

The fullest face belonged to a scowling fat man I knew as Stavo.

The other to a beautiful young brunette, her mysterious dark eyes smoldering like a Romanian campfire.

"Bingo?" Hazard asked.

I shook my head. "Bimbo."

CHAPTER 12

"Congratulations, Hackshaw. You've managed to piss off one of the nastiest gypsy clans in the state."

Just what I needed to hear, although my battered body already had a sneaking suspicion. Hazard took back the mug shots and held them up one at a time like flashcards.

"Stavo Wanka, age 52, 57, or 58, take your pick of birth dates. Baro of the Wanka clan, which means leader or chief. Basically Stavo sits around on his fat ass, laying bets at OTB when he isn't busy counting the money the women bring in from welfare fraud and fortune telling and every kind of swindle known to man."

Down went that photo set, up came the other.

"Bimbo Wanka, believed to be 21. Daughter of Stavo and Mary Wanka, who's also known as Queen Mary and Mother Sacajewea."

A chuckle escaped me at that last bit.

"I'm serious," Hazard said. "Mary was the queen of the boojo in her heyday. Boojo, that's what the gypsies call the old Jamaican switch. Used to pass herself off as an Indian mystic, could tell your fortune, cure you of evil spirits and bad luck. The suckers'd whine about how miserable their lives were, she'd tell `em the problem was their money was cursed and had to be blessed or cleansed. They'd bring in their life savings and hand it over and that'd be the last time they saw their money or Mary Wanka."

"How can people be so foolish?"

"We're talking about the same kinda folks go to palm readers and astrologers and faith healers. Once you get `em in the door, *wanting* to believe you've got the answers for `em, hell, the rest is just technique. The way Mary worked, she'd give the mark the spiel about their money being cursed, okay? Then she'd say `Gimme a ten dollar bill.' When they give, she wraps it up inside a handkerchief, says some mumbo–jumbo over it, and hands it back. `Sleep on the handkerchief, unopened, for three nights', she tells the mark, `and if the cure is working, your money will be doubled.' What the marks don't know is that Mary has already palmed their ten and replaced it with a twenty. So when they finally open the handkerchief in three days, they're hooked like a trout. Can't wait for Mother Sacajawea to do a miracle on the rest of their dough."

"What happens when they realize they've been swindled? Can't you make an arrest, get their money back?"

"Jesus, how small is that town you come from, man? It's the mark's word against Mary—and as many of her relatives as she wants to bring in to say how innocent she is, how the cops cooked up the whole thing to persecute a poor gypsy, yadda, yadda, yadda. You ain't heard wailin' till you get a room full of gyps tryin' to beat a rap." He shunted the photos aside and rested his arms on the desk. "And that's if the mark reports anything at all. Some are too embarrassed to come forward and a few—the terminally dumb ones—don't even realize they've been swindled, like if Mary pulls off a successful burn–up."

I hated confirming his opinion of me as a hopeless rube, but I had to ask. "What's a burn–up?"

"She gets a real gullible mark, she'll tell `em the curse is just too strong and the only thing to do with all that evil money is to burn it up. She pretends to wrap it up again—pulling a switch, naturally, for cut–up newspaper—and then she burns up the dummy wad in front of the mark, right there in the ofisa—that's what they call these hole–in–the–wall storefronts they operate from."

I had by this time taken the dual mug shots of Bimbo Wanka from the desk and was staring at the profile. "Where does this one figure into the mix?"

"Right in the middle, knowing her. Social Services put me onto Bimbo's tail the first time about four years back, for welfare fraud. That didn't stick, but I got her into court once for dipping—that's pickpocketing, to you." He frowned. "Judge let her go for a fine and a reprimand."

"Like sending a Hell's Angel to his room."

"Mm. So, you say Slow Eddie Williamson and Bimbo Wanka were doin' the wild thing together, huh? `Magine that. Stavo must've been climbing the walls, his daughter takin' up with a gadjo. Gypsies, they don't take to outsiders."

"So I've heard," I said. "I guess it's a predictable reaction, considering. Slob or not, every father has a soft spot for his little girl."

"Hah! Stavo Wanka's got plenty of soft spots, Hackshaw, but his heart ain't one of `em. His head neither. He's looking to get Bimbo back because she's one of his best meal tickets. He's probably grooming her to take over for Queen Mary. It's either that, or he's got a marriage contract lined up for her."

"Bimbo's supposedly already married to this guy named Toma," I reminded him.

"Yeah, that's probably true, given her age. The old man would've sold her long before she turned 21."

"*Sold?*"

"For big bucks, with her looks and talent. But we might not have a record of it; gypsies usually marry in their own ceremonies, not bothering with licenses." He got up and left the room again, returning in under two minutes this time. "Toma Kurts sounds like our man, although I wouldn't swear to that surname; they change last names the way the rest of us change our socks. He's thirty–six, been pinched locally on minor fraud beefs a couple times, blacktopping driveways with old crankcase oil and shit like that." He held up the sheet he was reading from, showing me a pair of mug shots stapled to the corner. "That the guy?"

I'd never forget that lizard–eyed face. "That's him."

"Well, like I say, I don't have much on him. If he's running with the Wankas and married to Bimbo, you can figure he's got some status. Or it could be his family paid a lot for the girl and wants either her or their dough back"

"Bad enough to kill?"

"That's the sixty–four–thousand dollar question, isn't it. I'm glad I don't have to figure out the answer. And in case you've got any ideas, my advice is to stay the hell away from the lot of `em."

"That's what I intend to do, if they'll only oblige. I take it the clan lives right around here some place?"

Hazard was nodding. "I couldn't give you an exact address at the moment—they move around a lot, depending on the season, but the Wanka clan always ends up back here part of the year. See, gypsies traditionally like to stay near an international border, the better to jump jurisdictions whenever there's too much heat—there's three bridges into Canada within five miles of here. And they like to work carnivals, amusement parks, any place you find tourists. You factor in that new Canadian casino, it makes Niagara Falls a regular Mecca, and not just for them, but for all kinds of grifters. The Wankas and the Williamsons are just the tip of the iceberg, believe me."

The sergeant had been looking furtively toward his crowded in–basket for the past several minutes and I decided it was time to take the hint. One last question, I said.

"How do I find Pete Williamson?"

* * *

Main Street in Niagara Falls looks like too many other main drags in too many other small American cities, which is to say neglected, tired, passed by. Most of the buildings are either grand old piles needing TLC or newish prefabs built on the cheap. The church Hazard had sent me to belonged in the first category.

The ceremony was still going on when I arrived, so I slipped my aching bones into a back pew next to a large matron in a pink Jackie Kennedy pillbox, who was honking as demurely as possible into a tissue.

She noticed me noticing and whispered sheepishly, "I just can't help myself, I always cry at weddings."

I cry when I get the invitation. Do you have any idea how much they're getting for a toaster these days? "A beautiful tradition, isn't it?" I told her.

Up front, the clergyman finished the vows, the blissful couple kissed, and a final blessing was intoned. Bride and groom did a reasonable about–face and marched back up the aisle, she glittering in a white gown with daring decolletage, he smiling tightly and scanning the crowd for a rough envelope count. A lovely pair, I couldn't help but notice, and the groom wasn't bad looking, either.

I waited out my man on the sidewalk at the bottom of the stone steps in front of the church. The camera equipment and all the contortions he was doing around the wedding party gave him away, but I would've known him anyway; he looked just like the guy in the picture I'd discovered in Eddie Williamson's junk drawer; all but the eyes.

He had me figured, too.

I caught up to him as he was loading his equipment into a dented Plymouth Horizon, the limo carrying the newlyweds having just driven off into the fragile sunshine. He sized me up with a casual glance and said, "You're the reporter Elgin called me about this morning, right?"

"Hackshaw." I shook the hand he offered. "I was hoping to talk to you for a few minutes. About Edgar."

He had shrugged into a long overcoat, the collar turned up against what was still a penetrating breeze, sun or no. Maybe that's what accounted for the slight tremor of his cheeks and jaw.

"I guess we could do that," he said after a moment. "I've got to rush over to the Wintergarden right now—more shots of the wedding party. Shouldn't take more than twenty minutes—you can come watch, if you want—and after that I've got about an hour and a half before the reception. There's a coffee shop in the hotel kitty–corner to the convention center."

He gave me directions and I helped him hoist the last camera bag into the back of the Horizon.

"I understand there's lots of weddings held here," I said, ice breaking. "You must stay busy."

"Yeah." His eyes drifted heavenward. "Sometimes I think if I hear Corinthians 13 one more time or *Alla Hornpipe* bellowing from a pipe organ, I swear I'll grab an assault rifle and climb the carillon."

For some reason, I liked him immediately.

* * *

"I just got sick and tired of the life, even before they put me away that last stretch. I'd never done any serious time before that and I don't plan to do any more."

Pete Williamson inhaled the last quarter inch of his cigarette and snubbed the butt into an ashtray. I took another grateful swallow of my hot chocolate.

It was more like forty minutes, but we had eventually made it over to the hotel coffee shop. The Wintergarden turned out to be a giant conservatory abutted to a small shopping center at the foot of Main; a soaring, angular glass house inside of which flourished tropical plants, ponds, even small waterfalls for those too lazy or jaded or, I suppose, warm–blooded to walk a few hundred yards to view the real thing.

I decided to brave the elements as long as I was there, and walked down to the Falls—capital F, to be sure—while Pete was delayed with the bridesmaids, whose collective mascara had run enroute in the teary cold, and the father of the bride, whose only resemblance to Spencer Tracy *or* Steve Martin was his unbridled anxiety. The rumbling rush of the Niagara River was as I remembered it from summer visits, but the look was different in winter; the ever–rising mists were luminous with hovering ice crystals and, far below the observation platform, the rocks and trees were coated with a frozen spray and great flowing mounds of white ice had formed a natural bridge between the American side and Canada's majestic Horseshoe Falls. The tourists, a surprising number given the season and the windchill, were mostly Asians, their teeth chattering in a dozen different languages. I shot some video footage for a smiling family of Japanese, thinking as I did so how trusting they were, how easy it would've been to distract them long enough to run off with Papa–san's pricey Sony camcorder.

They say it's the company you keep.

"Eddie, he was—" Pete sighed, wistful–cum–melancholy. "—I guess you'd say married to the life. He always figured there's three kinds of people; players, marks, and cops. See, he was raised to believe that if some chump could be duped out of his money, he deserved to be. I was, too. Like some kids come from a long line of bankers or lawyers and such, our family's been on the con since as far back as anybody could remember. We were the last, Eddie and me. And now it's just me."

It seemed a good time to remind him he was no longer on the con, just in case he was thinking of backsliding. "Speaking of cops, Sergeant Hazard really looks out for you."

"Yeah." He mulled it over for a few seconds while he nursed his coffee, then allowed himself a small, self–conscious smile. "I think we give each other hope."

Like his brother, he was tall, slender and blond, with only a hint of thinning hair above the temples. The color of the eyes was the same, too—gray-blue—but, as noted, the younger Williamson's lacked the merciless intensity I'd detected in Slow Eddie's photo. I'd already explained in diluted form my own posthumous connections to Eddie, and Pete had seemed to accept what I told him with the equanimity of one for whom life's ironies held few surprises. I wanted to know if he could tell me what Eddie and Bimbo Stavo were doing in Kirkville; what they had up their sleeves, besides selling phony shares in a riverboat gambling scheme or collecting rents on a house they didn't own. And what could possibly have gone so wrong that Eddie had wound up dead and Bimbo missing.

Pete had quite a bit to say on the subject of his brother but, boiled down, he didn't know what Eddie had been up to, either.

"But I'd be surprised if it wasn't just the same old bullshit. The yack—the phone con—and the rental scam, that'd fit Eddie's profile. Only this time something musta gone really sour before he could cop a heel. You gotta understand, Hackshaw, everybody's always talking about the big con, the million–dollar swindle. But it's like anybody else, a fishing nut dreaming about landing a record marlin off the Florida Keys, or a kid in a garage band landing a major record deal. People talk about it, yeah, but very few ever go for it, and even fewer ever succeed."

"Your brother was basically a small–timer, is what you're telling me, and was likely to stay that way."

"I'm not putting him down, it's just the way it was. Always was for us." He lit a new smoke. "If I could tell you something that'd help nail whoever did Eddie, I would. I mean, you make your play and you take your risks, but nothing Eddie ever did or ever would do deserved getting him killed, I'm sure of that."

"Maybe he'd changed," I suggested. "A man's been known to do some foolish things to impress a pretty young woman. If he was desperate to keep her—"

Pete laughed. "A woman might be able to drive you or me to do something we didn't wanna do, but not Eddie. Uh–uh. Sentiment, romance, whatever you wanna call it, big brother didn't believe in it. Sex, yes. A pretty young thing to rope for him, help him run his games, yeah. Beyond that, Eddie was the perfect lone wolf." He tried his coffee again. "Funny thing is, I introduced `em."

The previous autumn, he told me. Pete was working his day job at the time, clerking at a camera shop up the block from where we were sitting. Bimbo came in and tried to flim–flam him, making a small purchase and paying with a twenty, then asking for her change in various denominations in hopes of confusing him and walking away with her original twenty and another fifteen or sixteen dollars profit.

"She was damn good, I'll say that. She just picked the wrong mark. And when I finally called her on it, she just smiled as big as you've ever seen. You can bet that smile got her out of more than one jam."

They ended up having dinner together, and one more date after that. She was attractive, lively, funny, Pete said, and they had a lot in common. And that's what worried him.

"I liked her, but it was like a reformed drunk hangin' around saloons, y'know? She told me she wanted to get out of the life herself, but Bimbo's real good at tellin' people what she thinks they wanna hear. Anyway, Eddie and her both showed up at the photo shop one day, and I did the introduction bit, and it was like two peas in a pod. They started up together then and there."

"You weren't the least bit bitter?"

"Relieved is more like it. You know why they were at the shop that day? They both wanted to bum money off me."

"I was wondering. That photo of the two of them—"

He nodded. "I took it. With a little Canon 35 I keep in the car, in case I get a quick assignment from the PD or an insurance deal. That's the last time I saw either of them, a couple weeks before Thanksgiving. We made some noise about gettin' together over the holidays, but that was just talk. I knew Eddie'd be working some kind of play somewhere—folks get real sentimental around Christmas time and that makes them vulnerable." He shook his head ruefully, then added, "Truth is, it's just as much my fault we didn't connect. Keeping my distance from Eddie was about the best way I had of keeping straight."

Until Sergeant Hazard had called him about his brother's death, Pete hadn't even known he was in Kirkville. It was beginning to look as if the girl was the only person who could shed any light on Slow Eddie's demise. "You have any idea what could've become of Bimbo? Where she might go?"

"None. If she didn't go back to her family, my guess is she found someone to take her in. Another man, most likely."

"Maybe I'm overlooking the obvious. I mean, could it be Bimbo made herself scarce because *she* murdered Eddie?"

He thought it over, but not for long. "Anything's possible, but I really can't see her killing a man, not in cold blood," he said. "On the other hand, she wouldn't think twice about robbing the corpse."

CHAPTER 13

❀

"If you ass me, they should throw all those bums in jail until they rot."

"I wouldn't ass you if you were the last man on the cell block."

"Whaddya mean, ass me? You some kinda homo or somethin'?"

"It's a joke. You said `if you *ass* me' instead of `if you *ask* me.'"

"Hell I did."

"Hell you didn't. Didn't he, Hack?"

"I'll thank you to leave me out of this." I placed my glass of Twelve Horse precisely in the center of its little cardboard coaster, just to reassure myself I could.

"This", in its broader context, was what's become known as male bonding, but was in truth a handful of men sitting around a bar, drinking too much beer and waxing stupid. Philosophical, in my case.

I gave Tony Ioletta the squint eye. "Because if I ventured a comment of any kind, it would concern homophobia, Freudian slips, and the fact you just used `ass' and `bums' in the same sentence."

"I never said `ass'. Anyway, so what if I did?"

Lou Edelman grinned viciously. "He means you're suppressing homosexual impulses. Right, Hack?"

I was pleased one of us thought he knew what I was talking about, but not pleased enough to engage.

"I told you to leave me out of this discussion."

Women do the same thing, only with pina coladas; if their husbands should ask, they call it networking.

It was nearly midnight and we were down to three. We'd started the evening as a foursome, pairing off for euchre at one of the back tables while the Saturday night crowd swirled and ebbed and flowed past. Sometime around eleven, Dwight Philby had abruptly excused himself, mumbling he had to get up early to drive his mother to church. The guffaws from the rest of us increased in intensity when Lou Edelman pointed out that Melanie, the chunky waitress who worked the diner half of Norb's Nook, had retired her apron for the evening and was tapping a sneaker–clad toe near the front door. When she and Dwight exited not quite at the same instant, we were left to playing a few hands of cutthroat gin until Lou and I had cornered the market on Ioletta futures, at which point we adjourned to the bar to buy Tony a drink with his former money.

"All I was tryin' to say, f'chrissake, is anybody swindles old ladies deserves whatever they get. Somebody gassed that bastard Hackshaw wrote up in his paper, they should get a medal."

"Damn straight." That came from a soggy geezer two stools removed, who'd been trying to put his opinions in play for the past half hour. We continued to ignore him.

"You think what this Slow Eddie guy was up to was bad," Lou said, leaning over and lowering his voice so only half the bar could hear, "you know what Fritz Kohl told me?" Kohl is a lineman for Rochester Gas & Electric and a neighbor of Edelman's over in Port Erie. "Some guy dressed like a meter reader got into this fella's house a few days ago, right? He's got the blue hard hat, the blue work shirt with the company logo on the pocket—everything. Only once he's inside, he pulls a gun and ties up the guy and robs the place. RG&E's had to pull all its meter readers until the cops get a line on the bastard, Fritz says. Hell of a thing, with all the kilowatts people're burning up with all this cold weather."

"Television," Tony said emphatically into his glass.

"What?"

"Kids sit around watching all that violent crap on TV and their parents let `em. Then they wonder why little Johnny ends up stickin' up banks."

"You figure Jesse James watched a lot of TV, do you, Tone?"

I hadn't wanted to talk about, or think about, Slow Eddie Williamson in the first place. It was Dwight who had blabbed between euchre hands. I suppose he figured that since we were glibly solving all the world's other problems, we might as well take a flier at Hackshaw's latest aggravation. Booze makes us so wise, it's a wonder alcoholics aren't in charge of everything.

Buddy McCabe glided down the bar with his damp rag and volunteered a minority opinion.

"The problem is, crooks like this Williamson dude didn't grow up playin' sports. Or if they did, they didn't play team sports like football and basketball, they went in for individual stuff like tennis and golf."

"Hah!" Ioletta said, knowing Edelman was an avid linkster. "Now, golf, there's a game for homos."

"Bullshit."

"Lou's right, Tony," I said. "No self–respecting gay man would wear the clothes."

Buddy wasn't ready to yield the floor. He'd been a college football player himself until his knees went south on him and he never missed a chance to confuse real life with athletics. "I'm talkin' about teamwork, learnin' to cooperate with other people."

"Sharing your toys?"

"Go ahead and laugh."

We did, convincing Buddy to give up and do his job. His oversized index finger traced a circle in the airspace above our glasses. "Another round, gentlemen?"

Lou and I were both driving and, after a second's hesitation, decided large mugs of the alleged coffee Buddy keeps warming behind the bar would be in order, heavy on the cream and sugar. Tony, who was riding with Lou, stuck with Budweiser. They both finished ahead of me and, with slaps on the back my battered body didn't need, said their goodnights and departed. I took the warmup Buddy offered and sat there all on my lonely for a while, trying my best not to think about the Williamson mess and thinking about it anyway. It was the reason I'd ended up on a bar stool Saturday night instead of home where I belonged, resting bruises both physical and psychological; laying awake staring at the ceiling was even worse.

In case you're wondering, I doubt Slow Eddie was the phony RG&E man Lou mentioned. Even if Williamson hadn't already been dead before the incident occurred, guns didn't sound like his methodology and anyway, the hard hat Dwight had found in the trunk of the Mercury was white.

So armed home invasion was probably out. But it remained a very high possibility that *some* con Williamson had been working had backfired, leading to his death.

The other likely scenario, of course, was that Stavo's bunch had killed Williamson in retaliation for running off with Bimbo. Another reason sleep proved elusive; the recurring nightmare of Toma Kurtz stuffing me/Williamson into an idling Jeep/Mercury, then running a piece of drain hose from the exhaust pipe to one of the windows.

I took another sip and grimaced. Buddy saw and came grinning back.

"How's the coffee, Hack?"

"It should come with a dipstick and a viscosity rating."

"That's the idea—sober everybody up for happy motoring." His ebony face turned sober as well. "Tell you the truth, man, you don't look so hot, and I don't think the ale is what's ailin' you. Stoneman's not still tryin' to jack you up over this dead con man, is he?"

"Who knows?" That bothered me, too; Stoneman letting me walk on the supposed B&E at the Bing Road rental house. Normally he would've run me through the system, even if he knew a charge wouldn't stick. The sheer joy of harassment is what some of these tin flashers live for, after all. But he didn't, and that had me wondering. Could it be he knew about the girl, missing but presumed knowledgeable? And if he did, had he done the math; take one mysterious gypsy beauty, add one local newsie with a reputation for doomed romantic entanglements and hope it adds up to a pair? Let me run and hope I run straight to Williamson's missing girlfriend, was that the game?

"Let me ask you one," I said to Buddy, then described Bimbo Wanka. "You haven't seen or heard anything about a woman like that, I suppose?"

"Only in my dreams."

The guzzling geezer to my left added, "You and me both, brother." Like half the men in the place, his hair was pushed up on top and mushed down on the sides from wearing a knit watch cap too tight. When the temperature drops, fashion is the first casualty.

"So what's this babe got to do with anything?" Buddy wanted to know.

"I'll ask her if she turns up."

He gave me the standard you're–your–own–worst–enemy disclaimer, then went to fetch the geezer a new vodka. I decided to pack it in, but before the thought could work its way from my brain to my legs, an ill wind snuck in through the taproom's side door, blowing with it a trio of Darth Vadar wannabees.

That was the impression, anyway. Three figures in various sizes, but dressed nearly identically in heavy black boots, black nylon snowsuits with gray piping to show where all the zippers were, and shiny black helmets with dark tinted visors. Snowmobilers with attitudes.

They came straight for me, naturally. I don't know what it is.

The biggest one barked a muffled greeting that doesn't bear repeating, then unscrewed the helmet. Dutchie Prine.

"How they hangin', Hack–man."

"By a thread."

"Ouch." He shouted to Buddy for three brewskies—I'm quoting—then sucker punched my shoulder to show how much he liked me. "Hey, you shoulda been ridin' with us tonight, man. It's awesome out there."

Surf's up, dude. "Sorry I missed it, Dutch." Along with cholera and the Thirty Years War. Dutchie Prine was vice president or assistant warlock or something of the Gullywhumpers, as they called themselves. He used to be lower in the pecking order until the previous second–in–command had thought it would be neat to go night riding without permission across a nearby farm. Decapitation was the result; what enthusiasts call a barbwire smile. There are plenty of other reasons I wouldn't be caught dead riding with Prine or any of the others, but that's at the top of the list.

While he teetered off in search of a free table, the other two worked off their helmets. The middle–size one had big teeth and a fussy orange mustache. The short, stocky one I knew on sight.

"Hi, Stanley."

"I got a gripe with you, Hackshaw."

Stanley Grebwicz. He looked a lot like the young Brando, only shorter and with small, inset brown eyes. Some people call him Alphabet, but only behind his back, owing to the fact that the wit who first coined the nickname now had more elaborate bridgework than the River Kwai. Stanley's surname was pronounced just like it was spelled, provided you were both Polish and dyslexic; Gur–*veech*, if you're scoring.

You've probably heard that bullies are all cowards at heart; don't believe it. Some are, certainly, but there's also a large contingent who are absolutely indifferent to pain, their own or anyone else's. This may be because they were banged around so often growing up, they consider rage and violence as normal communication tools, but I'll leave the excuses to the sociologists. All I'm saying is one treads lightly when Stanley's in the building.

"The line forms at the left," I said, forcing up a smile.

"Ma got taken for fifteen hundred bucks, her whole bingo winnings, by a guy turns out to be your Edgar Williamson." Punctuating every word with a thrusting index finger. "Bought ten shares in a new gambling casino, or so she thought. Only the papers this guy gave her ain't worth shit and now he's dead and I wanna know who's gonna make good."

I expressed my sincerest regrets at Arlene Grebwicz's misfortune, all the while keeping one eye on the smarmy fellow with the geometric mustache, who was keeping both eyes studiously on me. Calculating my net worth, as it turned out.

"Who's this?"

He stuck out his hand. "Tad Reznik. Esquire."

I shook it anyway. "Any relation to the magazine?"

"He's my lawyer."

"Uh, actually, I'm acting more as a friend in this, giving Stan some legal advice."

"You mean he isn't paying you."

"Uh, right. It's a loyalty thing," he explained, "both of us being with the Gullywhumpers."

"Mm–hmm." Two improbabilities in a row. I flashed on an image of lawyers on Arctic Cats circling the Donner party, looking for litigation–minded survivors. "I hope you advised him that, sympathetic though I am, I'm in no way responsible, legally, morally, or otherwise, for his mother getting taken by a con man."

"I wouldn't be so sure. Under some of the newer interpretations of tort law, it's possible a derivative action could be ruled in order." He was warming to the subject like a snake on a sunny rock. "We might even be able to establish a product liability case from this, in that the product you sold Mrs. Grebwicz may have, no matter how inadvertently, caused her financial injury."

"What he means is if you didn't go and put it in the paper, that son of a bitch wouldn't a known to go after Ma in the first place."

"Your mother called me herself to tell me about winning the super jackpot. And so did Father Wirth—why don't you sue him." The pastor at St. Paul's; the Word of God is one thing, but word of mouth is better when promoting bingo. "They practically begged me to mention it in my column."

"Still, you have what might be considered a fiduciary duty to act in the best interest of your readers."

Jesus. "How about if you just stick a sock in it, okay?"

"Hey! I'll sock *you*, asswipe." Grebwicz, not the lawyer. His hands were reaching for my throat, on the verge of taking media bashing to a new level.

Lord knows I'm a peaceful, retiring sort, but I'd put up with enough in the last few days to stress out Mary Poppins. I slumped down on the stool a bit and managed to hook my leg behind Stanley's right stump, jerking hard as the back of my calf found the back of his knee. He spun a quarter turn, wobbled, arms flailing, then toppled over onto his back like a sea turtle.

While he struggled to right himself in the clumsy snowsuit, I filed a brief with his attorney—another phrase that doesn't bear repeating—and fled out the door.

CHAPTER 14

Some things can be done as well as others.

That snippet of nonsensical folk wisdom was the motto of Sam Patch, an early nineteenth–century daredevil extraordinaire who, accompanied by his pet bear, made his reputation jumping off high places into deep and dangerous waters. The pinnacle of his career, the stunt that rocketed him—plunged him, really—to his moment of national celebrity, was a spectacular leap off the cliffs of Niagara Falls into the frothing cauldron below.

They said it couldn't be done, they being the politicians and the pundits and, most important for the sporting crowds, the odds–makers. But Sam did it, and came up smiling in the bargain.

But that a showman and huckster survived a leap off Niagara Falls isn't what had me staring up at my bedroom ceiling late on Sunday morning. What put old rascal Sam in mind was what he did a week later, on a Friday the 13th in November, 1829, when he came like a one–man circus to our neck of the woods to jump the smaller but still impressive upper falls of the Genesee River, with its ninety–foot eternity from the limestone ledge to the deadly stew of hidden boulders and swirling foam. As seven thousand entertainment–starved spectators watched, man and bear ascended a wooden platform built special for the event, adding another dozen or so feet to the height of the stunt. After a few words of bravado—and, tradition has it, a few sips of fortifying home brew—Sam gave the balky bruin a push, then threw himself over after it, the pair of them dropping, tumbling, cannonballing into the whirlpool at the base of the falls.

The bodies were never recovered.

Sam Patch's Last Leap, as the locals still call it. A song or two has been written, and a play, and I think there's a plaque somewhere near the notorious spot on the west bank of the river, only a stone's throw from what was and still is downtown Rochester. Niagara Falls made him famous, we like to say, but the High Falls of the Genesee made him a legend. And all he had to do was die.

Pick your own moral:

Size isn't everything.

Don't push your luck.

Never jump to conclusions.

I clattered out of bed stiff as a parboiled lobster and eased into a steaming shower to finish the job. Two mugs of coffee and a toasted muffin later, I was surprised how human I felt under the circumstances. Half my body was still marred with ugly yellowed bruises, but the permeating ache was all but gone and I could move with reasonable agility, provided I was careful which parts I leaned on. Even my brain seemed to be functioning at near normal speed.

Which brings me to something else I'd thought about, staring up at that ceiling; Queen Mary Wanka, a.k.a. Mother Sacajewea. And daughter Bimbo, heir apparent, gone to ground.

I had a hunch, in other words. But a nuisance commitment to deal with first. Fortunately, it was on the way.

Money may buy good taste, but it doesn't confer it. The main advantage the rich have over the rest of us is the wherewithal to hire someone to do the things we don't do well ourselves. But sometimes success in one area deludes people into thinking they have the answers for everything else, i.e. the industrialist who, because he can afford a baseball team, thinks he knows how to manage one.

The ones you really have to watch are the professed self–made men who pride themselves on having created an empire out of a good idea and the sweat of their brows, often conveniently forgetting a six–figure inheritance from their fathers and a subsidized small business loan from their Uncle Sam.

The Greeks called it hubris.

The Tice place was depressing. Having gone over this ground once, I'll spare you the details. Suffice it to say the house was a mish-mash, not exactly contemporary and certainly not traditional, but a poor borrowing of both.

The sidewalk off the driveway was shoveled only as far as the service door next to the garage extension. Apparently the fancy front entry, with its barrel–vaulted portico and huge fanlight, was used seasonally, if at all. I pushed the side door's buzzer and waited, then pushed again and waited some more. I was about to go happily on my way when the door swung open.

"Hi. You're Hackshaw, right?"

Mrs. Tice, I presumed; she never did say. With a crook of her finger, she led me through a mudroom and into a crowded family room; crowded, that is, with a tuxedo sofa and fat upholstered chairs and a huge pine repro armoire with a big television in it, blaring cartoons. A talking sponge, as best I could figure. The room was higher than it was wide with a pair of blank skylights up near the peak, reminiscent of a silo. A bespectacled girl of around thirteen was in one of the chairs, the magazine supplement from the Sunday paper in front of her face. She ignored us relentlessly. I wish the same could be said of the other one, a little toe–headed boy, maybe six.

"Hey! It's the pizza dude," he hollered. He was wearing one of his father's ties around his noggin and waving a plastic sword with an illuminated orange blade, which he proceeded to poke at a place I don't care to be poked. "You're late, pepperoni face!"

"Trey," his mother said mildly. "Calm down."

The boy war–whooped and ran out of the room.

"He's ADD," Mrs. Tice explained matter–of–factly. "He's just had his Ritalin, so he should be slowing down soon."

I said, "Trey, as in the trey of hearts?"

"No, as in Webster Tice III." She was a frosty blond with a trim but sturdy figure, imperious cheekbones and compressed lips. The eyes were narrow chips of blue flint. Not the sort of woman to mess around with, even if she were to give you the chance.

"I guess I should tell you." She halted abruptly in the middle of the family room, arms crossed defensively. "It's all Web's idea to have work done on the house. I wouldn't mind a solarium addition, but the rest of it seems like a big inconvenience to me."

I let it go with a neutral nod. "Where is Web?"

"In his study, tweaking some numbers for an order he's trying to land with Cadillac." She sighed. "Gone are the good old days when you could pretty much phone in a bid to GM and they'd authorize."

"Mmm." I nodded knowingly and mumbled a few phrases I remembered from Harold's dinner party. "It's all about reengineering and TQM these days." I don't think she heard me; I could barely hear myself with the TV blaring.

"Web has to grovel like Gunga Din to get an order anymore, and even then they don't want you to make any profit. Anyway, he knows you're here, he'll be along in a minute hopefully."

The boy buzzed by and jabbed me again in passing. I looked expectantly to Mrs. Tice, but she was still busy ragging on hubby.

"He's constantly working. Sixty–hour weeks at the plant and another thirty at home on the computer. The children may as well come from a broken home. I swear, I have to be both mother and father."

And the Holy Ghost. I was about to fake commiseration when junior shouted, "Hey, are you the pizza dude, or what?" and stuck me yet again.

I figured the worse thing his mother could do was to order me to leave her house, which is what I wanted to do anyway. So I snatched the thing away and barked, "*No*, I am not the pizza dude, but if you don't stop poking me with this sparkler I may turn into the toy–smashing dude."

I don't know if it was the tone of my voice, the set of my jaw, or merely the novelty of hearing the word "no" for the first time in his life, but the little troll suddenly stopped bouncing around like a superball and stared up at me open–mouthed. For good measure, I reached over and switched off the television.

"Well, that's better," Mrs. Tice said, as if she'd thought of it herself.

Tice blew into the room just then, apologizing up and down for keeping me waiting, et cetera. While he was at it, Webster III pulled a flanking movement and punched the set back on, cackling triumphantly, and the missus tapped her foot, impatient with all of us. The daughter, whatever her name was, exhaled her displeasure as only a teenage girl is capable and dropped back behind her magazine. I almost apologized for intruding on everyone's quiet Sunday, but didn't because it was really them who were intruding on mine.

The tour of the house went as expected, unfortunately. Tice did the honors, with her ladyship shadowing us half a room back. He took great pride in explaining how he'd essentially designed the place himself, only calling on an architect to "cross a few tees and dot a few ayes" to make the blueprints official. Idiot. Every room was done in eggshell white except the one room where it would've made sense, the kitchen, which was heavy on expensive wood cabinets and Mexican tile. The living and dining rooms were huge spaces with proportionally high ceilings, but sterile; white everywhere but for the thick gray wall–to–wall carpeting that ran throughout the first floor. The whole place was about as lively as one of Drummond's clients.

"Adding custom trimwork throughout couldn't hurt," I allowed when we'd ground to a halt in the foyer, another silo. "Crown moldings in the formal rooms definitely, dadoed paneling for the study and half–walls in the dining room if you've got the budget, some nice tall milled baseboards everywhere. Good natural oak, set off with some large–patterned wallpapers and paint with strong deep colors." A few hundred board feet of woodwork wasn't going to help the shell one whit, but at least the inside could be saved. "You have hardwood floors under all this nylon?"

"Wait one minute." The missus. "Assuming we go ahead and add natural wood trim all over, dark paint and busy wallpaper is the last thing we'd want. You need the white walls even more, to counter the wood—"

"Absolutely wrong." I wasn't interested enough to go into detail with her, but what you want is a contrast—walls done in hunt green, say, or maybe sage—to bring out the honey richness and the graining in the wood. "You also need textures and more natural materials, things that don't look like they've been squeezed from a tube."

Mrs. Tice wasn't happy with my analysis. Hubby had `designed' the house, but she had `decorated' it, and who was I to tell her, and so on, and so on.

"Fine by me," I said, making to leave, but Webster II pulled me back.

"All I'm asking, Babs, is that you keep an open mind." *Babs*? No wonder she hadn't bothered to introduce herself. "Hackshaw here is the expert on these things, after all."

"On *Victorian* house restoration, maybe" she countered, somehow managing to pout and pounce at the same time. "Obviously not on contemporary interior design."

"She's got you there, Web." To be fair, the world is divided into two kinds of people, those who prefer modern design and those with good sense.

"And I'll tell you right now, I'm absolutely not interested in having my house turned into some drab and dreary old Victorian museum."

That got my hackles up a touch. "I wasn't suggesting you go Victorian in a house, uh, like this. Only that you incorporate an eclectic mix of *traditional* materials, colors, and furnishings to warm up the place. As for `drab and dreary,' that's a common misconception." I gestured up at the track lights above us. "Victorian interiors were intended to be seen in firelight and candlelight and by the flicker of a gas lamp, not a bank of hundred–watt bulbs. Many of the paints and wallpapers had a special luminescence that would reveal itself under the proper conditions. Very romantic stuff."

Tice looked confused at my speech, but vindicated. "You see, Babs? I told you Hackshaw was just the man to put a little character into this place."

I felt another domestic dispute about to erupt and I wanted no part of it. I also wanted no part of the job, even if it did promise a nice profit. Instead, I offered to give Tice the name of a good finish carpenter who could do the work for them, but he was insistent that I should supervise the project personally and Babs was equally adamant that all they needed was a solarium off the kitchen. They were still "discussing" it when I slipped back through the family room, deftly evaded a swipe from Tice Cubed, and let myself out.

For that matter, I knew where Webster Tice could special order all the fancy millwork he'd need, too.

Drive a long country block west from the Tice place, then south a mile to the Oatka Trail, and southwest another mile or so along the winding Trail. You'll see through the overhanging trees on your left a gentle cataract, then a spot where the creek widens into a popular trout pool, then narrows again, spanned by a small steel–decked bridge. Follow the rutted dirt road beyond the bridge and you'll have officially left the town of Kirkville, New York, and entered a nation unto itself, the Oatka Seneca Reserve.

Oatka Custom Hardwoods operates from a bulky corrugated–metal pole barn in a field behind the tribal council longhouse. I found a clear gravel patch fronting a snowbank and parked. The whine of a ripsaw guided me as I stepped out of the Jeep and let myself into the chilly shop. Chester Youngfoot was, as expected, hard at it, feeding a ten–foot length of oak through the saw's jig, aided at the opposite end by a younger man I didn't recognize.

Chester somehow spotted me using that three–hundred degree peripheral vision he'd perfected during two jungle tours in Southeast Asia. He flipped a switch and the saw whirred to a stop, leaving only an echo.

"*Nahwah–skayno*," he said approximately, removing his safety goggles. "Welcome, Man–Who–Honors–Tall–Houses."

I raised a flat palm, John Wayne western style. "How, Stoneface."

The hard set of his jaw softened around a grin. "If you don't know how by now, Hackshaw, you never will. This a social visit or d'ya have an order to place?"

Entrepreneurial capitalists are everywhere. "That'll be the day," I drawled. More John Wayne.

Chester said, "Buddy Holly, right?"

Introductions followed. The younger man was Jay Bearpaw, a Seneca who'd recently been laid off working the high steel downstate and had returned to the reservation to apprentice for Chester. He had copper skin and long braided hair and a broad face that smiled easily. His pony–tailed mentor, on the other hand, looked about as much like an Indian as Jeff Chandler. Chester Youngfoot is only half Seneca by blood, but that's another story, one I've told earlier and won't bother repeating here.

"How's your mom?" I asked him. It was Mary Youngfoot who'd hung me with the name The–Man–Who–Honors–Tall–Houses, only she could say it in the original Seneca Iroquois tongue. Other than a few words of greeting, Chester, like most of his contemporaries, had never learned the language.

"Doing fine. She's over at the house getting dinner ready. If you don't stay, she'll take it personal."

"In that case, how could I refuse?"

As I spoke, Chester's attention moved past my right shoulder. "Hi, Naomi. It's okay, c'mon in."

"Your mother says to come eat now."

"Yeah, we'll be right up. First I'd like you to meet a friend of ours."

I turned. She stayed rooted in the doorway, hesitating at the sight of me, presumably. Huddling inside an oversized wool overcoat, collar turned up and hiding half her face, black hair parted down the middle and paired into braids. But the eyes told the tale, those suspicious, ageless dark eyes.

I smiled. "Hello, Bimbo."

CHAPTER 15

The black eyes smoldered like a Romanian campfire.

"What choice you think a poor girl has, raised up to lie and steal from when she's a baby almost? Queen Mary, my mama, started teachin' me the boojo when I was seven. My father—" She looked about to spit. "—he sells me to Toma's family when I'm *thirteen.* Twenny thousand dollars Stavo got for me, and all I got was to live like a colored slave or somethin', waitin' hand and foot on Toma and his fat mama and the whole stinkin' family when they didn't have me out workin' games to make money for them. Pah!"

As I listened to her, I began to understand why gypsy men play violins. Not that it wasn't a tearjerker, much of it probably even true. But it raised one caveat: if she was really desperate to exchange the criminal life she'd been born into for the straight and narrow, why'd she hook up with Slow Eddie Williamson?

"You grew up as the daughter of your vitsa's baro, the tribal leader," I added, for the benefit of the others. "That makes you privileged among the Rom. So how bad could it have been for you?"

It was more than showing off, flaunting the few words I'd learned from Professor Blednau. If she thought I knew a lot about her people and their ways, I reasoned, there was a better chance she'd stay within shouting distance of the truth. I was mindful of something

Sergeant Hazard had said: Ask twenty gypsies a question and you'll get twenty different answers; ask one gypsy the same question twenty different times and you'll still get twenty different answers.

She was surprised, but recovered quickly.

"*Gadjo*," she hissed. "You think you know somethin' because you read it in a book? You don't know nothin'."

We were crowded into the tiny living room of Mary Youngfoot's Cape Cod by then, having at Mary's insistence finished a sturdy meal of roasted chicken, mashed potatoes and assorted boiled veggies before getting down to questions and answers. My revelation as to Bimbo's true identity had caught Chester flat–footed, but I think Mary had known all along that the young woman calling herself Naomi Silvercloud wasn't the itinerant Mohawk mystic she claimed to be. It was traditional Seneca hospitality, I'm sure—and curiosity—that had prompted Mary to offer up her spare bedroom.

I suppose Bimbo looked as much like a true Native American as most of the actors who played Indians in old B–movies, and certainly more so than Chester Youngfoot. In any case, she cut a fine figure with or without the braids and the turquoise baubles. Underneath the colorful long skirt and low–cut peasant blouse, she was as shapely as a well–turned baluster, and, I suspect, just as likely to give off splinters if not handled carefully. That said, it took no insight to see how both Williamson brothers—and Chester, too, apparently—could be enchanted by those pouty red lips and smooth cafe au lait skin and...

Don't worry. Having had my quota lately of loony lovelies and their pretty lies, I had no intention of falling prey to the charms of the larcenous Bimbo. I was still licking the wounds from my last misguided affair, with a New Age crystal gazer by the name of Hester DelGado. Still, a man can't help but notice.

"Let's get back to what happened to Eddie," I said. "What you know, or saw, that made you decide you'd better find a quiet spot to lay low."

"How'd you know I was here anyway?"

"An educated guess."

My deductive reasoning wasn't much, but it went like this: If Stavo Wanka believed his daughter was still in the area somewhere, she probably was. And if the mother's M.O. included masquerading as Indian nobility, mightn't Bimbo use the same ploy? If you're trying to hide a tree, what better place than a forest?

The television sleuths make it look so nail–biting hard, but it's really just common sense.

"If you're going to keep answering questions with questions," I continued, "we'll be here all night."

"C'mon, Hackshaw," Chester said, assuming the famous scowl that had earned him the moniker Stoneface. "She's had a tough time."

He was smitten, as I'd feared. Chester could demolish me, and most others, without breaking the slightest sweat. It had nothing to do with his heritage and everything to do with the Special Forces training he'd had drubbed into him many moons ago. Usually I'm obsequious in his presence, but anger gives courage.

"Not as tough a time as her *late* boyfriend," I calmly pointed out. "And it hasn't exactly been a cakewalk for me, either." I'd already filled them in on my interest in Bimbo and her recent past, emphasis on the Wanka clan beating me blue because they thought I was in league with her and Slow Eddie Williamson. "I'm trapped in the middle of this thing, Chester, through no fault of my own—" Well, very little, anyway. "—and I'm looking for the escape hatch. To find it, I need to know everything she knows."

He looked like he still wanted to be Bimbo's protector, but a few quiet words from Mary held him in check; her house, her rules, essentially. Bimbo seemed to accept the matriarch's prerogative, too, a cultural reflex, perhaps. After a few delaying swipes at the folds of her pleated skirt, she started to tell her story, a disjointed tale that paid no attention to chronology and God only knows how much to reality.

"It was Eddie give me the idea to come to this place," she said. "I don't mean like he *tole* me to come hide out here if there was trouble or nothin' like that. I mean he talked about this Oatka Indian Reservation one time, like how he was thinkin' about tellin' people they was gonna build a gambling casino here, the Indians, and how they was lookin' for investors to put up money."

I asked if by `people' she meant folks like the Pedersens and Arlene Grebwicz, potential and actual marks, but Bimbo dismissed it with, "Just people, is all. Anyway, he figured this place was too close by and everything, and some big hotel was in the papers talkin' about how they was plannin' to do riverboat gambling over by Buffalo, so Eddie used that instead."

Her accent, like the others in her clan, had the odd inflections and syntax of someone who'd grown up in a household where English was a second language, learned at street level. After half explaining how she'd ended up in Mary Youngfoot's spare room, she jumped back a few months to when she first hooked up with Eddie Williamson in Niagara Falls. Her recounting, predictably, held much more drama and pathos than the version Pete Williamson had told; how she had fled the house of her in–laws, determined to leave her worthless wife–beating husband, who she never loved no–how on account of it was like an arranged marriage.

"Love comes later, Stavo says. Pah!"

Our heroine was destitute and desperate (words to that effect), winter was coming on, Toma and Stavo were hunting her down, no doubt intent on tying her to a railroad track. That's when she met Eddie's brother, "a famous professional photographer of weddings and things like that", who fell in love with her immediately and begged her to marry him.

"I liked him very much, but I don't *love* him," she said, clutching at her blouse. "So I said said no, I can't marry somebody I don't deep down love, I'm sorry."

"Plus you're already married."

You could plow a field with the glower she gave me. "You wanna hear this or what?"

"I'm transfixed."

She started in again, after first fishing a pack of cigarettes and a lighter from somewhere in the depths of her bountiful cleavage.

Puff–puff. Pete, Eddie's brother, loved her so much he decided to help her get out of town, away from Mad Stavo and Toma the Terrible. Only Pete couldn't leave with her because, she said, his clients depend on him. (Parole violation might be another good reason, assuming any of this was true in the first place.) So Pete asked Eddie to take Bimbo with him on his "business trip" to the Rochester area.

"I didn't know Eddie's business was monkey business, not at first." Puff–puff. "And there wasn't no monkey business between me and Eddie, neither. Not at first."

"Love comes later," I said.

She shrugged. "Eddie was a good, strong man, I found out. I needed somebody like him, and he needed somebody like me, too. See, I was gonna help him change."

"Right. But first you helped him *make* some change."

"Damn it, Hackshaw!" Stoneface, rising.

"Chester!" His mom.

"Well, he's not giving her a chance!"

"I don't have time for Grimm's Fairy Tales."

Mary cut us both off, calling for a half–time break. "Chester, take Naomi—Bimbo, to the kitchen and make us a pot of tea, please. And bring some of those butter cookies from the supermarket."

While they were off doing their chores, Mary gently took me to the woodshed.

"Hackshaw," her soft voice chided, "so hostile today. You're like the hungry bear who stands in the middle of the stream and slaps at the water, hoping its claws will sooner or later snatch a passing trout. Then there's the clever raccoon, who carefully picks his spot, then waits, still and patient, for the fish to come to him."

I hate it when she regales me with parables from the animal kingdom. Even more so because she's always somehow right. I never know if it's true native wisdom bubbling behind that beatific tarnished–copper face, those tranquil brown eyes, or if she's really no different than any other thoughtful elder biding time in any other afghan–draped easy chair from here to Asia Minor.

"How should we play it, Mary?"

"Tell me now what you know, what you suspect, and what you need to find out. If I ask, she may talk freely, and Chester won't feel he's competing with you for her favor."

"He isn't," I insisted. "Her charms are wasted on me."

"Hackshaw," she clucked. Brown, white, black, it made no difference; gender is what allows them to see right through a man.

By the time Chester and Bimbo brought in the hot tea and nibblies, Mary and I were in synch. And it worked fairly well. Bimbo knew she was being good–cop–bad–copped, but she seemed much more comfortable directing her story to the room's surrogate mom. I already knew, from Mary, that `Naomi' had arrived at the reservation the previous Monday, having hitched a ride in a teen–aged farmhand's pickup, bringing nothing but a small suitcase jammed with a few items of clothing, jewelry and makeup, and an old clock radio. Bimbo backtracked a bit and picked up the tale, as the Lit majors say, *in medias res.*

When they arrived in Kirkville the day before New Years, Eddie decided to rent a small house for them to use as a business address. (Good move; it's the only way to get the phone company to assign a number.) He soon concluded, however, that a fixed address would make it too easy for the Wankas to track down Bimbo, so they decided to sublet the house and stay in the camper. (To how many people they decided to sublet the house, Bimbo didn't say.)

The business, of course, was selling speculative (phony) shares in a riverboat gambling casino to local high, medium and even low rollers; anyone with gold dust in their eyes and cash in their pockets. (Scabbing off my columns like they were tip sheets,) Eddie would contact prospective `clients' by phone and make his pitch. If the potential mark showed any interest, a `prospectus' Eddie had had knocked off at a Port Erie quick–print shop would be hand delivered; by Eddie if the mark was female, by Bimbo, posing as his administrative assistant, if the mark was male.

I tried not to, but I had to interrupt on that point.

"You? Administrative assistant to a supposedly respectable financial adviser?"

Chester looked ready to launch, but Bimbo handled me herself. "I'm sure you don't mean to imply," she said, her voice suddenly news anchor precise, "that I'm unqualified for the position?"

"Damn." She was good.

"Go on, Bimbo," Mary said.

And she did, slipping effortlessly back into her street argot. (Acting is overrated; wives and husbands do it constantly.)

"Mostly Eddie'd sit by the phone, makin' calls or takin' calls from the clients or sometimes somebody who maybe'd wanna rent the house. Me he'd leave stuck way the hell out in that trailer all day, makin' meals, unless he needs me to deliver papers to the clients. I only did that one time." She pointed a red–tipped finger at me. "Don't ask. Then sometimes he takes me to the house with him and leaves me to handle the phone all day, like I'm his assistant, right? This is like when he's got to go out hisself someplace. He tells me what to say if somebody calls, that I should take down their number and say Mr. Smith, that was like his business name, would call `em back. Only he was talkin' about gettin' one a those machines, whaddyacallit."

"Answering machine."

"Yeah. I don't read or write too good, okay? Rom people, we don't go in much for school." She flapped her hand dismissively. "Eddie, he'd get mad because I couldn't always remember everything people said. I go, hey, if I ain't good enough, hire a real sec'atary, see if she takes care a your meals and…other stuff."

Other than that, things went okay the first couple of weeks. Money came in—Bimbo wouldn't say how much or from whom—and Eddie was talking about what they might do next, where they might go, after he closed down the Kirkville operation at the end of January. (When, of course, all those duped renters would be trying to move into the Bing Road house en masse.) Then, one night when he got back to the camping trailer, Eddie was all fired up about something; a big score, he told Bimbo, if he set it up right.

"What was it?" Mary blurted. So much for your stoic native peoples. I'll bet she watches *Survivor* when nobody's looking.

"I dunno." Bimbo's lovely bare shoulders rose and fell. "He never told me. It was like on Thursday or Friday, he starts talkin' about this big idea he got. Only he don't wanna say too much till he checks it out better. `Who says you can't make money sittin' around on your ass', he tells me, but that's all. Then Saturday night he don't come back to the trailer and I'm thinkin', like, that's okay. Maybe he got drunk someplace to celebrate, right? Because he figured out his big plan, I mean. But he don't come back on Sunday, neither, and I'm gettin' worried out there at that campgrounds all by myself, for more reasons than one."

That morning, she'd seen a big old Lincoln twice cruise slowly past the entrance of the campground, but it had apparently left when a state trooper came through on park patrol. Bimbo was certain it belonged to one of Stavo's underlings. She packed up her few things and talked some weekend campers from Rochester into dropping her off in Kirkville on their way home. Once back in the village, she finagled a ride out to the Bing Road rental from "some square–head bozo" who I'd bet was Dutchie Prine.

The house was empty, naturally—Slow Eddie had been dead for some twenty–four hours by then—but Bimbo still didn't know that, she claimed. She finally found out late that night, while camping out in the living room, listening to a news report on her radio.

"When I heard, my body shaked like I was possessed or somethin'. Eddie was a good driver, y'know? It didn't make no sense, he drove off no cliff."

Monday morning she braided her hair, put on the turquoise jewelry she owned "for certain occasions", and started hitching again, catching a ride out to the Oatka Trail with a farm hand. Scared, broke, and confused, she was only looking for a place to hide out until she could decide what to do next.

And that was all she could tell me. She hadn't even known for sure that Eddie's death hadn't been accidental until I came along.

She said.

"What happened to all the money Eddie took in from the rental and casino scams?"

"I dunno. I'd be in Sarasota or someplace hot like that if I had it, believe me."

For once, I did. "What about a bank account some place?" As gullible as Eddie's marks may've been, I couldn't see many of them handing over cash, either to buy casino shares or as a rental deposit. He had to have a way to clear checks.

"Yeah, he opened up an account at that little bank in the village, whatchacallit." Kirkville Trust. "Only he didn't keep money in there for very long—just in and out like."

"How far would your father and Toma go to get you back?"

She repeated her cigarette ritual—mesmerizing—before answering. "Toma's crazy, I tell you that. One time he takes his knife, says he's gonna cut me up `cause I wouldn't wear my scarf . A married woman is supposed to wear the headscarf all the time, okay? You think he wouldn't kill some guy he thinks I been, you know, stayin' with?"

"What about Stavo? Would he help Toma?"

"To kill somebody?" She shook her head adamantly, the braids whipsawing. "No, no. The Wankas don't kill nobody, no how. Toma, yeah, his whole family's crazy like that, I swear it to a judge. But Stavo Wanka, no. For him, everythin' is just business."

CHAPTER 16

❁

Sunday night. An icy wind rattled the carriage house dormers, the scented red candle on the nightstand guttered in the sudden draft. And Jackie Plummer shivered.

"It's scary is all I'm saying, Hackshaw. All these murders lately in peaceful little Kirkville."

"*Three* murders in three years. Old man Jenkins, Elton Venable and now Williamson. Who, let's face it, was asking for trouble."

"Five. You're forgetting that Morrison man—"

"Another one who was asking for it."

"—and Chester's cousin, Calvin Hemlock."

"Doesn't count. He was killed in Chilton."

"Well, same thing. He was *from* Kirkville."

"Lincoln was from Illinois, but that doesn't mean they claim him in their crime statistics."

Her bare leg drew away from mine under the quilt. "You know what I mean. We're no longer a rural village, not with suburbia encroaching from the east, the city fifteen minutes away by expressway."

Fifteen minutes if you've been shot from a cannon. I swear commuters are enough to scare Mario Andretti off the road. "Cities didn't invent violence, they merely figured out how to do it wholesale."

"Maybe you can afford to be cavalier about it, but I've got a teenage daughter at home. Two women living alone—I've been thinking about buying a handgun."

I wormed my way up into a sitting position. "If you're really concerned, get a monitored security system. That way you won't accidentally shoot me if I show up unannounced on your porch some night."

"Don't worry, I'd keep it tucked away someplace safe, like high up in my bedroom closet. Just in case some nut should break in—"

"You can't find your cordless phone in broad daylight half the time, yet you think you'd be able to get to a gun hidden in your closet in the black of night with a maniac in the house? Look, dearheart, get a good security system. With your pottery studio there on the property, you could probably write off most of the cost as a business expense."

"Maybe you're right."

"It had to happen sooner or later."

We slipped back into thoughtful silence. A blue half–moon was frozen in place outside the window, the bed sheets were fresh that morning from Mrs. Johnson's dryer; you could still smell the fabric softener. It would've been a perfect way to end a weekend, if only I'd ever learned how to talk in my sleep.

My lids were at half–mast when she started in again.

"I can't believe you're really planning to give Cosmo's Acropolis a favorable review, after that meal."

"It wasn't so bad."

"Puh–lease. The lamb chops should've come with shoelaces. And that screwtop wine—"

"I warned you to stick with the sandwich menu, didn't I?" Cosmo Costas's restaurant was nothing more than a glorified Greek diner tucked into a South Chilton shopping strip. He'd gotten big ideas when he expanded his dining room into the empty hardware store next door and secured a wine and beer license, but he forgot to hire a new chef while he was at it. "Mine was fine." Turkey club, creamy coleslaw, cottage fries; it might even have been good if I hadn't still been full from Mary Youngblood's table.

"Your toast was burnt. The silverware was spotty, and so was the service."

"What d'ya want for free?" The deal is I get dinner for two at various eateries in the tri–town area in exchange for a flattering write–up in the *Advertiser*. It's not as hopelessly corrupt as it sounds. As a for instance, I use lots of flowery but empty phraseology, like "the finest establishment on Colby Street" for a little pizza place that happens to be the only establishment on Colby Street. Or in Cosmo's case, I'd probably say something like "The turkey club plate at the Acropolis lives up to its name" and let the readers figure out what that means. Everything's caveat emptor in this world. I mean, if I say the pie was just like Mom's homemade, our readers have to realize my mother was a lousy cook, God bless her soul. Anyway, the review column was Ruth's idea.

"It's just it's all so beneath you. The phony restaurant write–ups, the self–serving editorials. And those ridiculous `book reviews' you do of Harold Morecock's so–called novels."

She wouldn't think those were so ridiculous if she knew how much Harold pays me. "It's my nineteenth century sensibilities. I'm trying to bring back yellow journalism. `You provide the pictures, I'll provide the war.'" Hearst probably never actually said that, but that's my point. People believe what they want to believe, so what's the diff?

Jackie wasn't through saving me from perdition.

"Maybe you should try your hand at writing a book yourself."

"Yet another business best seller?"

"Don't be silly. You have no business sense whatever."

"Since when is that a disqualifier?"

Her chilly toes found mine. "Stick with something that suits your talents. Maybe an off–beat romantic novel."

"Ah. *The Bridges of Monroe County.*"

All of this was leading up to something; I just didn't know what. Then she told me.

"If you ask me, that's why you can't let go of this con man business. It smacks of real reporting and you need that. You're bored, Hackshaw." She considered, then added, "That, and you'd like to outsmart Investigator Stoneman again so you can rub his nose in it."

If men were capable of multiple orgasm, you'd never hear a peep out of us, but women can't seem to leave well enough alone. I decided it was time to get angry.

"One, I didn't ask you. Two, maybe you should mind your own business. And three, I *told* you to stay away from the goddam lamb chops."

"How dare you speak to me like that!"

Tears welled, but I didn't care. Hadn't she just impugned my reputation, my livelihood—and after eating nearly every last morsel of that terrible free dinner and then draining the sap out of me as if I were one of her backyard sugar maples? I jumped out of bed and stood defiantly naked in the cold draft. "I'll tell you what this is about. It's the girl, isn't it? I mention one word about a beautiful young gypsy—"

"Why, you—you stupid, conceited bastard!" Her short chestnut bob bobbed in counterpoint to each word. "It's your safety I'm thinking of. Just look at you, all bruised and battered. I'm worried about you, God knows why!"

I dropped my chin to my chest; half shame, half inventory. They make you feel small sometimes. Shriveled, even.

"Umm..."

"Save it, Hackshaw." She was up now, too, trailing that nice clean sheet across my dusty hook rug. "Just let me get dressed and drive me home."

It was my own fault for answering honestly when Jackie asked if Bimbo was attractive. But if I'd lied and said ugly as a potato, the two would've conspired to bump into each other on a street corner ten minutes later and I'd be dead meat for lying. Believe me, I've been there.

I sighed for all I was worth and turned toward the wall, shoulders slumped. Tragically pathetic. (Married couples aren't the only thespians.)

"I should've known you'd see right through me," I emoted. "This obsession with the Williamson story. I guess I tried to fool myself into thinking I worked on a real newspaper, not a chintzy weekly shopper."

"Oh, now." Her voice inched closer.

"I suppose I must be having a mid–life crisis." Another Vesuvial sigh. "You know, almost forty—"

"Almost?"

Inconsiderate snot. No matter the specifics, I'd always be two years younger than her. She was standing right behind me by then. I shuddered—from the cold, but she could interpret it however she liked—and whirled, taking her into my arms and, in the process, grabbing myself a substantial portion of that nice warm sheet.

"I have no right to take my problems out on you, sweetness," I murmured, my nose nuzzling that spot behind the ear where she dabs her Chanel. "I hope you can forgive me."

I may have gone too far; neither of us was sure. She pulled away slightly.

"Get dressed, Hackshaw, and make coffee. We'll talk."

Damn.

"Good idea." I squeezed her bare shoulders. "Thanks for being there for me."

We ended up sharing the living area's wicker love seat, Jackie with her feet snugged in behind my rump despite the heat radiating from the woodstove. There was no point in trying to convince her that my continuing interest in Slow Eddie's demise was purely defensive. Ditto for my interest in Bimbo Wanka. Instead, I hewed to the facts of the case as I understood them, weaving in conjectures and educated guesses at the appropriate pauses. The plan was to drone on until she got sick of it or dozed off, but I have to admit, talking the thing out didn't hurt.

First, common knowledge. Slow Eddie Williamson, a Niagara Falls con artist, had spent the first three weeks of January in Kirkville, working various scams on the locals. Persons unknown had, a week ago Saturday, poisoned Eddie to death using carbon monoxide and subsequently, several hours later on pre–dawn Sunday, had driven, towed, or pushed Eddie's Mercury over to Park Road and, with Eddie's lifeless body propped behind the wheel, ran it off Black Creek Bluff.

This much Jackie already knew from reading it in the piece I did for the *Advertiser*. Some of the rest she knew, too, from our dinner conversation, either last week at Harold's or tonight at Cosmo's Acropolis.

More facts, not widely known: Williamson was accompanied and assisted by his nominal girlfriend, Bimbo Wanka. Bimbo claimed she had beat it for the hills as soon as she learned he was dead, and all she knew was that Eddie was working on "something big"—maybe, maybe not. Meanwhile, Bimbo's father and husband and assorted gypsy flunkies were out scouring the vicinity for her and, in the process, displaying a propensity for violence; exhibit A, the bruises all over yours truly. Toma's reasons for wanting Bimbo back seemed obvious; she was his wife, as well as his meal ticket. In some ways, she might qualify as Stavo's meal ticket, too, or his reasoning could be more complicated than that. Fear of ghosts, for instance, and a guilty conscience a la Poe's *The Tell–Tale Heart*.

"And that's just the gypsy side of the ledger," I said. "God knows how many angry citizens there are out there who might've done in Slow Eddie for cheating them. The killers could be almost anyone."

"You keep saying killers. Are you sure there was more than one?"

"Reasonably." The logistics of faking the car accident, I said, suggests at least two people, one to drive Williamson's Mercury to the accident scene and someone else to drive them away from it.

"Well, I think you're making this too difficult. I mean, it's obvious what happened," Sherlock Plummer declared imperiously. "Those gypsies, Tommy and Stova—"

"Toma and Stavo."

"—tracked down Eddie Williamson at the rental house and tried to get him to tell where Bimbo was. He didn't talk, so they killed him somehow, using carbon monoxide, then they arranged the car accident. Then they went back to trying to find Bimbo."

"That's my first impression, too, dearheart," I said. "But the more I think about it, the less likely it seems. For one thing, Eddie doesn't strike me as the heroic type. If Stavo and the boys had him cornered, he would've given Bimbo up in a New York minute to save himself. And another thing; the gypsies would've stolen everything in that Mercury that wasn't nailed down, especially the printing press and laminator."

But that led to another question, I told her. What happened to the evidence of Williamson's phony stock offering? The extra copies of stock certificates and prospecti that he was peddling? Bimbo claimed she hadn't gotten rid of any papers, yet they weren't in the trunk of the Mercury with the portable press and the laminator, and they weren't in the rental house or the camping trailer. I also didn't think Stoneman had found them with the body; at least he'd made no indications he had. So who had taken them? And why? Why take items that have no intrinsic value and leave behind items that are worth at least a few bucks?

"Maybe they just overlooked those things," Jackie suggested. "I mean, if you've just killed somebody and you're trying to clean up after yourself, you're liable to do something hasty like that. Maybe whoever killed him forgot to look in the trunk, and that could be just as true for the gypsies as for anybody else."

"Hmm. Or maybe the press and stuff didn't matter. Maybe the killers didn't care if it became known that the dead man was a con man, provided no one knew what he'd been up to *specifically*."

"I don't understand the distinction."

"For instance, the phony stock sale could produce a paper trail for the police to follow," I said. "A trail which could lead them eventually to Williamson's marks, see? So if it was a couple of the marks who killed him—"

"They'd try to eliminate the paper trail, but wouldn't necessarily care about anything else."

"Right." I nodded, but a bit uncertainly. "So it could well be that someone Williamson duped with his riverboat gambling scheme killed him."

She sniffed. "Unless your gypsy princess took the phony documents herself before lighting out for the Indian reserve, to eliminate as much incriminating evidence about their little scam as possible. She couldn't take the things in the car's trunk, because it was already gone by then."

Also possible, I conceded with a weary nod.

"So," Jackie said, hoping to sound merely curious, "she's beautiful, this gypsy of yours."

"*Not* mine. And I didn't say beautiful, I said attractive. In a crude sort of way."

"As attractive as Hester DelGado?"

The New Age crystal gazer I'd briefly dallied with the previous summer. "Not even close."

I thought it was the correct response, but there's no such thing when a woman insists on being unreasonable. Jackie's big toe nearly punctured my kidney.

"*Ow!* Jesus, what was that for?"

"For being a man."

You see what I mean?

❧ ❧ ❧

I really meant to go straight back to bed after I dropped Jackie at her place, but somehow I ended up wide awake on a stool at the Nook—her fault for stirring up my brain in the first place. A couple of cold drafts, I've found, is the second best thing to cure insomnia.

I took a large swallow of Twelve Horse, in a hurry to get home to what I hoped would be a dreamless sleep. But people just won't leave you alone.

"Take my advice and slow down, Hackshaw." Doc Gordon slipped onto the adjacent stool. "You'll live longer and enjoy it more."

"Is that a medical opinion or purely a philosophical observation?"

"Mostly the latter. I drink, therefore I am." He signaled Mickey, the part–time weekend barkeep, for a double Dewar's. "Still poking around in the Williamson investigation?"

"No." It was the last thing I wanted to talk about under the circumstances; the late hour, my mood, the morose company. But it's like telling yourself not to think about elephants, if you see what I mean. "Why do you ask?"

"Oh, nothing important." He took a grateful tug on the scotch. "Mmm—ambrosia. That serologist friend of mine at the medical examiner's lab? He faxed me a copy of the post–mort report the other day, a sort of professional courtesy."

He stopped to sip, naturally, leaving me to say, petulantly, "And?"

He shrugged. "A slight oddity. The toxicology readings turned up traces of formaldehyde and ammonia. Not that either chemical had anything to do with his death. It was definitely c.m. poisoning that killed your con man."

"Hmph." This time we sipped in tandem. "I wonder where he'd come into contact with stuff like that."

"Ordinarily I'd say it was probably job–related, something he may've absorbed through the skin from prolonged low–level exposure. Ammonia and formalin—the liquid equivalent of formaldehyde—have lots of industrial applications. Do you know if Williamson worked in a dry cleaning plant or somewhere like that? When he wasn't out ripping off people, I mean?"

"Not that I know of." I signaled for another round; I'd never get to sleep anyway. "The autopsy tell you anything else interesting about dear old Slow Eddie?"

"Yeah, he wore cheap shoes."

"Cheap shoes?"

"Well, inappropriate to conditions, anyway. Your man's toes showed mild frostbite damage, as if he'd spent some time recently tramping around outside in wet street shoes."

CHAPTER 17

❀

"It's about time you showed up, Elias."

You know that party game where they ask if you were an inanimate object, what would you be? My sister would be a broken record.

"I've been a bit sluggish lately, possibly an iron deficiency," I told her. "My doctor ordered me to slow down."

Well, it was true, in a way. Ruthie refused to cancel the ambush. She'd been standing there waiting for me at the threshold of the newsroom late–ish Monday morning, armed with doleful brown eyes and a fistful of yellow memo slips.

"I just want you to know I have better things to do than read you a bunch of phone messages."

She didn't have to, of course; she could've just handed them over and let me read them myself. But martyrdom demands the personal touch. So:

"In no particular order." She slipped her glasses down to the end of her nose. "A Mr. Reed Postelwaith called to take issue with your crediting Winston Churchill with inventing the army tank."

"Do tell."

"He seems to think the credit should go to H. G. Wells. Possibly even the Trojans, if you trace the logic back far enough."

"In the long run," I said, apropos of nothing, "we'll all be dead."

Remember those presumably interesting factoids I mentioned way back when? The did–you–know tidbits I sometimes insert into my column to bulk it up to the needed length? This was one of those. Churchill, while serving in World War I as Britain's first lord of the Admiralty, came up with the idea of designing and building heavily armored tractors with caterpillar treads as a way to overrun the German trenches and to act as a vanguard for advancing infantry troops. To mislead spies it was decided to spread the word they were building mobile water carriers. A Churchill aide suggested they shorten this to "tanks" and the name stuck. Just something I'd run across while browsing through the library's reference shelf, don't ask me when or why.

"Tell Mr. Paperweight his argument is with the *Encyclopedia Britannica*."

"Postelwaith. And you can tell him yourself." She handed over the memo and went on to the next one. "An Arnold Clapper called twice."

"The name rings a bell." I couldn't resist; Ruthie could.

"Apparently he wants you to locate some doors for him?"

"Oh, right." Clapper was renovating a Port Erie Folk Victorian, hoping to open a bed and breakfast, I think. He needed several four–panel interior doors in oak or possibly chestnut. I took that slip from her eagerly. "I've got at least three stored at the carriage house that might do."

"And yet another message from Webster Tice, wanting to know when you can meet with him again about his remodeling project. Something about owing you a consulting fee, too." Exasperation jetted out her nostrils. "You know, Elias, we all get a little tired of taking endless non–work related messages for you. When are you going to get an answering machine for your home phone?"

"When am I going to get a raise?"

"When this newspaper of ours begins to turn a profit. If ever." She consulted the penultimate memo. "Sister Maggie says to tell you your laundry is ready."

"Bless her." The Sisters of Perpetual Devotion operate a second–hand store in Chilton, profits from which go to their numerous charitable activities. What happened is I was there one day to do a short feature on the place and I noticed they were selling used men's shirts and slacks for a dollar per item. I further noticed every item had been freshly washed and pressed. Now, it occurred to me that the laundry in Kirkville was charging me a buck and a half for my good work shirts and two bucks for slacks. So what I did is, I brought in a pile of my dirty clothes later that week and "donated" them to the sisters. The next day, I went in and bought everything back at the going rate, saving myself a total of six dollars on six fresh–cleaned cotton shirts and three likewise pairs of pleated pants.

The nuns caught on after a week or two, but you don't get into the mercy business if you don't have a sense of humor. The upshot is we reached a mutually satisfying agreement; they do my laundry at a dollar per and I make damn sure a mention of each and every charity event they hold makes it into the paper. A match made in heaven, if you ask me. The good ladies naturally prefer the Latin: *quid pro quo*.

"This call was actually intended for me." Ruth was holding up the last memo, no doubt expecting a drumroll. "Before I call back, I need to know— what, exactly, have you done to upset Bud and Marion Koon?"

"Nothing." I plucked it away and read. The memo was written in Liz Fleegle's loopy, flowing script. At least it was legible. Ruth's handwriting was almost as bad as a man's and Mrs. Hobarth wrote in tiny, square characters that dented the paper as if they'd been chiseled onto stone tablets. "This is complete garbage."

The jist of the Koon's message was that I had invaded the privacy of their home, been rude and abusive and generally uncivilized, and should I ever darken their door again, et cetera, et cetera.

"Christ. All I did was ask Mrs. Koon a few questions about their former tenant." I explained about Slow Eddie Williamson renting the Bing Road house, then re–renting it.

Ruth was peering suspiciously. "Mrs. Hobarth also had several calls last Friday from Stanley Grebwicz, looking for you. His tone was so offensive, she didn't bother writing any of it down, but it had to do with this Williamson man, too. What's going on, Elias?"

"Nothing. Really. I'm just looking into the possibility of a follow–up on last week's exclusive." I came down hard on "exclusive", but the reminder didn't phase Ruth.

"On what grounds?"

"On the grounds Slow Eddie apparently bilked several of our readers in recent weeks, including Stanley Grebwicz's mother, and I think people should be warned about this sort of thing, if only so they'll know better next time." Not a bad idea, now that I'd thought of it.

"You're not interfering with the murder investigation, I hope."

"Not at all." If anything, it was interfering with me.

"Well, I suppose, under the circumstances, an FYI–type piece might be in order."

Timing is everything, even when it's lousy. Just when I had Ruth appeased, her hubby Ron decided to scurry into the newsroom and complicate things.

"Hackshaw, what the heck is going on with this dead con man of yours?" Ron Barrence has sad brown eyes, too. He reminds me a lot of Jimmy Stewart from his *Mr. Smith Goes To Washington* period, only more earnest. As brothers–in–law go, I could do worse, and I'd say that even if he didn't own and operate the printing shop that made the *Advertiser* possible. Normally he stays out of the newsroom side of the building and lets Ruth handle the badgering.

"I just explained all that to your wife," I said, maneuvering to my desk.

"Well, now you can explain it to me. Starting with why Mel Stoneman came into the shop this morning and confiscated that portable press you sold me."

He and Ruth surrounded the desk and glared down like gargoyles.

I muttered something scatological. "What'd Stoneman tell you?"

"That he needed it for evidence. Evidence of what, he didn't say—but he did say you were `being looked at' for possible obstruction of justice charges."

"That old catch–all." It was the charge that had landed me in the hoosegow previously; that one–night stand I mentioned earlier. "He couldn't make it stick before and he won't make it stick this time," I said confidently, hoping to convince all of us.

"He also wanted to know if you've been squiring any pretty young brunettes around town recently. Early twenties, about five–two, shapely."

"Oh, *Elias*."

More mumbled scatology from me, of the self–pitying sort. There was no point in simply denying I had any romantic connections to Bimbo Wanka; I could barely believe it myself. I had no choice but to begin at the beginning—the previous Monday morning at Dwight Philby's garage—and lay out the series of misunderstandings and coincidences that had followed. While I was at it, the remainder of the *Advertiser's* editorial staff drifted in and joined the jury, Alan Harvey first, followed a few minutes later by our social events specialist (gossip columnist), Liz Fleegle. When I finished, the gang of four took turns offering verdicts. The consensus was that I should've gone straight to the police the minute I learned about Williamson's camper trailer and certainly after I'd been battered by Stavo's gypsy band.

"Going straight to the police means going straight to Stoneman," I reminded them. "It's his case. And the only reason he's breaking a sweat on it is because he smells a chance to get me."

"I thought Jackie cleared you?"

"She alibis me for the time of the murder, but that doesn't prove I wasn't involved with Williamson beforehand—that's the spin Stoneman's liable to put on it," I said. "As for Stavo and Toma beating on me, it's my word against theirs. And speaking of my word, I promised Bimbo I wouldn't reveal her whereabouts to anyone. For the time being."

"Well, what *are* you going to do," Ron wanted to know.

"I don't know," I admitted. "Keep on the trail, I suppose, tidying as I go and looking for an out."

Ruth gnawed at her lower lip. "I don't like this, Elias. It's not just obstruction of justice charges you have to worry about. There's a killer or killers at the heart of this. Those gypsies sound deranged. It seems to me they're the prime suspects right now, or they would be if the police knew about them and what they've been up to. Not only is it your civic duty to tell Investigator Stoneman about them—and about that ridiculous Bimbo woman—it's the best way to protect yourself. If Stoneman is out chasing the gypsies around, that doesn't give either one of them much time to go after you."

Everyone was nodding agreement, with one exception.

"I don't know, Ruth," Alan said. "Hackshaw may be right. He'd need to present some kind of evidence, something irrefutable, to force that Stoneman creep to back off. I mean, the guy's got this really intense, irrational hatred for your brother."

I showed solidarity with a nod in Alan's direction. He was young, but he knew all about intense, irrational haters. But Ruth wasn't quite out of breath.

"I realize Mr. Stoneman isn't an ideal human being, Elias, but I still say cooperation is your best option."

"There's one other," I said. "The first amendment."

After all, I pointed out, this Williamson boondoggle was a legitimate news story and we were a legitimate newsgathering organization, under the tolerant interpretation of the Constitution if not in the eyes of the Pulitzer Prize committee. I had a right to protect my sources, even if—especially if—the principal source was me. My rationale may have been a bit convoluted, I'll admit, but it played well around the room, particularly with Ruth, who loved to hear the *Advertiser* compared even tacitly with the likes of the *Washington Post* and the *Philadelphia Inquirer*.

(All right. I know what old Sam Johnson said, about patriotism being the last refuge of a scoundrel, and maybe it should apply to constitutional protections as well. But if the Supreme Court of the United States figures it's better to err on the side of the Fourth Estate in these matters, who am I—or you—to quibble? Anyway, I could counter your Johnson with a dose of Jefferson on the critical importance of a free press, but I see your eyes are glazing, so I won't.)

Ruth was obviously still conflicted between being a publisher and model member of the community and being my sister, but blood had the edge. "Since you won't listen to reason, Elias, I suppose all we can do is stay out of your way and hope for the best. But for goodness sake, be careful—you know how these things tend to snowball on you."

Ron had some parting wisdom, too. "Play it your own way, Hackshaw—you will anyway," he said. "Just don't come running to us if those gypsies break both your legs."

"That I can guarantee."

Eventually everyone drifted back to doing whatever it is they do, leaving me to do whatever it is I do. First, the phone messages. I tossed the ones from my laundering nuns, with a mental note to swing by later, and from the Winston Churchill nitpicker, who was free to waste his time if he liked, but not mine. Arnold Clapper I called back immediately, but found myself talking to his machine. I told it how I had been searching high and low for appropriate doors for Clapper's Folk Victorian, how I'd managed to chase down three so far (hiding in my garage, I forgot to mention) and that I'd bring them by later in the week. Lastly, I called Webster Tice at his place of business in Kirkville.

He burst onto the line the millisecond his receptionist put me through. "Hackshaw, thanks for getting back to me. Listen, guy, I owe you a consulting fee for coming out to the house yesterday; seventy–five dollars, wasn't it? And I thought maybe we could meet again at my place tonight after dinner and go over the project some more. In fact, come for dinner, why don't you?"

"No! I can't today." Imagine eating dinner surrounded by Lady Tice and TV Trey and Sulky Sis; I'd end up on Ritalin myself. I pleaded a previous engagement, work–related, and suggested he mail me a check for the consultation.

"It's just I thought you might want the money in cash—you know, for tax purposes," he said. "Besides, I really do want to get moving on this remodeling work, Hackshaw, and I need your input. I'll make it worth your while."

"First things first," I said, trying to forget about the money to be made and concentrate on the depressing realities of the project. "Have you managed to convince, uh, Babs yet?"

"She's coming around."

Well, I wasn't, I told him. Not that night, anyway. That's the problem with these business types, with their quarterly–profits mindset; they're too impetuous, too myopically focused on the short term and "getting things done." Which probably explains how Tice's house had turned into such an expensive mess in the first place.

I got rid of him with, "Have your wife call me herself when you've both decided what it is you want." Just before hanging up, I added, "And a check will be fine, thank you."

That out of the way, I rolled a sheet of three–ply into my vintage Royal manual and hammered out seven inches on the Kirkville Lutherans' fish fry fundraiser the previous Friday and, to avoid a holy war, five more column inches on the Catholics' upcoming baked goods sale. Then I followed with a few short items for that week's Ramblings, and a snippet on a guy who'd recently opened an electronics repair shop in Kirkville (and even more recently begun running a weekly boxed ad in the *Advertiser*), and a longish piece on the Port Erie school district's annual budget battles, cribbed from several press releases I'd received on the subject, both pro and con. Interspersed with all this industry were several incoming calls from people wanting this or that publicized, or who had a bone to pick with something or other I'd written, or who simply wanted to vent their diseased spleens on someone. (I always refer the latter to talk radio; those call–in shows where the narrow–minded get to reassure each other that the world was indeed a better place before the advent of civil rights, women's suffrage, Medicare, child labor laws, et cetera.)

By the time I came up for air, it was mid–afternoon. Ruth was out somewhere hawking ad space to the local retailers. Alan, who had just come in from a go–fer task, was shmoozing with Liz at her desk in the opposite corner. I managed to catch a few phrases about "runway queens" and a night spot called Midget's Green Door before my approach caused them to downshift into conspiratorial smirks and low giggles.

"Did I miss something amusing?" I asked.

Liz gave out a condescending smile that, with her long narrow face and three–tone blond hair, reminded me of Lassie growling. "Alan was just telling me about the, um, floor show at a city club he and some of his friends go to."

"Sounds interesting. The Green Door, did I hear you say?"

"I don't think it's your cup of tea, Hackshaw," Alan said quickly. "It's a very avante garde kind of a place."

"Uh–huh." Young people think they discovered everything, have you noticed?

Midget's Green Door is a place on Rochester's post–industrial north side where men of Alan's persuasion go to eat, drink and be Mary. I remember back when it was the Green Door Tavern, a place where blue collar types gathered to guzzle beer, listen to Tammy Wynette, and speculate on the prospects of various football and hockey teams. But the factories had all downsized and the warehouses had emptied of manufactured goods, eventually filling up again with cheap studio space and loft apartments. The neighborhood now swarms with struggling young artists and artisans and their patrons, all orientations well represented; God love `em, they're giving all those magnificent old brick piles, including the Green Door, new life.

I said, "Does it still have that magnificent circular mahogany bar?"

"Well, uh, yeah, it does." Alan went into near–gape mode.

Liz was intrigued, hoping for dirt. "You continue to surprise, Hackshaw. How is it that you know about Midget's Green Door?"

"How is it that you don't? I thought everyone who was in the know knew about it." That set her molars grinding. Actually, I heard about the tavern's reincarnation from Jackie Plummer, whose pottery business keeps her current with the local arts crowd. I ignored Liz's follow–up and turned to Alan. "I have an assignment for you, if you have wheels available."

He assured me his battered Datsun was roadworthy again and I filled him in. I wanted him to interview Mary Margaret Hoos, the woman who appeared in my Ramblings column for winning a million dollars in the state lottery. I also wanted him to drive out to Bing Road to quiz the neighbors again, including the house I'd visited where there'd been no answer to my knock. I gave him a list of questions to ask in each instance and sent him off in his floppy galoshes and greatcoat. Then I slipped into my pea jacket and headed out with my own to–do list.

I got as far as the parking lot and my Jeep, keys at the ready, when a large Lincoln rolled up behind me. I hurried to unlock the Jeep's door, but my hand was shaking so badly—from the cold, I mean—I couldn't get the damn key in the hole. It was hopeless by then, but I kept at it, fumbling pathetically even as I heard a car door creak open and a mocking voice say, "Maybe if it had hair around it, huh, Hackshaw?"

CHAPTER 18

Toma Kurts, cowboy hat and all. Flanking him were the grinning twins from before, both dressed again—or still—in leather jackets, bandanas, loud flared polyester pants, and black pointed shoes.

Toma jerked a thumb toward the Lincoln. "Get in. Somebody wants to talk to you."

If I hadn't been preoccupied with terror, the scene would've reminded me of one of those clunky cop shows from the 1970s; men in salmon leisure suits and hair spray and music tracks that sound like disco for Mormons.

Unfortunately these weren't nice, friendly Mormons, nor was there a director on hand to yell cut and return everything to reality. I bluffed courage.

"I wish you people would call first. I have a previous appointment—"

Toma cracked his knuckles, a neat trick in leather gloves. "Quit screwin' around and get in, Hackshaw. Or do we gotta persuade you of our sincerity again."

You know how people say they'd rather be dead than paralyzed or brain damaged? Put me down for none of the above. I got in.

The Lincoln was seventies vintage, too, messy with fast-food wrappers and empty beer cans, but roomy as a condo and with more horsepower than the Calgary Stampede. That was all I was allowed to observe before Toma climbed into the back beside me and ordered one of the curly–haired look–alikes to remove his neckerchief.

"Just so's you don't get any cute ideas about blowin' us in later," he said as he tied the thing over my eyes.

That "later" part at least reassured me somewhat that this wasn't to be a one–way trip. We took off with a thrust that threw me back against the seat. I couldn't see a thing through the blindfold, but it didn't matter; this was my turf, not theirs. I knew by the turns and stops and relative distances that we were heading south on Union Street, then southwest on what had to be Deming Road, with a final left turn onto a bumpy country lane that my sacroiliac remembered from previous assignments: Old Mill Road, one of South Chilton's rural–most byways. The whole trip took less than ten minutes and ended with a few closing moments of sizzling gravel. When the car stopped and the bandana came off, we were parked in the lee of a rotting cow barn I recognized as part of the former Terwilliger dairy farm, now dormant and looking for a buyer to develop it into tract housing.

I blinked wildly and said, "Where are we?"

"Shuddup." Toma leaned across and shoved open the door. "Get out."

The Lincoln was eased in next to a newer Cadillac bearing Alabama plates, which in turn was snuggled beside a big travel trailer more than twice the size of Eddie Williamson's Nomad. A heavy–duty electrical cord ran from the trailer to an adjacent utility pole; someone had rigged a set of alligator clips to tap into the drop line that had once serviced the barn.

The bruise brothers stayed in the front seat of the Lincoln, engine idling, while Toma herded me across packed snow to the door of the camper with a series of unnecessary jabs. I climbed the fold–down step, knocked tentatively, then hurriedly let myself in at Toma's angry command.

"Ah, Hackshaw. You made it, huh?" Stavo Wanka, pretending I'd had a choice in the matter. "Come. Sit." Doing Marlon Brando doing Vito Corleone. His Obeseness was spread out over a built–in bench-seat in the living area in the front part of the trailer. There were two plump upholstered chairs and a low table between us. The floor was layered with Turkish rugs in various sizes.

I sat, or started to.

"Nah–nah–nah, not there. Toma, bring the guest chair, that's a good boy."

The voice came from behind me and turned out to be female. I'm not sure if she truly outweighed Stavo or if being half a foot shorter merely made it look that way. She moved ponderously past me—I couldn't avoid a whiff of jasmine mixed up with fried onions—and eased herself into one of the club chairs. Meanwhile, Toma came out from the back with the guest chair, a Samsonite folding job. He set it up in the only open space left, pointed me into it, and took the second club chair for himself.

Stavo cleared his throat and said, somewhat formally, "Hackshaw, this here is my wife, Queen Mary."

Like the ship, I almost said.

Her smile had port holes. "Call me Mary."

Call me a cab. "A pleasure to meet you, ma'am."

"God's luck and health, and welcome to our home."

Some welcome. Bits and pieces of what Professor Blednau had told me began filtering back, including how gypsies often keep one so–called marimay chair on hand, so gadje visitors won't contaminate the good furniture.

Her Regalness was dressed in an ankle–length burgundy skirt and a colorful shawl wrapped over a low–cut blouse that gave away more than any reasonable man could possibly want, and decades late at that. A necklace of ancient gold coins spanned the crevasse of her bosom like a suspension bridge. Her long, gray–streaked hair was pulled back and covered with a headscarf; gold disks dangled from her ears. Her black eyes, like pits embedded within that round olive–skinned face, studied me.

Stavo did most of the talking, but it was clear where the real center of power resided.

"So, Hackshaw, you found our girl, huh?"

"Huh?"

He rocked forward as best he could, elbows resting on the knees of his baggy chalk striped suit. "Bimbo. We hear you found out where she's keepin' herself."

"Where'd you hear that?" I was guessing they were only guessing, and I guess I was right. Stavo shot a glance at the missus, then came back at me.

"I told you before, we Rom got our ways."

"Well, you're mistaken this time." At Toma's low growl, I added, "Not that I haven't been trying, leaving no stone unturned."

"*Lying bastard.*" Toma whipped off his cowboy hat and swatted me with it. "You prob'ly know where she's been hidin' all along."

"Toma!" the old lady barked, followed by a stream of Romany invective. Toma slumped, pouting, into his chair. Stavo eyed him contemptuously, then shrugged.

"You gotta make allowances for my son–in–law," he said. "He forgets sometimes he don't run things."

"Texans have a saying," I said. "All hat and no cattle."

Stavo jiggled with mirth. "`At's a good one. I gotta remember that."

Toma was less amused, but contented himself with muted mutterings and murderous looks. Queen Mary looked bored with the pace of the proceedings, but her husband was determined to pretend everything was civilized.

"Lemme tell you what I think the problem is here, Hackshaw," he said amiably. "What we got here is a misunderstanding, huh?"

"Failure to communicate."

"Yeah. Like that. You think because we maybe lost our tempers a little before, that means we're bad guys, huh? And you say to yourself, uh–uh, I ain't tellin' those gypsy hardasses nothin' about some poor runaway girl." He held out open palms. "This is an honorable thing, Hackshaw, to protect a woman. I respect that. But see, you got us wrong. This is our *daughter* we're talkin' about here—Toma's wife, huh? We just wanna get our girl back with her family where she belongs, is all, like any good mama and papa wants, now, you can understand that." He sat back and waited. It was my turn.

I summoned as much innocence as I was capable of, adding a touch of whine for flavor. "It's just you expect too much from a guy. I mean, if you people can't find one of your own, how do you expect me to?"

"`You people'?" Stavo erupted, hands flying, imploring the ceiling. "I'm tryin' to talk man to man here and you give me `you people'? You think I don't know what t' hell you mean? `You damn stinkin' worthless gypsy people'—why you don't just say what you mean?"

His performance was as flawlessly calculated as Greenwich Mean Time. Something else I remembered from the professor's tutorial; sudden histrionics were part of the profile. If you can't trick or wheedle or beg your quarry into doing what you want, outshout him, create a scene. If the pattern held true, threats were not far down the road, and if those didn't work—Blednau hadn't wished to prejudge, but then he didn't have my bruises.

"You Americans," Stavo ranted on, "you think you know it all, huh? Lemme tell you somethin', the Rom, we go back to the dawn of civilization."

I wish they'd go back somewhere, the sooner the better.

"I got copper pots in the kitchen there been in my family since before your George Washington was big enough to wipe his own ass. Me and Mary, our fathers and our grandfathers even, we was all born here, but you think that makes it any different for poor gypsies? *Pah.* Every place we go for hunnerds of years, it's the same. The Moslems chase us out, the damn pope chase us out, the czar—you know how many Rom got gassed by those Nazi crazies in the war? A million of us, easy."

Blednau said possibly half a million, but still—

"—but all anybody hears about is the poor damn Jews, like us good Rom people don't even count." He abruptly changed pace, his tone dropping back to a conversational level. "Whaddya think'd happen, Hackshaw, if you went around sayin' stuff like you jewed down the price on a car or somethin' like that? But you tell somebody how you got *gypped* buyin' that car, nobody'd think nothin' of it, huh? Jews, colored, cripples—nobody gets put down like that no more, `cept us gypsies."

I almost mentioned dutch treats, welshing on a bet, and scotching a deal, but decided the timing was wrong. If I was to have a Chinaman's chance of getting out of there in one piece, sucking up seemed the way to go.

"Look, Stavo—may I call you Stavo? I meant no disrespect to you, and certainly not to your lovely wife." Toma could go fish. "But I can't give you what I don't have, can I?"

"You speck me to believe you could figure out where Bimbo and this Williamson was livin' before, way the hell out at that park campground—"

"That was a lucky guess, as I tried to explain—"

"—and here you are anyway, this big–deal newspaperman, always goin' around askin' people questions for a livin', and you can't find out where one little girl is stayin' in your own town?" He threw up the hands again and turned to HMS Mary. "*Pah.* I give up with this gadjo."

"Bring him here," she said, too calmly.

Before the words were half out of her mouth, Toma had me by the back of the neck. He pushed me out of the folding chair and bullied me across the layered Turkish rugs on all fours. I thought about depositing an elbow in his crotch and beating it out of there, until I remembered the bopsy twins idling in the Lincoln. Anyway, by the time I reviewed the options, there weren't any; I was kneeling at Queen Mary's skirted feet, my wrists held fast by her surprising grip, my free will held even faster by the force of her personality.

"How you want me to do him," she asked hubby. "The hands or the ball?"

I didn't like the sound of that one little bit and began to struggle, but the combination of her steel grasp and Toma's knee at my back kept me in place.

"I dunno," Stavo said. "Where's the ball at anyway?"

"Packed in a box under the bed, I think. Maybe one a the kitchen cabinets."

My brain registered *crystal* ball and I stopped struggling.

"So, do the hands then," Stavo grumbled. "It don't matter, you got the power either way, huh?"

"Of course."

She turned my wrists and commanded me to uncurl my fingers, then oohed and ahhed and mumbled for several seconds while she examined my palms.

"Long life line, hmm?"

"Hah. If some woman's man don't get to you first."

That brought another growl from Toma. Mary said, "I gonna let go now, Hackshaw. Be a good boy, okay? I want you to hold my hands real tight and look right up here into my eyes. Don't think about nothin' `cept the color of my eyes."

That was easy—the hard part was not laughing. They were black; black as a con artist's heart. Black as...deep space...deep as infinity...pitiless black holes hidden in the great cosmos...swirling, irresistible, swallowing up all energy...

After an eternity, a voice said, "You can let go now, Hackshaw. *Hackshaw*."

"What?" Somehow I ended up back on the folding chair, wishing it were a chaise longue. Sleepy as hell...

"So?" I heard Stavo ask gruffly. "He's lyin', huh? He knows where Bimbo is at."

I forced myself to sit up straight and pay attention. Mary was still staring at me. Deciding. My fate was entirely up to her, I knew. Stavo and Toma would buy whatever she told them. They *believed* in her power, and I was beginning to understand why.

Queen Mary stared. "Women, Hackshaw. Everywhere you turn, they're your joy and your curse."

"Yeah, well…" Common knowledge, really. All she had to do was ask around. Ditto for the next bit.

"You like the old houses, too, huh? Fixin' `em up."

"A sideline," I admitted.

"Stay away from new houses, Hackshaw. New projects. I see trouble that way."

I flashed on Webster Tice and his contemporary monstrosity, then silently chided myself for such foolishness. It's how they work; make a ballpark guess and let our eager, overworked imaginations fill in the blanks.

Toma was ready to bash. "C'mon, Mama, does he know where she is or don't he?"

Her great heavy jaw shook minutely. "No."

CHAPTER 19

❀

The men blistered the air with bilingual profanity.

"You *sure* he don't know?" Stavo demanded.

Mary answered with a majestic arc of eyebrow. "I said so, didn't I? It's like he knows, but he don't know."

"How could he know but he don't know?" Toma. "Give him to me and the boys a few minutes—"

"Nah, nah, nah." She wagged a finger at the goon. "It's like this. Inside his head, he got all the pieces floatin' around to tell him where our Bimbo is at, okay? But he ain't been able to make everythin' fit together yet, maybe because he can't think too good when he's all black and blue and worryin' about what somebody's gonna do next."

I sat there taking it all in with fascination and qualified relief, and just a touch of totally irrational disappointment. I mean, that Queen Mary had guessed wrong was all to my benefit, but that she'd had to guess at all, just when I was starting to think maybe there really was something to this clairvoyance business—like I said, totally irrational. Mostly I was overjoyed at the turn of events. But not Stavo.

"Huh. What the hell somebody's gonna do next, that's a goddam good question."

"You ask me, we tie him to the trailer hitch on the Lincoln and—"

"Nobody's askin' you. Go. Go outside with the boys. You, too, Stavo. I gotta work with Hackshaw, make him relax so's he can think."

"Leave you alone with this—this gadjo?"

"It's okay. You wouldn't lay a finger on me, would you, Hackshaw."

"No, ma'am." I was starting to like the old butterball, but not nearly that much.

"While youse are all waitin'," she said to her husband, "why don't you send the boys over to that SuperDuper, pick me up a package of Sara Lee cinnamon buns or somethin'."

Without thinking, I volunteered, "There's a nice bakery closer by. Just tell the boys to head back up to the main road and take a right…and drive…" Stupid. See what being neighborly gets you?

They were all staring now, of course; Stavo bemused, Toma livid, Queen Mary inscrutable.

"Didn't I tell you dummies to blindfold him?"

"We did. He musta figured it out."

"Now we gotta move the goddam caravan again."

"Never mind. Go find this bakery and bring me back somethin' good. With white icing."

"It's in a little shopping strip on South Chilton Avenue," I said, in for a penny. "Turn right on Union, drive a mile and a half, then a left. You'll see it."

Toma thanked me with a kick at the side of my chair, but followed Stavo out. Mary, meanwhile, worked her bulk up from her chair and motioned me to the adjacent kitchen. It occupied the center section of the trailer with, I assumed, a bedroom and bath through the door at the other end. A booth–style dinette took up most of one wall, with cabinets and appliances, including a double sink and a microwave, stretching along the opposite wall and wrapping around into a short–ended el. Everything neat and clean.

"Siddown, Hackshaw. I'm gonna have a bite. You hungry?"

"I could eat." It wasn't polite to refuse food, and besides, one of the items on my to–do list had been a late lunch, and now it was really late. "You sure you don't want me to bring in the marimay chair?"

Her eyes widened, but then she gave out another gap–toothed smile. "Nah, I think you prob'ly got a little gypsy blood in you someplace. Anyway, those seats there're vinyl, they wipe down real easy."

I slid into the booth and watched as she puttered around the tiny kitchen like anybody's mom, if you overlooked the exotic clothes and the clanking of gold jewelry.

"Mmm, sarmi, you gonna like these. And what's this here?" She was bent over in front of the open refrigerator, pulling out plastic–wrapped dishes, checking the contents, putting the winners on the adjacent countertop. "You like a good ragout?"

"Ragu? Like the jar sauce?"

"Like a spicy stew; y'know, a little meat, some vegetables, nice red wine."

"Sounds delicious."

"Yah. It's like what they call a Hungarian goulash, only they stole the idea from us Rom." While the food heated in the microwave, she laid out plates and raved on about thieving Hungarians and sneaky Poles and a few other nationalities. When everything was ready, she pulled a low stool out of a cubbyhole and placed it at the open end of the dinette table, gingerly settling onto it.

"Try the sarmi, see what you think."

I took a tentative bite, then a bolder one. "Mmm." It was a cabbage roll, stuffed with pork, onions, peppers, some rice and tomatoes; a little greasy, but very tasty.

"Is a dish all Rom women make, like for special celebrations. Very important tradition." She shook her head. "Bimbo, she can't make decent sarmi to save her butt. She just don't care about these things. Makes Toma crazy. Your drink's okay?"

"Fine." I took a sip; a can of Genesee beer for me, sweet–smelling tea for Mary.

"So, Hackshaw, what'd Bimbo tell you about us? How everybody beat her, make her work like a ox?"

I finished chewing and swallowed. Mary, I noticed, wasn't eating much at all, just picking and watching me.

"How could Bimbo tell me anything—?"

"Hackshaw." As if I'd wounded her. "We both know you found my girl. She's stayin' with some woodsman and an old woman, like me, right? Someplace not far away from here."

I covered my surprise with a spoonful of the ragout. It went in smooth and delicious, then detonated halfway down my throat. "*Christ.*" A liberal dose of beer quelled the fire. "Whew, when you say spicy—"

"I know you ain't gonna tell me where she is, okay? But you can tell me *how* she is, can't you? Her own mother?"

I flashed on another Mary—Mary Youngfoot. Take away a few pounds of flesh and jewelry and this one could almost be her twin. Evil twin. I risked another bite of the stew rather than look her in the eye, and held silent.

"You think if you tell me anythin', I go `ah, hah' and call Stavo and the boys back in so they can beat the rest out of you, huh?"

Maybe she was clairvoyant after all.

"But I think you too stubborn. Even a good beating won't make you talk."

But not infallible.

"So I'm gonna make you a deal, Hackshaw, and I swear a curse on my dead father's head if I ever try to double–cross you," she said solemnly.

One more thing came back to me from my visit to Professor Blednau. As a rule, the Rom show unwavering respect for elders and tribal leaders, he told me, especially departed ones. Not unlike Mary Youngfoot's people.

Maybe that's why I decided to believe her.

"What's the deal?"

She sighed, the Brobdingnagian bosom quivering with relief. "Tell me how Bimbo is, what she gonna do now. And take a message to her from me and her papa—we wanna talk to her, that's all. Promise you'll do this much, and I have Stavo take you back where the boys picked you up."

I let it ride for a few seconds, working on another sarmi. Then:

"All right, Mary. If you answer some questions for me first."

"Whaddya wanna know?"

I took a flier. "You seem to have the second sight—tell me who killed Slow Eddie Williamson."

She flinched visibly at the name, but shook her head. "I don't know nothin' about that. I heard that—*American* killed hisself in a car wreck."

"You know better than that. He was dead from poison gas hours before his car went into the creek."

"Poison gas?"

"Carbon monoxide poisoning, like from a faulty exhaust system on an old car."

"Huh. That's what killed him? I don't know nothin' about that."

"All right." For now. "Tell me what the deal is with Stavo and Toma. Why're they both in such a sweat to get Bimbo back? I can't believe it's just the money."

"Money?" Innocence incarnate.

"The money she brings into the vitsa with her scams. And the twenty thousand dollars Toma's family paid to get her."

"Twenty thousand—she told you that much? Whadda liar, that Bimbo." Said more with maternal pride than anything. "Fourteen-five Stavo got for her, is all, and some of that was Canadian."

"Whatever." Not for the first time, I had the passing feeling I was caught in a time warp, trapped in the Carpathian Mountains circa

1650. "This has to be about more than a few thousand bucks and a broken marriage contract."

"Money's always important, Hackshaw. But not so important as blood. You Americans, you think mixin' up is okay. Like some Italian marry some Swede, or French marry English, even maybe white marry black. So long as it's love, huh? But love don't matter. Love—"

"Comes later."

A wistful little grin formed at the corner of her mouth. "Maybe yes, maybe no. What I'm sayin' is us Rom, we got our own ways. We gotta stick together, marry our own, otherwise pretty soon we stop bein' Rom. You see?"

"So daughters get sold off young to marry into safe Rom families," I said, "and all the children, to keep them away from outside influences, are held out of school, never learning to read and write—"

"Bimbo told you that?" She frowned. "About sendin' the children to school?"

"As a matter of fact, I heard about it somewhere else. But it's true, isn't it?"

She flapped her bejeweled fingers. "You're a gadjo, Hackshaw, nobody speck you to understand us. I tell you what's the truth. What Stavo said about hunnerds of years of bein' persecuted, that's the truth us Rom know."

"I don't doubt the persecution, Mary. But haven't the Rom been their own worst enemy in some ways, with the traditions of fortune-telling scams, the boojo—"

"We got a right to make a livin', don't we," she said irritably. Then she told me, with apparent sincerity, the story of Christ on the Cross and the stolen nail that supposedly earned the Rom a special dispensation to steal.

"Is in the Bible," she insisted. "And I tell you somethin' else is in there. `He who steals my purse steals trash.'" The grin returned, sly this time. "I guess that makes us like trash collectors, huh?"

She was right about one thing; I'd never understand them. "Let's get back to Stavo and Toma and their search for Bimbo. I've got a theory to run by you."

"Okay."

"I think they're worried about a mulo."

Her shiny olive complexion turned a shade or two lighter and a string of Romany hissed from between her lips. For a second there, I thought she might topple off the little stool. "How'd you know—what d'you know about stuff like that?"

"I know that a mulo is supposed to be the spirit of someone who died too young. And I know it's a malevolent spirit that the Rom believe can attach itself to a vitsa and bring a plague of bad luck."

She tried to cover her distress with an evasion. "I can't talk to you about such things—is against my religion."

"I know something else, too. Your people usually travel south to warmer weather this time of year. For all of you to hang around out here in the sticks, in the dead of a hard winter, something's driving Stavo and I think I know what. Slow Eddie Williamson's mulo is tormenting your vitsa and Stavo's responsible—"

"No!"

"—because he killed Williamson himself, or had Toma and the boys do it."

"No! Not Stavo, or Toma. You got it wrong, Hackshaw, but—not so wrong." The sudden slump of her shoulders signaled surrender. "Stavo…he thinks I killed the gadjo."

"*You*?"

I realized I'd been leaning in closer, on the attack, and now I sat back, surprised at the turn of events. Frankly, coming in I'd only half believed the mulo theory myself.

Mary quickly recovered some of her old spunk. "Who knows, maybe I did kill him. See, I put a curse on him. I don't mean no ofisa jive for the tourists, I'm talkin' about a sacred Rom death curse on his stinkin' blond head." She shrugged. "Sometimes it works, sometimes it don't."

What do you say to something like that?

"Doesn't Stavo realize it was carbon monoxide poisoning that killed Williamson?"

"So what? You put a curse on somebody, maybe they have a heart attack a week later, maybe they crash a car—the thing is they die, okay? How don't matter." She reached over and stroked the back of my hand. "For Stavo to change his mind, somebody else gotta say it was them killed the gadjo, for some reason got nothin' to do with us. That way we get rid of the mulo, okay? But first somebody gotta find out who this other somebody *is*. See?"

I did see; why Mary was stroking me, why I was sitting with her in the comfy travel trailer instead of outside getting kicked through the snow. She was hoping I'd figure out who really killed Slow Eddie and take her family off the hook. Which might also explain something else.

"Is that why Bimbo is so important? Stavo thinks she may know what actually happened to Eddie?"

"Nah, nah. I told you, Stavo thinks my curse killed the American. He wanna get Bimbo back because she's our daughter, huh? And she belongs with her people. That's one reason."

"What's the other reason?"

"The kris—you know what's a kris? The old men of the vitsa, like judges. Somebody breaks the rules or is marimay, the kris tells `em what they gotta do to get clean again, see? Stavo, he's baro, like the bossman for the vitsa, but he still gotta do what the kris tell him, like everybody."

"And the kris ordered him to bring back Bimbo."

"Yah. There's some things we can do, like sacred Rom rituals, I mean, that maybe could free us from the mulo and take away all this bad luck we been havin'." She rolled her eyes. "Things been tough, Hackshaw, ever since Bimbo run off with that stinkin' blond pretty boy. Could be because the economy ain't that good around Niagara Falls these days, but could be this other thing, too."

Somehow, I'd managed to polish off most of the grub while we talked. Mary got up from the stool and began clearing the dishes. "Now it's time you tell me about Bimbo. The boys'll be back soon."

I sipped my beer and told her what little Bimbo had told me about her situation, careful not to mention the Youngbloods or anything else that might give away her whereabouts. Mary kept on cleaning up, but listened intently, pleased to hear her daughter was in good health and feisty spirits, but disappointed I could tell her so little about Bimbo's future plans. Disappointed even more that Bimbo appeared to know nothing about how Slow Eddie had gotten himself murdered. But Mary's heart proved to be as stout as the rest of her.

"So, I guess that's that," she said. "You still gotta talk to her for me, Hackshaw. Let her know about the kris and everything, huh? Tell her mama's gonna work things out so it'll be okay."

"How do I find you to let you know—?"

"She knows how to get a message to us." There was an impatient rap on the trailer door. Mary shouted, "In a minute," then to me said, "If you don't have no more questions, I get Stavo to take you back."

"Just one." I had to ask. "How'd you decide to name your daughter Bimbo?"

"Hah—that was Stavo's idea, to please his mama. See, she was a Bimbo. I mean her last name."

"Ah." I got up and followed her lead to the door. When we got there she turned and looked up at me.

"I almost forgot. Gimme ten dollars, Hackshaw."

I began a protest, but then I remembered the old Jamaican switch—impressing the gadje by making a ten dollar bill "miraculously" metamorphose into a twenty. So I grinned and dug a bill from my wallet.

"God's luck and health," she said, as she took the money and stuffed it down her blouse.

"Wait a minute, aren't you going to wrap that up and have me put it under my pillow for three days?"

"Nah, this is what I charge for tellin' your fortune, warnin' you off new projects." She chuckled. "I think you too smart for Queen Mary's boojo tricks, anyway."

Obviously not smart enough.

CHAPTER 20

I was feeling a tad more optimistic about things when I got back to Chilton Center, and not only because Stavo dropped me at my Jeep unscathed.

After all, eliminating a possibility always simplifies things. If the gypsies didn't kill Slow Eddie, then somebody else did it, someone who'd been victimized in one of his scams, just as I'd suspected originally; maybe this "big score" he was working on.

Or possibly someone who was *in* on one of Eddie's cons, but became disenchanted for some reason. Or someone nursing an old grudge that had nothing to do with Eddie's final days in Kirkville.

Or even, I suddenly realized, some of the gypsies acting on their own, like Toma and the boys.

But, no. Queen Mary was too perceptive to miss something like that; if Toma killed Eddie, Mary would know.

Unless she was lying.

Damn. It's little wonder so many people never even try to be smart; being dumb is so much easier.

But I didn't think Mary had lied to me. I could be wrong, of course—*probably* was wrong, if track records are any indicator—but you have to trust someone sometime, even if it turns out to be an old gypsy swindler.

I unlocked and climbed in behind the wheel, the Jeep groaning and creaky stiff after half a day sitting unused in the cold of the parking lot. I urged the engine awake and let it warm while I sat and shivered and waited for the heater to heat. I was tired of thinking and the radio hasn't worked in years, so I had nothing better to do than idly gaze out the frost–blurred windows at my surroundings.

That's how I happened to notice the birddog on my tail.

Usually I'm too preoccupied or dense to pay attention to something as mundane as a dull gray late–model Chevrolet sedan parked all the way on the other side of the lot. But this one earned a second look for sitting half hidden alongside the bank building on the far end of the Chilton Plaza, a white cloud of exhaust billowing out the back. And a third look when it began to nose out of its hiding place, then inched back again when the driver determined my Jeep wasn't yet ready to depart.

Not that it was a purely serendipitous observation on my part; I had been forewarned. When Mel Stoneman quizzed my brother–in–law that morning about me squiring a pretty brunette, he had to know Ron would tell me all about it. Which meant Stoneman didn't care if I knew. Which further meant he actually wanted me to know he knew about the girl—or *a* girl.

The thought process was a bit sophisticated for Stoneman, but every dog has his day. The idea probably was to see if I'd panic and go running to warn my supposed girlfriend the minute I learned the intrepid Investigator Stoneman was on the trail, thereby leading the intrepid Investigator Stoneman right to the lady's hiding place.

He was getting nowhere on the case, in other words, and was desperate.

Time to test my theory. I put the Jeep in gear and drove slowly down the parking lane toward the Buffalo Road exit, adjusting my rearview mirror accordingly. As expected the gray Chevy—too innocuous to be anything but an unmarked police car—eased out from beside the bank and followed, keeping well back.

It took forever to make a left turn onto Buffalo Road, giving me time to decide on a course of action. I could simply proceed on to a couple of the innocent errands on my to–do list; picking up my laundry from the Sisters of Perpetual Devotion and swinging by the Chilton Town Hall to interview the town clerk about her new computerized filing system. But there was something else that needed doing and I didn't want a police escort along when I did it.

I had an idea how I could beat Stoneman at this little game, but there was one other thing to consider first.

Had he been sitting out there earlier, when Toma and the boys whisked me away in the Lincoln? And if he was, had he followed us out to Old Mill Road? That would complicate matters, but it didn't seem likely. With Stoneman's take–no–prisoners approach to law enforcement, he would've called in backup, surrounded the trailer, and arrested everyone in it on suspicion of being suspicious.

Okay, then.

I made my left, then a right onto Union Street at the traffic light. I was a mile south on Union before I could confirm he was still with me, but he was, hanging back a couple hundred yards, cruising steadily along behind an old van. I went east on Chilton Avenue, then south again on Beaver Road. It was nearly ten miles to my destination, at the very southeastern corner of the town of Chilton, but he stayed with me the whole way, closing up fast when he realized where I was leading him.

The Sheriff's Department substation occupies an older, one–story brick building that had been a kindergarten before the Chilton and Kirkville districts had unified. A cynic might note the irony, and I often have.

I dithered choosing a parking spot, giving Stoneman plenty of time to dump the Chevy sedan off in the staff lot behind the building and get himself inside through the back door. I walked through the main entrance just in time to see his trench coated backside ducking into a door at the far end of a narrow, green–tiled corridor. I smiled and nodded to the woman at the front desk and kept walking as if I knew what I was doing.

As I drew near the office Stoneman had entered, I could read the sign extending from the wall above the door: Captain Schulz, Chief of Station.

All the better.

I took a breath and strode brazenly into the office. The head honcho, blue uniform starched and pressed, sat behind the desk, fingers steepled, in mellow tones passing wisdom down from on high. Stoneman, seated in one of two side chairs, was nodding attentively, but his tapping toe gave away his impatience. Both men were taken aback at my unannounced arrival.

"Afternoon, Captain. Excuse the interruption, but I've got a deadline to meet. All right, Stoneman, who is she?"

"What the—?"

"The woman seen aiding and abetting that dead con man of yours, Eddie Williams."

"William*son*."

"Right, whatever." I helped myself to the third chair and took out my notepad. "Look, I know you guys have a job to do, confidential investigation, blah, blah, but I've got a job to do, too. And more important, the people have a right to know." Move over, John Peter Zenger. "So what's the woman's name? And where is she? Is she a suspect at this point, or just a key witness? Is that it? You've got her under protective custody?"

"Wait one minute." The captain. "What's going on here? Who is this, Mel?"

"He's Hackshaw, that newspaperman I was telling you about," Stoneman mumbled out of the side of his mouth, apparently trying to keep me from finding out my identity.

"Oh! The one who…" Irritation gave way to confusion. "But I thought he already knew about—"

"Uh, can we get back to that later, Cap? In private?"

"Hmm? Oh, right. Certainly."

This might be a good time to explain about the county sheriff's department. Like most places, we elect our sheriff, which means he's at least as much a politician as he is a law enforcement officer. That makes him super sensitive to a little thing called public relations, and the attitude tends to filter down through the ranks. After all, captains may come under civil service, but deputy undersheriffs don't, if you see what I mean. Patronage is the word I'm searching for, and ambition. (Note the word competence is conspicuously absent.) Show me a captain stuck in a small, out–of–the–way substation and I'll show you a career administrator daydreaming about a bigger desk downtown at the Public Safety Building. And they're even friendlier since this community policing craze hit.

I squinted at his name tag and began writing. "Captain Schulz, no t. And the R stands for?"

"Uh, Richard." He smiled professionally. "Folks call me Dick."

Little wonder. I smiled back. "You should hear some of the things they call me."

Stoneman refused to get into the spirit. "Just what in hell are you up to, Hackshaw, barging in here?"

"I thought I'd made that very clear, Mel. I'm doing an FYI piece on con artists for the *Advertiser*. You know, using the example of this Williams character—"

"Uh, I believe it's William*son*," the captain corrected.

"Right, right. Don't know why I can't keep that straight." I jotted a triangle in my pad. "Anyway, we're trying to expose the tricks of the trade these con artists use to prey on people so our readers will know what to look for. Now, we naturally thought we'd build the piece around this—" I glanced down at the triangle. "—Edgar Williamson and what he and his accomplice were up to recently."

Have you ever seen a dog trying to catch a butterfly? Stoneman's face held the same expression. Captain Dick, on the other hand, was cautiously enthused.

"I think that's an excellent idea, Mr. Hackshaw. The first thing people should do to avoid being defrauded is to deal strictly with reputable, established businesspeople located right here in the county. You can quote me on that, if you like."

"Very good." I jotted for real this time.

"But as far as the specifics of the Williamson case goes, I'll have to remind you that it *is* an ongoing homicide investigation. Officially, on the record, we can tell you only that we have some leads and are following up on them."

"Uh–huh. So unofficially, off the record, what's the deal with this mystery woman of Williamson's?"

"Well, uh—how'd you hear about that?"

"Same way you guys did, I expect. Interviewing the neighbors out on Bing Road, talking to some of the folks Williamson and his girlfriend tried to scam. Shortish, mid to late twenties, dark haired, possibly Italian–American, attractive and well–spoken. Sound about right?"

"That's—very much like the profile we have," he said, after a confirming glance toward Stoneman. "But you yourself have no, uh, personal knowledge of this woman?"

"Me? Why would I need to drive all the way down here to ask you guys about her if I already knew the answers?"

Stoneman wanted to blow so bad his eyes were seeping blood, but he couldn't lay a glove on me in front of Schulz. It was like confronting the neighborhood bully when he's with his parents. I couldn't resist tweaking his nose.

"So, Mel, have you developed any theories on who killed Edgar Williamson, or why?"

"Yeah. I think he was working this area with an inside man to help line up the marks." Just like Sherri Lewis, his lips hardly moved. "Only the partnership soured, maybe over the brunette bimbo, and Slow Eddie ended up dead."

"Interesting." I nearly choked when he said bimbo, but recognized the lower–case in time. "But wouldn't it make more sense if the killer was somebody Williamson was trying to cheat, or had cheated previously?"

He was slow to answer. "It's a possibility. I'm looking into that angle, too."

"We're pursuing all avenues," his superior added hastily. "But don't you think the murder angle is a bit—off the subject for your purposes anyway?" Hint, hint.

"Good point, Captain. After all, it's an FYI piece, right?" I homed in on Stoneman. "So, Mel, can you give me the pertinent names and a dollar count? The people Williamson ripped off locally, I mean, and for how much? I understand Arlene Grebwicz lost fifteen hundred."

"I can't go into that. People got a right to privacy, Hackshaw. They don't wanna do something stupid like this and then have everybody reading about it in the papers."

"That's very true," Schulz agreed. "However, I don't see any problem in releasing the total dollar amount. People need to know we're still talking about relatively small sums here. We're not dealing with the crime of the century, right? Go ahead and fill him in, Mel."

Williamson's three–week take came to just over five thousand dollars, as best they could tell, Stoneman said. About half of that was from a couple of people duped into investing in phony stock certificates, the other half from three couples who had each put down nine hundred dollar deposits (first month and security) on the Koon rental. I tried again to coax the names out of them, but it was no go.

Still, mission accomplished, as far as I was concerned. At the very least I'd sown the seeds of doubt concerning my own culpability in the Williamson affair, if not in Stoneman's mind then in the mind of his superior.

I started to pack away my pad and pen, but Captain Schulz insisted on giving me more tips on how to avoid being ripped off by con artists, which I dutifully recorded. ("Lock your doors"?) When he ran out of breath, I hopped up from the chair and pleaded a pressing assignment across town, mostly so I could get well away while Stoneman was still digging himself out with the boss.

Halfway out of the office, I turned back.

"Thanks a lot, Dick."

"You're very welcome."

"I was talking to Mel."

CHAPTER 21

❀

"You promise you won't use our names?" she said.

"Scout's honor."

"It's just we don't wanna look foolish in the papers," he said, adding ruefully, "Not that we don't deserve to."

"You shouldn't blame yourselves, Rolly. Williamson was a professional con man. You two weren't the first folks he bamboozled."

"Just the last." He managed a slight grin. "I guess that's somethin' anyway."

"It's all my fault, Rolly," she insisted. "If I hadn't gone and told you about Mr. Smith's offer—Williamson, I mean—you wouldn't have lost all your savings."

"Now, now, deary." He patted her hand, resting on the sofa beside him. "Truth is I practically begged the no–good son to take my money. Imagine, Hackshaw, I was worried he'd turn me down `cause I couldn't come up with the whole fifteen hundred, like Arlene here."

She sighed. "It's almost enough to make you lose faith in people."

Almost? I thought, studying with wonder her open, innocent face.

Arlene Grebwicz is a soft–spoken, lovely woman in her sixties; the sort who's had more than her share of hard luck and misery in her life, but who always has a kind word and an encouraging smile for everyone else. Just the sort of person who gets taken advantage of regularly.

It was early evening by the time I made it to Arlene's small bungalow in Kirkville. What little afternoon was left after the episode with Stavo's gypsies had been eaten up by my cat–and–mouse game with Stoneman. I had managed to squeeze in a quick interview with the Chilton Town Clerk and her new computer system and to pick up my laundry, but it was after five before I could call Arlene to verify she'd be home and willing to talk to me. It was then, over the phone, that I learned it was Arlene's friend, Rolly Keller, who was the second victim of Eddie Williamson's stock scam. Rolly has a tiny efficiency apartment in a converted house on Buffalo Road, just around the corner from Arlene's dead–end street. He's a ruggedly handsome, friendly guy of around sixty, with thick, wavy gray hair and a well–seamed face. He's also a very simple man who never made it past the eighth grade and who's spent a lifetime eeking out a living at a dozen different forms of manual labor. A thousand dollars may sound like a small amount, but in Rolly's circumstance, it's a fortune.

The sofa Arlene and Rolly shared and the chair I was seated in were draped with lacey old antimacassars. Spread across the low butler's table that separated us were the remnants of fresh coffee and a delectable spice cake with cream cheese frosting; dessert for them, dinner for me.

"It seemed like such a lucky coincidence at the time," Arlene was saying. "My winning that fifteen–hundred dollar superjackpot at St. Paul's, then out of the blue getting an offer to buy shares in a riverboat casino for exactly that same amount. Of course, I know now it wasn't a coincidence at all. This Williamson man knew just how much money I had from reading it in your newspaper column."

It was said without rancor, but I felt my defenses rise anyway. "I don't mean to rub it in, Arlene, but you did *ask* me to run that item."

"Oh, I'm not saying you did anything wrong, Hackshaw. I was pleased to see my name in the paper—I even clipped it out and put it up on the side of the refrigerator. It's Stanley who started talking like it was partly your fault, after we read your article about Williamson dying and how he was just a con man, and here I'd just gone and thrown all that money away. Stanley was mad as the dickens and looking for somebody to blame."

Speaking of no–good sons. "Well, I hope you'll set him and his lawyer straight."

"I've been trying, but he never listens to me. If it's any comfort, I think his friend from the snowmobilers club advised him to forget about trying to take you to court."

That was good to know, although I hoped Mr. Tad Reznik, esquire, had also advised his non–client to forget about trying to rearrange my face for me.

"Arlene was thinking we might wanna hire this lawyer ourselves," Rolly said. "Just to see if we'd have any chance of gettin' some satisfaction from Williamson's estate. I don't know about such things, but it sounds to me like we'd just be throwin' good money after bad."

"You're probably right. I doubt Slow Eddie left much of an estate anyway, but if you're both agreeable, I could talk to Bob Lebran for you, see what he thinks. I'm pretty sure he'd give me a consultation gratis. Without charging a fee," I clarified, in answer to Rolly's quizzical frown.

Unlike the reptilian Reznick, Lebran was one of those rare legal eagles who was always threatening to give the profession a good name. He also owed me a favor, or believed he did, which in his case amounted to the same thing.

"That'd be wonderful if Mr. Lebran could do that for us," Arlene said.

"Long as he understands I can't pay him anything up front," Rolly said. "If he can get some of our money back, that's different. Or maybe if he'd wait awhile, till I pick up some work."

"You're not working for CLF anymore?"

"Nope. Got laid off four, five months ago. Things been awful slow down there the last few years—ever since old Mr. Tice left, if you ask me. Young Tice, he's real interested in cuttin' the payroll, hirin' temporaries to fill in the gaps. Workin' lean, he calls it." He frowned and shook his head. "I guess he figures there's no percentage in payin' me a full–time wage and benefits when he can hire an outside cleaning crew to come in, or sign up the Hemford boys to work the shipping dock whenever he's got a truckload of fifty–fives comin' in or goin' out. Tell you the truth, Hackshaw, I'm gettin' a little long in the tooth to wrestle those big old steel drums anyhow."

By then, I was frowning myself. The old Mr. Tice Rolly was referring to was the company's founder, long–since retired to Boca Raton. Webster Tice was his nephew. Interesting that Tice was cutting back at his leather fabricating operation at the same time he was planning to spend thousands remodeling his house. Apparently belt–tightening was reserved for the rank and file.

"You say he's hired the Hemfords for dock work?"

Rolly nodded. "Earl and his boy. Not regular, but off and on for the last two, three years. They get called in say if there's a shipment of solvents to unload."

"Hmm." You're probably way ahead of me, but I'm the type who needs to let things simmer before I can make sense of them. At the time, hearing about the Hemfords' connections to Tice produced no more than a nagging, distant bell tinkling in the farthest recesses of my brain. And I had too many other things competing for attention.

"Anyway," Rolly was saying, "I've been lookin' for work, but the unemployment lady keeps tryin' to send me to job interviews in the city, and I don't have my own car anymore. Thing is my benefits run out in a few more weeks, so I guess I'll end up with no choice but puttin' on a paper hat at one of those fast–food joints over in Chilton—"

"Don't you even think it," Arlene said, her hand finding his. "Something more suitable will turn up sooner or later, you'll see. Something here in town."

Arlene and Rolly were more than neighbors, and more than good friends. She'd been widowed for several years now, living in simple comfort on her late husband's railroad pension. Marriage, or at least moving in together, would probably solve all of Rolly's problems except one—pride. But I suspected the bigger stumbling block was Arlene's son. Stanley Grebwicz had been married and divorced twice and, last I knew, had moved back in with his mother in the cramped bungalow. If you ask me, Arlene should try a little tough love and send Stanley packing, get on with her own happiness while she still can. Of course, nobody asked me.

"Uh, have you tried the IGA?" I asked Rolly. "I think they might be looking for a new produce man." I felt a touch guilty bringing it up, what with poor Judd Ames lying paralyzed in a hospital bed after wracking up his hot rod. But *somebody* stood to benefit from his bad luck and it might as well be Rolly Keller.

He and Arlene were all for it, after first tempering their enthusiasm with the appropriate sympathies for Ames. "I'll go by to see the manager first thing in the morning. Thanks, Hackshaw."

"Thank me if it works out." My circuits were beginning to overload on good will. "Now, you think we could get back to Edgar Williamson?"

There were no surprises in their stories; I hardly even took a note. Williamson, calling himself Edwin Smith, had called Arlene out of the blue one afternoon and explained that his "investment firm" had been authorized to handle "an initial public offering of stock futures" for a riverboat gambling venture due to begin operations next summer on the Niagara River near Buffalo. Under rules established by the State Gaming Commission, he said, this golden opportunity was being made available first to residents of New York State. Any unsold shares would later be made available to the general public at market prices considerably higher. The standard minimum purchase, he told her, was for ten shares at one–hundred and fifty dollars per, for a total of fifteen hundred dollars. And would she like him to stop by the house to explain the prospectus?

I asked if she still had the prospectus and had her dig it out from the cardboard file box she keeps under her bed. It never would've fooled an experienced investor like Bud Koon or Dave Pedersen, but it was easy to see how a guileless widow living on a fixed income could be impressed. The "prospectus" was a pastiche of *Wall Street Journal* and *Business Week* articles on the steady, often spectacular rise in casino and riverboat gambling stocks in recent years, juxtaposed with bar charts and columns of price/earnings ratios and so on; verifiable statistics on legitimate stocks, each and every one. The stickler was that none of the companies mentioned or stocks listed had anything to do with the Niagara River venture Williamson purported to represent. Sadly, to a person like Arlene, the distinction was like spotting broken glass in a diamond mine.

"I really wasn't that interested over the phone—I was just being polite—but when I met him, he seemed like such a nice young man. Neat, well–spoken." She blushed. "I remember wishing Stanley could be more like that."

The more she listened to Williamson, the more Arlene thought it might be Kismet; a chance to build her lucky bingo winnings into a substantial nest egg. And when she told Rolly about it, he was eager to get in on the action.

"I talked to this Smith—Williamson—on the phone and told him how I only could come up with a thousand dollars, but he explained how he could write it up so it was what he called a group sale. Me and Arlene poolin' our resources is how he put it." He shrugged. "Next thing I know, he sends his Gal Friday around to my place—pretty little thing, sweet as a mouthful of honey—and I'm handin' over a check for every last cent I got."

✤ ✤ ✤

The drive home to the carriage house was as cold and dark as my mood. You can stand back and look at something and know that it's wrong, but until you step in close, close enough to see the faces of the victims, you can't fully appreciate how wrong. I'd just about had it with dead con men and blustery gypsies and bullying cops. As far as I was concerned, Slow Eddie Williamson had gotten himself killed strictly on merit. I didn't believe for a moment that either Arlene or Rolly had anything to do with the murder, but I wouldn't blame them if they had.

By the time I was climbing the stairs to my crib, I'd decided to wash my hands of the whole slimey Williamson affair. Let the chips fall where they may. I'd write up the FYI piece for the *Advertiser*, because both Ruth and Captain Dick were expecting it. And I'd talk to Bob Lebran for Arlene and Rolly. Other than that, I had only one obligation left and I figured I could fulfill it with a phone call.

Chester Youngblood answered the second ring.

"It's Hackshaw," I said. "Let me speak to Little Stormcloud."

"Jesus, Hack, I was hoping you'd call." He was already half whispering, but he dropped another few decibels. "You making any headway straightening this thing out with Bimbo's people? I mean, we don't mind helping her out, but, man, she's starting to drive me nuts."

"Her allure is wearing a bit thin?"

He muttered a non–sacred oath. "She heard about Turning Point from one of the young guys over here, right? How much money the Oneidas are raking in with that damn casino of theirs." The Oneida branch of the old Iroquois Confederacy operates a gambling casino on tribal land east of Syracuse. No alcohol or slots, but plenty of roulette, craps, poker, and blackjack, and plenty of eager customers. "Now she's stirring up talk around here, saying how we should turn the Oakta into a Seneca version of Atlantic City. `We', she says, like she's starting to believe she really is Indian. What's worse, some of the young ones are starting to listen to her."

"I can't promise anything, but I think her family might be ready to deal on her terms, if I'm reading the situation right. And if Bimbo's interested in dealing. Put her on."

Her familiar voice filled the line and I was subjected to two minutes of non–stop jabber punctuated at regular intervals with snapping gum. How boring it was around there and how she had such a good idea for livening things up and making some money, but Chester was too hardheaded to listen to reason. She eventually shut up long enough for me to relate my latest encounter with the senior Wankas and to pass on Queen Mary's plea for a face–to–face talk.

"They need me, huh, because the Kris says so?" She chuckled softly. "That's good to know. Gives me like an edge, y'know? But that don't mean I'm just gonna walk into a room someplace, let Toma and Stavo and the Kaslof brothers haul me home by the hair, I don't care what Mama says."

"Look, you and yours will have to hash that out between you. I delivered the message, now you do what you want. Meet or don't meet. Work something out with Stavo, take a powder, it's up to you. But make up your mind in the next twenty–four hours. After that, if Toma and the boys come after me again—"

"You wouldn't tell `em where I was!"

"The mood I'm in," I said, "I'd draw `em a map."

"So what's got you so pissed off all a sudden?"

"I just got done talking to a couple of your marks."

"I…dunno what you mean."

"I mean Arlene Grebwicz and Rolly Keller. A kindly little widow and a sixty–year–old man living off his unemployment checks. Ring any bells?"

She was silent for two seconds, probably a personal record. Then, "Lookit, all I ever did was pick up a check from somebody like Eddie told me, so I dunno why you should be so mad at me."

"Because Williamson is too dead to holler at and you're the only one who's left. And because this hear–no–evil, see–no–evil routine of yours is a load of bullshit. Cheating, stealing, taking all comers for whatever you can get—it's what you do, Bimbo, and you've been doing it since you were old enough to tell a convincing lie."

A sharp intake of breath was followed by a sob. "Sure I been doin' it since I was a little kid. I didn't know no better, Hackshaw. You think a seven–year–old's s'posed to stand up to her papa and her mama when alls they teach her is—"

"Save the nature versus nurture crap for somebody who's interested. If anyone has a right to cry right now, it's Arlene Grebwicz—and she's got too much class."

There was a longer pause this time; when Bimbo finally spoke again, her voice oozed petulant defiance. "I was gonna tell you somethin' I remembered about Eddie, somethin' that maybe could be important. But if all you can do is be mean to me, Hackshaw, you can just kiss my gypsy ass."

The connection broke with a clatter.

I slammed the receiver back in place and bounced some pointless epithets off the apartment walls. I calmed down a few minutes later, aided by a bowl of pipe tobacco and a silent heart–to–heart with yours truly.

The important thing, I reminded myself, is that I was out of it. Or almost. If Toma and Stavo came after me, I'd simply tell them what they wanted to know and that would be that. As for Stoneman, if he'd hung his entire so–called investigation on dogging me in hopes I'd convict myself, well, he was every bit as dumb as I suspected and, thus, no more a threat than he'd ever been. That was the new theory, anyway.

If I felt bad about anything, it was for Arlene and Rolly, and to some extent the folks who'd lost their rental deposits...but, no. That wasn't my responsibility. I mean, that's the real reason Justice is blindfolded, isn't it? She doesn't want to see the looks on the faces of all those plain, honest folk she's let down.

So move on, Hackshaw. Leave mystery to the Brits and tragedy to the Greeks; your niche is journalism, the comfortable, non–threatening, name–dropping variety.

I felt my shoulders sag. With relief, I'm sure.

Then Fate came knocking again. Unquestionably a female rat–tat–tat on the downstairs door.

My brain threw in the towel and followed my feet down the narrow stairs. When I pulled back the door, she fairly flew across the threshold, a whimpering, overly–fragrant dervish of encircling arms and swaying cleavage.

"Oh, Hackshaw, thank God!"

But before I could thank anyone, I was up to my eyeballs in Delia Hemford.

CHAPTER 22

She hustled me back up the stairs, in every sense of the word.

"I was afraid you'd be out cattin' or somethin' and I'd miss you," she said breathily, still clinging to my arm.

"Delia, what's this all—?" In the full light and relative calm of the apartment, I could see her clearly, including the mouse under her left eye. "Earl beat you up?"

"What, this?" Her fingers found the bruise; I winced, afraid she might puncture her eye with one of those long, sparkly silver glue–on nails. "Damn right the son of a bitch beat on me. Think I'd be used to it by now, wouldn'tcha? But this time was different. This time I got to thinkin' about things, how it don't have to be like this. And I got you to thank for it."

"You do?"

"When you came around the other day, it reminded me how a real gentleman acts with a woman. Polite, I mean. Considerate and fun and nice, and not talkin' filth half the time like that asshole husband of mine." Her cotton candy hairdo was tickling my nose. "So when he starts whalin' on me tonight, I said, lady, you don't have to put up with this shit anymore. There's men out there know how to treat a woman. Like you, Hackshaw."

"Well, I—"

The rest was obliterated when Delia's mouth encircled mine. I swear she could open an aspirin bottle with that tongue of hers. It took all my strength and what little willpower I had to back her off to arm's length.

"Listen, you were right to leave him," I said, gasping for air. "If you let me make a couple of calls, I'll find a place you can stay, maybe a program that can help. There's a shelter over in Chilton—"

"You're all the shelter I need tonight, baby. We can talk about that other stuff in the mornin'."

"Now, Delia—"

"*Now*, Hackshaw." She whipped off the ankle–length fake fur she was wearing and threw it on the floor. "Right now."

She looked like one of those cartoon femme fatales from the L'il Abner comic strip. The skin–tight scoop–neck jersey barely containing the impossible cantelope breasts; a ragged pair of denim cut–offs and high–heeled black leather boots; the lemon chiffon hair and ruby red bee sting lips and fluttery fake eyelashes and eyeliner thick as stucco.

I wanted her so bad my thighs quivered.

Appropriately enough, we ended up writhing on the love seat, Delia more or less on top, powerful wet kisses drowning me, two pairs of hands maniacally searching for contours and fasteners, our trembling voices a holy duet praising the Lord for the bounty we were about to receive.

Pathetic, I know, but try to put yourself in my position. Figuratively, I mean. I'd lusted for Delia ever since high school, when she was Delia Dunkle, the girl most likely to. She'd single–handedly inspired the principal to mandate a dress code outlawing miniskirts, hot pants, spike heels, and fishnet stockings—and this when she was a *sophmore*. Every male in the school, from the guidance counselor on down to the pimpliest freshman, followed Delia's every move through the hallways like a Wall Street analyst follows the Dow Jones

Average. (Miss Hardy, the girls gym teacher, gave up the profession altogether and joined the Marine Corps, make of it what you will.)

And now, twenty years later, it was as if an angel had descended to grant me one last shot at fulfilling my fondest adolescent fantasy.

"Slow down, Hackshaw, you're gonna rip my blouse."

"Sorry, Delia love."

"It ain't a race, honey."

Too bad, seeing as how I was a mortal lock to finish first.

"Scoot up a little, baby, so I can get at your belt buckle."

I scooted. "God, Delia, you're so—*ee–ahh*! Careful with the press–on fingernails, sweetness." She could neuter a horse with those things.

"Sorry, baby. They're just so big and clunky." She probably meant the nails. "How's that? Better?"

"Oh, yeah. Ohhh, yeahhh."

I began to slip away, eyes half shut, head lolled back over the arm of the love seat. Sinking toward ecstasy. Sinking…sinking…

Then I heard it.

A low, drawn–out squeak. Out in the stairwell, fourth step from the top. I know exactly, because I'd been meaning to fix it for years. What you have to do is, you get at the tread from underneath with some wood shims—never mind. I sat up fast and pulled Delia's hand away.

"Shush. Did you hear that?" I whispered.

"Hear what? C'mon, baby." She resumed groping.

Then I heard it again. Third step from the landing this time, louder and higher in pitch. Always reminded me of stepping on a cat's tail.

"There! Hear it?"

She had to that time.

But she didn't. She wrapped her arms around me. "Please, honey, we're just gettin' started—"

But she had to.

Which could only mean one thing.

In that last sliver of a second, just as I saw the door knob begin to slowly rotate, my mind again flashed back twenty–something years to Delia Dunkle, Delia the Dream, sashaying down the high school corridors on the arm of this or that greasy haired, leather jacketed, self–tattooed, pointy shoed hood. Drawn even then to the toughest, dumbest, most dangerous lowbrow losers she could find.

And I realized why guys like me, guys who edited the school paper or ran cross–country or voluntarily took driver's ed, had only our dreams to sustain us all these years; because Delia wouldn't give a one of us the time of day. And I realized, too, that girls who wear leopard skin leotards rarely change their spots.

It was the old badger game, of course.

With me as the Boy and Delia as the Girl and, starring as the pseudo–enraged Husband bursting in at the critical moment, who else but—

"Earl!"

The door slammed against the side wall and there he was, spread–legged in the doorway, cold gray eyes bugged out, hands balled, teeth clenched, every major vein in his head standing out in bas relief.

"I'm gonna *kill* you!"

I was struggling to my feet, but it wasn't easy with Delia draped around me, in the throes of her performance.

"Oh, Lord, don't let him get me, Hackshaw!"

"He was talking to *me*, you stupid—" I wrenched her hands from my shirt and, with all my might, shoved her backward into the path of the onrushing Earl. They both started to go down, but whether they made it all the way to the floor, I couldn't say. I was too busy running in the opposite direction, into my bedroom.

It was a dead–end. No doors out and no time to pry open the balky window. I heard a roar immediately behind me and dove under the bed—

"Come outa there, you chickenshit cocksucker!"

—and rolled out the other side again, brandishing a baseball bat. I keep it under there to deter housebreakers and other unwanted guests. It's an Easton softball bat, actually, one of those metal things that ping on contact and never break. Earl was impressed enough to stop jumping on the mattress.

"Whoa. What the hell you think you're gonna do with that, dickhead?"

"Fungo your face." I took a practice swing, nearly taking out a lamp. "If you don't pack up your wife and get out of here."

If bad judgment were brains, Earl Hemford would be a Nobel laureate. Rather than retreat, he telegraphed his intentions with a twisted grimace and an equally twisted curse. He also forgot to account for the extra thrust provided by the mattress, so when he leaped at me, I easily sidestepped and watched, awed, as he flew headfirst into the wallpaper.

"Unnghh."

His Lordship the Earl of Asinine lay in ruins along the baseboard. I figured that was the end of it until the other royal pain in the ass rushed in and began haranguing me for allegedly bludgeoning her meal ticket.

"You coulda killed him with that thing!"

"I never even touched the idiot."

"Lyin' bastard!" Her fists came up, but I waggled the bat to let her know I was an equal–opportunity slugger.

"Takes one to know one, Delia," I said. "I'd like to believe you got that black eye for trying to talk him out of this little charade."

"I don't know what you're talkin' about, Hackshaw, and neither do you."

"You can't possibly *enjoy* getting knocked around."

She puffed out her chest, overkill if ever there was. "I give as good as I get, and it's none of your damn business anyway."

Then it turned into a movie we've all seen. You know the one—where the obnoxious teenagers stand around congratulating themselves until the bullet–riddled ax killer miraculously springs to life for one last cheap scare? Earl's hand suddenly shot out and grabbed me by the ankle. This time I did bash him one.

"*Yee–aahhh*! Jesus Christ, you broke my fuckin' hand!"

I resisted the obvious joke that follows a set–up line like that and instead said, "If it was really broken, you wouldn't be able to flex your fingers like that. Now get up and get out—help him, Delia. Come on, *move*."

It took awhile, but I got them both to the door, Delia staring darts as she yanked on her faux fur, Earl shambling along and muttering obscenities like a poster boy for Tourette's syndrome. When they reached the bottom of the stairs, he turned, faceless in the gloom, and looked back up at me.

"Don't think this is the end of it, Hackshaw."

Once they were out the door, I went around to my kitchen window and watched them climb into a dented Plymouth. They hadn't even bothered with two cars; Earl must've been crouching in the back seat the whole time, estimating that Delia would have me half undressed and slobbering for more in under five minutes. For once in his life he was right.

Make that twice. This *wasn't* the end of it.

I boiled water for tea and repacked my briar and tuned my vintage stereo to an oldies station, the volume low. Then I sat and brooded, trying to block out the self–pity of paradise lost in order to concentrate on the implications of the evening's passion play.

I was still examining the pieces when the phone rang.

"Hackshaw, I decided to forgive you." Bimbo.

"Gee, thanks." I hung up on her.

She called back.

"Okay, now we're even. You gonna listen or what?"

"Listen to what?"

"I told you before, I remembered somethin' maybe could be important. Maybe it'd help you figure out this big play Eddie was talkin' about and you could find out who killed him. Maybe even what happened to those people's money he took. I dunno, but maybe."

"What is it you remembered?"

"First you gotta do me a favor, okay?"

I sighed.

"It's no big deal, Hackshaw. I need you to go back to Mama and Stavo again, is all, to like set up some ground rules for us to meet."

"Look, can't you handle this over the phone or something? Queen Mary said you'd know how to get in touch—"

"Yeah, but that's like through the gypsy grapevine, y'know? And I don't trust those people—they're all family. They do what Stavo tells `em."

I took a few puffs on my pipe. I was going to agree, but that didn't mean I had to make it too easy for her. Finally, I said, "All right. I'll be your go-between."

"Word of honor? You swear on your father's head?"

"Yes, Bimbo. I swear on my father's head."

Still she hesitated. "Your father—he's alive or dead?"

"Dead."

"Ah, that's good then. Okay, I tell you what I remembered about Eddie. After that, you write down what I tell you to tell Mama and Stavo and tomorrow you go find Stavo and give him the message."

"How'm I supposed to find Stavo?"

"I know where to look. If he ain't in one place, he'll be in the other one, sooner or later. Okay?"

"Fine. Now, about Eddie's big score?"

She remembered an item Eddie had taken from the camping trailer about a week before he'd first told her he might be onto something big.

"Thing is, they weren't at the house when I got over there on Sunday night—"

"`They'?"

"—and you didn't say nothin' about `em bein' in the trunk of his car with all his other junk."

"For Christ's sake, Bimbo, get to the point!"

"Didn't I mention? It's his binoculars."

CHAPTER 23

Robert Lebran's office is above the IGA on Kirkville's main drag. I had just stopped in downstairs at the grocery store to put in a good word for Rolly Keller with the manager and I decided, since I was there, to complete my commitment to him and Arlene by talking to Lebran about their situation.

It was while going up the stairs that I ran into Bud and Marion Koon, coming down.

"I'd say good morning," I said, as we passed. "But I'm afraid it may be construed as verbal harassment."

"Coming from you it might well be," Bud Koon said, in a feckless stab at wit. "You're probably as skilled at slander as you are at libel, Hackshaw."

"I know it when I hear it," I said. "Would you like to repeat that comment in front of witnesses?"

He stopped three steps below me and turned, ready to make an angry retort, but his wife gave a cautionary tug on his overcoat.

"We don't have time for this, dear. We have that other thing, and remember you have to be back downtown to the office by noon."

"I know, I know."

"Busy, busy," I said. "Between your investment portfolio and your rental properties, I'm surprised you have any time left to work for the county's taxpayers."

"I'm here on *personal* time, if it's any of your business."

"It's not," Marion interjected. "He's just trying to goad you."

She was right; I was still nettled by the nuisance complaint they'd called in to Ruth. And I've got just as much right to be petty as they do. We glared at each other for a few more seconds. The stairwell smelled faintly of oranges and fresh baked goods, I noticed. Also of anxiety.

"This is pointless," Marion said eventually. As often happens in these silly macho stand–offs, it takes a woman's touch to defuse things. "Look, Mr. Hackshaw, if we've been unduly harsh with you, then we're sorry. It's just that we feel we've been victimized, too. We've invested a lot of time and hard work into our properties and we've always tried to deal honestly and fairly—"

"Marion." He gripped her elbow. "Don't give him the satisfaction."

"If he's planning to write any more stories about that swindler, he should at least know that we've acted in good faith." She stared at her husband a moment; then, at his shrug, looked back up at me. "We've paid back out of our own pockets two of the three deposits Edgar Williamson illegally collected on our Bing Road property, a total of eighteen hundred dollars. And we've effectively absorbed the other nine hundred by agreeing to allow the third depositor to move in on February 1 without paying us first month's rent or security."

"Satisfied?" Koon asked.

What else could I say? "Yeah. I think you did the right thing by those folks. If I *do* write anything else about the incident, I'll see that you get the proper credit."

"Thank you." They turned as one to go.

"Long as I've got your ear," I said. "There is one other thing I wanted to ask you about. You had other tenants in the house up until last fall—a black family, was it?" I vaguely remembered one of the neighbors referring to `coloreds'.

"They were Brazilians," Koon said. "The husband was a civil engineer, here temporarily to do some post–grad work at Rochester Institute of Technology. Excellent tenants. We wish they'd stayed on."

"I was wondering if they might've ever commented to you about any strange goings–on at any of the adjoining properties. Maybe late at night—"

"No, they never complained about anything," Bud Koon said. "Like I told you, they were excellent tenants."

✦ ✦ ✦

Bob Lebran raked the fingers of his right hand through his rust beard and grinned. "You're fishing, Hack."

"What? All I did was ask if you had a productive meeting with the Koons."

He nodded. "Implying casual interest only. But how did you know the Koons had come by to see *me*, instead of, say, Winters across the hall, if you hadn't already been out checking up on them?"

I'd forgotten all about Mark Winters, the C.P.A. who occupies the back half of the floor. "It's a special form of intuition we journalists have," I said. "Anyway, I was just curious. If you think you need to be circumspect about it, fine. I was only making conversation."

Which was true. We had covered the reason for my visit—Arlene Grebwicz and Rolly Keller's situation—in the first five minutes. (He didn't think there was much he could do under the circumstances, but he agreed to run a check through Niagara County court records to see if Williamson had a will in probate, "in case there's anything there worth liening on.") Now we were merely making chit–chat while we finished the large mugs of coffee provided by Jeanie, Lebran's lovely wife/receptionist/paralegal. I'd brought up the Koons because I was looking for something to talk about and they were fresh in my mind. And I'm nosy.

"Oh, it's not a big deal or anything," he said. "I mean, they're not even my clients in this—I'm representing the town—and even at that, the whole business is little more than a legal formality."

"Which business?" If lawyers knew how to get straight to the point, we wouldn't need so damn many of them.

"Bud Koon filed request applications several months ago to have town services extended to some property they own out on Bing Road. But now they've decided to put the property up for sale, so they're withdrawing the applications and they want the unused portions of their application fees refunded."

"This property, you're talking about a small pre–fab ranch house they own out there?"

He shook his head. "A couple of acres of vacant land that came with it, I think. It's an L–shaped parcel that runs off Bing. The Koons were planning to build like a mini–tract on it, four or five houses on a cul–de–sac. They had to put up a couple thousand dollars in fees when they filed for the extension of services to the site, but now that they're canceling, they'll get all but about ten percent of it back. I'm on retainer to the town board, so I have to review the documents. It's pro forma stuff."

"Did the Koons say why they decided to sell instead of developing the land?"

"The town engineer ruled the land's partially on a flood plain, so the lots would have to be graded a certain way and the houses would have to be built with a more complex drainage system around the foundations. I guess the extra cost scared 'em off." He shrugged. "Building houses on speculation is always a risky—hey, I just thought of something. Isn't that the house that con artist was renting? The guy you wrote about last week?"

"As a matter of fact—"

"Hah! I knew you had ulterior motives, Hackshaw. What's going on?"

I sipped my coffee. "Good question."

❧ ❧ ❧

I didn't have an answer; not when it came to the Koons, anyway.

If I had to guess, I'd opt for the obvious. Their house–building scheme had grown too expensive and potentially bureaucratic, as Lebran had indicated, so they decided to cut their losses. Add to that the bitter taste left by their experience with Slow Eddie Williamson's rental scam and they may've been even more eager to put the Bing Road property out of sight and out of mind. After all, for a couple of self–described straight arrows like Bud and Marion Koon, even a whiff of scandal was too much.

That was probably all there was to it. I *hoped* that was all there was to it, because the only alternative I could think of created complexities I didn't need.

It had taken a couple hours of lying awake in bed the previous night to calm down from my near–midair collision with Earl Hemford, not to mention my near–bliss with his wife. A couple of hours to consider what Rolly Keller had told me—about Webster Tice's cost–cutting moves over at CLF and his hiring the Hemfords, pater and fil, to handle loading dock grunt work—and to examine these new bits alongside other, seemingly unconnected snatches of information I'd gleaned along the way.

I needed to check out a couple more things before I'd know with any certainty. But if what I'd hypothesized was right, it explained why Slow Eddie thought he'd stumbled onto the score of his life—and it gave Tice and the Hemfords a powerful reason to snuff out that life.

But all my nocturnal cogitating hadn't factored in a role for the Koons and, frankly, I didn't see where they could possibly fit into the picture. The Koons in cahoots with the Hemfords? It would make for the oddest of odd couples, the uptight, overachieving, image–conscious Koons and the profane, slothful, lowlife Hemfords. I mean, picture Ozzie and Harriet playing bridge with Bonnie and Clyde.

There was just no way such an alliance made sense…

"Elias? I said `good morning."

"Huh? Oh. Morning, Ruthie."

It's amazing how the body can put itself on automatic pilot sometimes while the brain is busy elsewhere. I scarcely recalled making the drive from Kirkville to the *Advertiser* office in Chilton Center, but there I was.

"You look a little haggard, Elias. I hope you weren't out at one of your dusk to dawn poker marathons."

"Did I mention I was suffering from a slight iron deficiency?"

"Oh! Yes, you did, but I thought…" Guilt flushed her lovely face. "Did Dr. Gordon prescribe anything? Vitamin supplements?"

"It's mostly a case of the winter blahs, Sis, don't worry about it. Has Alan been in?"

She shook her head. "Noonish. He has morning classes on Tuesdays, remember? Listen, we're a little light on ad space, I'm afraid, so we'll need to cut the news hole accordingly. Do you know how long Ramblings will run this week? And your informational piece on con artists, will that be ready, and how long do you think it will take to…"

Amazing, too, how the rest of the world goes on about its business no matter what.

I spent a solid ninety minutes doing the work for which I'm marginally paid; editing Liz Fleegle's saccharine social notes column, fleshing out Ramblings, reviewing photo art and cutlines with Ruth. I was about to peruse the notes I'd taken in my `interview' with Captain Dick, seeing how much of it I could actually use for an FYI piece on ripoff avoidance, when Alan showed up.

I waited for Ruth to leave for lunch, then motioned him over to my desk.

"Any luck with the assignment I gave you yesterday?"

"Well, not really." He pushed a lock of hair away from his eye, but it flopped down again. "She's quite a character, I'll say that."

"Who?"

"The woman who won the Lottery, Mary Margaret Hoos." He rolled his eyes at my hopeless stupidity. "She didn't seem to know anything about the Williamson thing. I take it she's had so many crackpots calling up since she won that million dollars, she's had to get an unlisted phone *and* an answering machine. Anyway, we chatted quite awhile—she was very outgoing once she realized I wasn't trying to sell her anything. You'll never guess what she told me, it's so cliched. She's planning to keep her waitressing job! Of course, she's going to take additional time off, for excursions to Las Vegas and Vatican City—"

"I didn't mean Mary Margaret Hoos," I managed to say, working it in edgewise. "I meant the other assignment."

"Oh. The Bing Road thing?"

"That very thing."

"It was a waste of time pretty much. I stopped at four or five houses, talked to three hausfraus and a retired graybeard who reminded me of my grandfather, right down to his red suspenders and bourbon breath—"

"*Alan*," I said sharply. "Focus. Stay on subject, remember?" I'd had to remind him about the same tendency in his writing, this meandering of his. He tried to argue it was a new cutting–edge style of journalism, but it was merely too much adolescent exposure to MTV and Nintendo.

He spent a moment composing himself, counting to ten, whatever. Then, with a sigh, "I tried that green house you told me about first, the one where no one was home when you stopped by? That's where I spoke with the old man. Urbell, I think—I've got the name in my notes. Anyway, he didn't know anything about Edgar Williamson except what he read in the paper. Said he minded his own business and expected his neighbors to do the same. And that's essentially what the three women I talked to said, too."

"What about the illegal truck traffic along Bing Road?"

"Well, yeah, Mr. Urbell knew what I was talking about, and one of the women, too. They both recall hearing noises from a large truck, like a big engine and grinding gears and stuff, maybe once a week or every two weeks."

"What time of day?"

"Late. Always late in the evening, they said. Which makes sense, right? If some trucker's taking shortcuts down a restricted back road?"

"Anybody ever get a look at one of these trucks?"

"Mr. Urbell said he did once, but not too clearly. Said it was like a big flatbed truck with high removable side rails. Something like a cattle hauler, I think he said. I wrote it all down."

I had him get his notebook and read me the particulars. Then I went through it with him again, double–checking exactly which homeowners at which addresses recalled hearing trucks and which didn't.

When we were finished, and I had Alan thoroughly confused, I gave him a new assignment and shooed him out. As for me, I had one last question to answer, which I was able to handle with a phone call to the library. Just as I was hanging up, Ruth returned, toting a white paper bag.

"What's that?" I sniffed her way. "Anything good?"

"Your lunch." She reached inside and deposited the contents on my desk; a plastic take–out bowl with a clear lid. "Spinach salad with a vinaigrette dressing. For your iron deficiency." She was actually smiling, so pleased was she with her thoughtful blessed self.

There was nothing to say but, "Yum."

CHAPTER 24

It was the missing binoculars that did it.

By the time Earl and Delia had cleared out of my apartment Monday evening, I had a general idea what was going on. Thanks to Rolly Keller tipping me to the Hemford boys working for Webster Tice, that is, and Doc Gordon telling me about the medical examiner finding traces of formaldehyde and ammonia in—or on—Slow Eddie's body.

But it was Bimbo Wanka remembering the binoculars that provided the connecting thread.

If you've already raced far ahead, fine, you're smarter than me. Or maybe you just don't have other distractions, like crazed husbands, gypsy and otherwise, threatening to dismantle you. Anyway, I never said I was particulary good at this sort of thing, did I? Just better than Mel Stoneman, which, as you may've noticed, ain't bragging.

The theory goes like this: Slow Eddie Williamson, sitting one evening in the Bing Road kitchenette and monitoring the phones, notices headlights bobbing through the woods that run well back behind the rental house. He's curious, not to mention bored, so he decides to bring the binoculars from the camper trailer the next day. He sits at the table, he waits, he answers the phone, he scans the woods, perhaps seeing nothing for the next several days.

Then, a week or so later, the lights return. Maybe he cracks open a window and hears the grinding of the truck gears as it moves over the bumpy, snowy terrain. He tries the glasses, but it's too dark and there are too many trees to make out anything definitive. So the next day, he hikes across the back lot and over the fence into the woods, trying to pinpoint the spot where he saw the lights stop. And he does find it, slipping and sliding and sinking to the tops of his thoroughly inappropriate street shoes into a toxic snowcone of frozen mush laced with liquid ammonia and formalin and probably half a dozen other chemicals. Chemicals that, according to the city library's science department, are commonly used in industrial applications, such as tanning and fabricating leather.

Alan's information had been just as informative. The households that had complained about illegal truck traffic were all sited along Bing Road between Kirkville Road—which leads due north from the village—and the Hemford Road turnoff. The two homeowners who lived well past the turnoff couldn't recall hearing any late–night trucks. Obvious conclusion: the trucks were coming up from the village and turning onto the Hemford's dead–end road.

And then there was the description of a large flatbed with side rails; CLF, Inc. had a truck just like that.

Of course, Eddie didn't automatically know the stuff was being trucked over from Webster Tice's auto upholstery operation; he had no idea where it was coming from. But he knew where it was ending up, and a minimum of research at the town clerk's office would've told him whose land it is.

Thus Slow Eddie's potential big score was not a con, but plain, old–fashioned blackmail. He contacts the Hemfords, tells them what he knows about the illegal dumping on their land, and demands hush money. They arrange to meet with him that fateful Saturday, probably Earl and his eldest boy, Early. They overpower Williamson or hold him at gunpoint, whatever. Then they either truss him up or knock him out and stick him in his car with the engine running, in an enclosed building, most likely the small barn that doubles as the Hemford's garage. Eddie succumbs sometime early Saturday evening, but to be on the safe side, the Hemfords leave the old Mercury in the barn until the wee hours of morning, when the Saturday night drunks have all gone home and the Sunday pious are not yet stirring. Then one of them drives car and body over to Park Road while the other follows. Fifty yards or so short of the dangerous curve, they prop Eddie behind the wheel, slip the car into the appropriate gear—mechanical, I'm not—and play bumper cars, using the Hemford's vehicle to push the Mercury along until it gathers enough momentum to overshoot the curve and travel another thirty feet, to and over Black Creek Bluff.

Tice may've been told about the extortion attempt beforehand and may've helped murder Eddie. Or he might've been kept in the dark until after the deed was done. But he *knew*—that much seemed certain. His aggressiveness in trying to hire me for an expensive remodeling job on his crappy house, over the objections of his wife, made no sense from the first. But now it did. He'd been informed by the Hemfords that I'd come snooping around, asking about Williamson and, even worse, about trucks illegally using Bing Road. Hoping to divert me from investigating any further, he tried to co–opt my time by throwing money and a big contracting job at me. When I put him off, the Hemfords decided to put me out of action their way, by staging the badger game so that Earl could pound me into a hospital bed.

Had to be.

Now the question was, what do I do about it?

I know what you're thinking. Go to the police, Hackshaw. Do an end run around Stoneman and lay the whole shebang at the feet of Captain Schulz.

Make myself a hero, right?

Maybe. Maybe not.

Look. The law doesn't deal in theories; it has this nagging insistence for tangible evidence, facts, eyewitnesses. What I had, in the main, was a lot of well–reasoned conjecture. What I needed was proof, and supporting testimony from someone in the know. This is where Bimbo comes in.

I needed her, to corroborate that Eddie had talked about setting up a big score only days before he turned up dead, and to attest to Eddie's routine out at the rental house, sitting at the card table and staring out the window for hours on end. And I needed her to verify that Eddie had taken a pair of binoculars out to the house, binoculars that had gone missing.

If I could keep some control over Bimbo until the time was right to call in the Sheriff's Department, there was a good chance her testimony, along with an inspection of the dump site and the medical examiner's report on the body and all the other bits I'd collected, would be enough to convince the police, a prosecutor, and, hopefully, a jury.

Because, now more than ever, I didn't want to blow it and see the bad guys walk away. Now it was personal.

Let's face it, neither the world nor I would lose any sleep if Slow Eddie's murder went unsolved. He was a cold–hearted predator who fed on the weak and the gullible, whose idea of upward mobility was to graduate to blackmail. But nailing Tice and the Hemfords for poisoning a patch of my town, now that was a worthy objective. Not to mention paying back the bastards for all the aggravation they'd put me through.

All right, then. The first thing I had to do was keep Bimbo in tow, so I could find her when I needed her. And that was an impending problem. From what she'd told me on the phone the night before, it sounded as if she was in a bargaining mode, ready to strike a deal with Stavo and Queen Mary. She'd asked me to tell her parents she'd meet with them on neutral ground to discuss how to deal with the mulo, provided Stavo would swear on his dead father's head that

Toma and the twin terrors, the Kasloff brothers, would be kept in the dark about the meeting. She might also be willing to consider returning to the family, she'd said, under certain conditions. I couldn't tell you exactly what Bimbo had in mind—she'd never confide completely in a gadjo, any more than the rest of her people would—but my impression was she was angling for two things; a release from her marriage to Toma, and a bigger say in how Stavo divvies up the money she brings in with her scams.

But if I made the arrangements for the meet, and if Stavo agreed to her demands, you could bet dollars to donuts the bunch of them would pack up their caravan and head south to join the rest of the clan for what was left of the winter. And I'd have lost my key witness.

Which meant I'd just have to string along both Bimbo and her family long enough to put together a solid case against Tice and the Hemfords.

That was the second thing I needed; hard evidence. And I had an idea how to go about getting it.

But first things first.

❧ ❧ ❧

The Bauhaus crowd would've been pleased with the new Off–Track Betting parlor in Chilton. It's a square, nearly windowless one–story building constructed of bland brown cast–concrete blocks, banded around the middle with a course of green blocks like a Christmas ribbon on a shoebox.

Bimbo had been very clear on one point; most afternoons Stavo could be found either at the closest OTB parlor or at any smoky bar-room that had cheap booze, a pay phone and a handy back door. I'd already tried the Nook, grabbing a quick ale while I was there to wash the taste of Ruth's spinach salad out of my mouth. My second stop proved to be the charm.

A familiar Cadillac bearing Alabama plates was idling in a fire lane out front of the betting parlor. One of the Kasloff boys was behind the wheel, watching me with that chimpanzee smile. Queen Mary was in the back seat, working overtime on a cruller. I waved and went inside the building.

There was a line of betting windows on my left as I entered, half a dozen clerks behind tinted glass dispensing bet receipts and Lotto tickets. To the right was a small snack area with vending machines. It opened onto a larger space, maybe thirty by thirty, where about two dozen people of all sizes and circumstances milled around or studied the racing cards posted along the walls or simply sat and stared intently at a trio of television monitors. Watching, not a field of horses racing around a track, but a series of arcane numbers crawling across the screen. Little pieces of paper littered the floor everywhere.

I found Stavo in a separate room reserved for smokers. He was overflowing a small, molded plastic chair, a stub of cigar plugged into the corner of his mouth, his eyes panning from a sheet of paper he was holding to the TV monitors mounted in the corner. He seemed glad to see me.

"Hackshaw, how ya doin'? Sit." He held out the sheet. "Listen, what's that say right there, for the seven horse?"

I squinted. "Lorene's Legend."

"Huh. Musta been a scratch. Fuckin' Aqueduct, they're always messin' me up."

I almost asked how he could negotiate a racing form if he couldn't read, but caught myself in time. The Rom have their ways, as with all things, and anyway, I wasn't there on behalf of Literacy Volunteers. Stavo got to the point first, however.

"Mary said you'd be around today. Bimbo sent you, right?"

"Right." I glanced to my left; a wrinkled old guy was leaning our way, hoping to steal a tip. "We need to talk, Stavo. Maybe we could find a less distracting atmosphere?"

"What, you don't like the ponies?"

"I like the ponies just fine. It's the jockeys, trainers, and owners I distrust." At least with cards, I'm the master of my own destruction.

"Okay. C'mon." He rose with the ease of a zeppelin and led me back outside to the Caddy. When she saw us come out, Queen Mary shoved open the door and weighed anchor to the far side of the back seat. I climbed in, with Stavo right behind. Mary wished God's luck and health on me and offered a cruller.

"I just had a big lunch."

"Me, too." She took a dainty nibble, crumbs falling to join others on the lambs wool lapel of her black winter coat. "So, what's our little girl got to say, Hackshaw?"

"Um—" I nodded toward the back of the driver's head. "She stipulated I was to deal only with you and Stavo."

"You mean Jimmy? Is okay, he's family."

"Not immediate family. Anyway, I gave her my word."

Both Wankas adjusted position slightly, the better to scrutinize me and exchange glances with each other. The car was too warm and claustrophobic and smelled of sweets and garlic; I felt like the sauce in a meatball sandwich. As usual, a decision was reached in a manner impenetrable to an outsider.

Stavo caught Jimmy's eye in the rearview mirror. "Take a walk or somethin'."

"Toma told me to—"

"And *I* told you to take a walk, huh?"

Jimmy shrugged his leather shoulders and got out. We watched him enter the betting parlor.

"They got no respect no more," Stavo muttered. His wife said something to him in Romany and, with a concessionary nod, he brought his attention back to me.

"So. Bimbo's ready to talk with us, huh?"

"Not so fast. She has conditions."

"Conditions! I got some goddam conditions for that little—" Stavo went off on a thirty–second tirade, with Mary clucking disapproval. When hubby settled to a simmer, she said, "Let's hear what she's got to say first, okay? What kinda conditions we talkin' about, Hackshaw?"

I related Bimbo's demands verbatim.

"Huh," Stavo grunted petulantly. "Ever'body thinks they can push me around anymore."

Mary elbowed my ribs. "She didn't say nothin' about the babies?"

"Uh, I'm trying to recall exactly." *Babies*? "Oh, you mean about getting custody from Toma?" Educated guess; I'd never pictured Bimbo with children for some reason.

"Custody?" She snorted. "Nah, nah. In the vitsa, ever'body takes care of the little ones. I'm talkin' about Rose and Stefano goin' to school."

"Mama!" More sharp Romany from Stavo.

"Is too late to worry how much Hackshaw knows our business," she told him. To me: "Bimbo got it in her head her babies oughta go to American school. She didn't tell you this?"

My opinion of Bimbo went up several notches. "I think she was lumping that in with her general demand for having more say in family decision–making."

Stavo again went ballistic. "How I'm s'posed to keep the vitsa together we don't stick to the old ways, huh? She speck the whole family to wait around all winter while the kids go to school, learnin' how to disrespect their parents, give up gypsy ways? Already I got half my people gone south without me and the rest tryin' to make a livin' over to Niagara Falls, freezin' their asses with no business comin' in to the ofisas. I gotta face the kris on Saturday and still I don't have my own goddam daughter—"

"Enough!" Mary reached across me and backhanded his arm. "Just because Hackshaw knows some stuff, that don't mean you gotta make a speech. If we don't work things out with Bimbo, you gonna lose ever'body anyway. You know it's true, Stavo."

"Huh. That don't mean I gotta like it."

Things calmed down to a brooding silence for a few moments. I bided time watching the windows fog over.

Stavo seemed several sizes smaller when he finally spoke again. "You tell Bimbo we gotta talk. She wants schoolin' for Rosie and Stefano, okay. We work somethin' out about the family business, too—you tell her I swear it on Old Santo."

"What about Toma?"

"That ain't so easy. I took his family's money; he's got his rights."

"Well, couldn't you pay them back or something?"

He heaved his shoulders, the left one bouncing me off Mary. "In better times? Maybe. Right now I got whatcha call a cash flow problem, huh? It's this stinkin' mu—this stinkin' bad luck's been doggin' the vitsa."

"Hmm." I simulated deep thought. "Listen, Stavo, if you'll give me another forty–eight hours, I think I can prove that neither you nor Queen Mary had anything to do with Eddie Williamson's death."

Mary said, "You can do this?"

"If you folks back off for two days, just sit tight and don't follow me around to get at Bimbo. And if you can keep Toma off my back."

Stavo's hand closed like a vise on my thigh. "You wouldn't be runnin' no game on me, huh, Hackshaw?"

"I swear," I gasped. I'd have indents for a week. "On my dead father's head."

The pressure eased. "That's good. It'd be better if you was Rom, but okay. But you gotta prove it to me that somebody else did that stinkin' Williamson, you understand? I gotta hear it for myself, so I'll know."

I sighed. "You mean a verbal confession?"

That's when we spotted Toma coming down the walkway from the parking lot, shoulders hunched against the chilly breeze and one hand holding onto the cowboy hat.

"This one's gonna be the problem," Stavo said grimly. "He wants to know where Bimbo's hidin', and he ain't gonna let you just walk away this time."

I'd been thinking about that. Toma was the wild card. If only I could put him out of circulation…

"Let me out so I can talk to him," I said. "I think I may be able to deal with him."

"Whaddya gonna tell him?"

"The truth. More or less."

Mama beamed. "Didn't I say you got some gypsy in you, Hackshaw?"

CHAPTER 25

"Your luck's run out, Hackshaw."

Toma's tone was as frosty as the windchill. He'd collared me as soon as I cleared the Cadillac and, with help from Jimmy and the other bopsy, had hustled me around to the rear of the OTB building, out of sight of prying eyes. Now he had me backed up against some sort of recessed metal service door, pinning me in place with his forearm.

"Here's how it's gonna be," he said, his crooked teeth clenched. "You're gonna tell me where Bimbo's at, I mean right now, or me and the boys here are gonna take you dancin' again. You remember the last time? All my fancy footwork? Hurt some, didn't it? But you know what? We wasn't even tryin'. This time's gonna be different."

I feigned terror at the prospect. (It wasn't difficult.) "I think you should talk to Stavo. He's already agreed to give me a few more days—"

"*Screw* Stavo. I ain't waitin' on that scared old man no more."

"I'm just saying, if you'd only be patient—"

The forearm smashed upward against my chin, banging my head into the door, and was followed by a punch to the solar plexus. Somehow I ended up on my knees, head bowed, retching pitifully. If I'd had a decent lunch, I could've gained a measure of revenge by puking all over his Tony Lama's, but spinach simply has no residual value.

"You wanna do it this way," he said dispassionately, "it's okay by me. Or you can save us some time and tell me what I wanna know. Up to you."

I'd've been ready to talk, even if I hadn't been sandbagging from the get–go.

"Okay," I croaked to the salted patch of concrete I was staring at. "Just don't hit me anymore."

Jimmy and his near–twin hauled me back to my feet and replanted my back against the door.

Toma stared from the shadow of his cowboy hat like some Third World Clint Eastwood. "You're a real candy ass, y'know that? So where's Bimbo at?"

"You'll leave me alone if I tell you? Let me walk away here and now—and swear a curse on your father's head if you're lying?"

"Jesus, you been hangin' around the old folks too long, Hackshaw."

"You better hurry it up, Toma," Jimmy said. "Somebody gonna come along sooner or later and, anyway, man, I'm freezin' my nuts off out here."

Toma considered me a moment longer and shrugged. "Okay, yeah, I'll let you walk, and put a curse on my father's head if I'm lyin.'"

The pledge meant nothing coming from him, but I could see the Kosloffs were at least slightly impressed. I made them swear, too, on the theory they were more orthodox or whatever and would see to it Toma kept his word.

Then I ratted on Bimbo.

"She's hiding out at the Oatka Seneca Reserve, passing herself off as a Mohawk mystic named Naomi Silvercloud. I can give you directions how to find it." Which I proceeded to do, right down to the last turn.

Toma was nodding. "Yeah, that sounds like her, all right. She always liked that Indian scam." He aimed his rigid index finger at my nose. "But I'm warnin' you, if she ain't there, you and me'll still have that dance."

"She's there, she's there." I made cow eyes. "Just one thing more, the people she's staying with? They're a couple of real nice folks. The son, Chester, runs a sawmill, like a job training program for the Indian youth."

"What's he, some kinda fuckin' social worker?"

"Exactly. Go easy with him, is all I'm asking."

"He gives me what I'm after, I won't have to lay a finger on the punk."

"Good. Tell him that," I said. "And wear the hat. That's sure to impress him."

* * *

Five minutes after Toma and the boys took off for the reservation, I was back at my desk, dialing.

"Oatka Custom Hardwoods."

"It's Hackshaw. You've got company on the way." I described the advancing horde. Chester was sanguine, to say the least. I'd counted on that.

"Tough guys, huh? Shit, I haven't had a good brawl since I gave up firewater."

"Listen, don't let the Sal Mineo clones distract you. It's Toma you wanna home in on, the mouthy one in the bad Stetson. Throw some of that fancy Green Beret stuff at him and the other two shouldn't be a problem."

"They won't be a problem either way."

"And, Chester? I know how much you want to see Bimbo gone and I'm working on that—I might be able to move her by tomorrow or the next day. But in the meantime, it sure would help if Toma was on the shelf. You know, like laid up with a broken leg or something?"

He chuckled. "Only just the one?"

I hung up the phone and let the air rush out of me. I was exhausted already from all the mental gymnastics. My gut was beginning to hurt from Toma's punch, or possibly the spinach salad. The afternoon was half gone.

And miles to go before I sleep.

Like I said, I had a plan. Sort of. Riddled with more `ifs' than a Rudyard Kipling ode, but still a plan. So many calls to make, people to talk to, details to work out...

"Elias, have you seen Alan?" Ruth, hurrying in from the adjoining print shop.

"I gave him a couple of errands earlier."

"Well, I hope he gets back soon. I have a few layout chores that need attention and Liz phoned in, one of the kids is sick again. I suppose it's almost a good thing we're so light on ads this week, we'll need that much less copy. In fact, we may have to drop a complete sheet—"

"Let's not decide to do that yet." A sheet is office jargon for a four–page section of the paper; when display advertising is down enough, we often have to reduce the paper's overall page count. Ruth was eyeballing me quizzically, about to form a question. "My FYI on con artists looks like it could run long," I explained.

"Certainly not *that* long." Her phone rang. "Well, we've got time to figure that out later."

While she was busy with her call, I made one of my own. Long distance.

"Hello?"

"Great, you're there. I wasn't sure I'd catch you. It's Hackshaw," I added.

"Oh, yeah." Pete Williamson; he sounded half asleep. "Well, what can I do you for, Hackshaw?"

"I was wondering if you meant what you told me before, about wishing you could do something about your brother's murder."

"Sure I meant it. I mean, we had our problems, but he was my brother. If there's anything I can do..."

❧ ❧ ❧

Midnight.

I took another look at the Budweiser clock behind the bar and shook my head, hoping to shake loose the cobwebs.

"Man, this place sucks worse than the Nook," Buddy McCabe said, and he'd know. "I can't believe I let you talk me into this."

"Friendship has its price." You'd think I'd asked him to donate a kidney instead of leave work a few hours early to help me out. "Think of it like a sort of safari, with me as the great white hunter and you as a trusty native pack bearer."

"Hmmph, that's about what I feel like, some of the looks I'm gettin' from these redneck peckerwoods. If I wasn't so big, we'd both be dead by now."

He was overstating, but still, it was the main argument for bringing him along. The place Buddy was complaining about is called Country Joe's Wayfarer Lounge, a shot–and–a–beer backroads bar that features sawdust on the floor and Johnny Paycheck on the jukebox. It sits across the county line southwest of Kirkville, a few miles out of our circulation area—both mine and the paper's. Apparently its chief attractions, at least in winter, were the acres of surrounding empty fields and the abandoned railroad right–of–way across the road. The combination, according to Buddy, had made the dive a popular pit stop for snowmobile fanatics on their nightly and weekend cross–country runs. The regular clientele seemed to consist of a limited assortment of scratch farmers and low–skill laborers with permanent grease stains under their nails and permanent chips on their shoulders; types who watch stock car racing for the crashes and automatically hate unions, although they're not sure why.

"It does look a bit like a membership drive for the Aryan Brotherhood in here," I admitted.

"Fifteen more minutes," Buddy murmured over the lip of his glass. "If Alphabet doesn't show by then, we're outa here. You'll just have to try and catch him at his mom's place in the morning."

I was too tired to argue. In addition to a dozen normal tasks that had to be done to ready the *Advertiser* for Thursday delivery, I had spent much of the late afternoon and early evening writing up a long story; what I knew and what I suspected about Eddie Williamson and the illegal dumping out at the Hemford place. I tucked the piece in my desk, along with a copy in an envelope addressed to Captain Schulz at the Sheriff's Department.

Don't be alarmed; it wasn't death, merely deadlines I was concerned about. See, with a weekly, you rarely have the opportunity to break a real news story, unless it just happens to fall into your lap the night before publication, which in our case is Wednesday evening. And I planned to be busy with other things Wednesday evening, not to mention most of the day. So, on the off–chance my scheming worked—and sooner rather than later—I wanted to have the story ready to go. Altruism is fine, but a possible front page exclusive is even better.

And speaking of the scheme, in between all my frantic newspapering I had those other details to handle. The phone call to Pete Williamson, securing his cooperation, was only the first of several. I also called Berk Savage, the guy who'd recently opened an electronics repair shop in Kirkville, and Jackie Plummer, to break an informal dinner date. I only wish she'd been half as cooperative as the electronics man.

"Yeah, I've got some refurbished answering machines I could sell you," Savage had said. "What sorta modifications did you have in mind?"

"As I understand it, those things are basically just tape recorders hooked to telephones, right?" I described what I was after in general terms, hoping he could sort out the technicalities.

"Yeah, that would work," he said. "It's just a matter of switching one of the circuits, maybe rerouting a couple of wires from the speaker phone, or maybe I could jerryrig a small mike. I don't know about having it ready for you by noon tomorrow, though. I'm kinda busy."

"Did I mention I was giving you a plug in this week's Rambling's column, Berk?"

Noon wouldn't be a problem after all, he decided.

My final call of the day went to Arlene Grebwicz. It was Stanley I needed to talk to, but he'd already come home from work and gone out again, Arlene said, off somewhere to meet up with some of the other Gullywhumpers and not expected back home until late.

I started my search at the Nook first, naturally, but when Stanley and his snow buddies failed to appear by nine, Buddy pointed out that they could be riding out to the west, along the old Erie–Lackawanna right–of–way. If they went out there, Buddy said, they were apt to stop at one of two places for refreshment.

We'd first tried the Turnin Tavern, a southwest Kirkville honky–tonk, with no luck. Country Joe's Wayfarer Lounge was our last hope, as it appeared to be for most of the other patrons.

Buddy chuckled softly. "So you really sent those three idiots out to try and hassle Stoneface, huh, Hack?"

I sipped. "Uh–huh."

"Man, I'd pay money to see that."

Buddy packs two–hundred and sixty pounds of mostly genial muscle, a good eighty pounds heavier than Chester Youngfoot. But the two had gone toe–to–toe once several years back, when Chester was still drinking and periodically busting up joints like the Nook. The result had been the bloodiest flat–out draw since the Korean War.

"Couldn't happen to a nicer bunch of boys," I said.

"Tell me again what it is you're tryin' to set up with Stanley and those others?"

I started to outline my strategy once more, but before I got very far, the noise level suddenly rose as half a dozen of the Gullywhumpers whooped through the door.

"Hey, Hackman, Budster!" Dutchie Prine, moving like a robot in his heavy black boots and snowmobile suit. "What're you guys up to, slumming?"

"We are now," Buddy said.

I was busy looking over the Dutchman's shoulder, sorting out the other five sociopaths as they stamped their feet and worked their zippers. Stanley was the last one in. He spotted me about the same time and waddled over, working up a scowl along the way.

"Just the guy I wanted to see." I offered the vacant stool next to mine. "I need a favor, Stanley."

"Oh, yeah?" He ordered a depth charge from the bartender; a shot glass filled with Wild Turkey dropped into a mug of ale. Apparently his brain cells weren't dying off fast enough as it was. "And why in hell should I do you any favors, Hackshaw?"

"Because it could help me prove who killed Slow Eddie Williamson, and whoever killed Williamson probably ended up with your mother's fifteen hundred dollars. Besides," I added, "you'll like this. It's right up your alley."

CHAPTER 26

❁

Bimbo Wanka gobbled down the last of her corn muffin and impatiently pushed aside the plate.

"What d'ya mean—" She frowned. "—a diversion?"

We were hunkered around Mary Youngfoot's kitchen table late Wednesday morning, Bimbo, Pete Williamson, and I. Outside, a light snowfall; inside, a thickening fog.

I tried to determine if she was being deliberately obtuse, but couldn't make up my mind. "A diversion: to divert attention from one thing by drawing the eye to something else. Misdirection, the magicians call it, and don't tell me you haven't used the ploy for any number of your little scams."

"I know what it *means*, Hackshaw, I ain't stupid. What I mean is, why d'ya figure you gotta have me and Pete bring off this diversion so's your plan will work? And why do I gotta be in on it in the first place?"

You'd think it was nuclear physics. "As I've already explained, the idea is for me to sneak onto the Hemford property tonight and see if I can find evidence they've been using those woods as an illegal dumpsite for toxic waste. I'd like to be able to accomplish it without Earl Hemford noticing and coming after me with a shotgun, okay? So I thought I'd create a *diversion* by stationing you two up at the

Bing Road rental house, lights blazing, and Pete here sitting in the kitchenette's bay window with a pair of binoculars."

It was one of Professor Blednau's factoids, about gypsy girls and the Jericho flower con, that had started me thinking; how they beguile their way into a potential mark's home by demonstrating the miraculous powers of the lumpish little plant, seemingly dead until submersion in a cup of water brings it back to life. While the mark watches in fascination as the one gypsy girl puts on a show with the Jericho flower, you'll remember, the other girl is busy plundering the silver; classic misdirection.

"Pete's perfect for this because from a distance he's the spitting image of Eddie," I said. "The Hemfords aren't the most sophisticated people on the planet. Presented with the sight of the man they murdered come back to haunt them, I'm betting they'll go from shocked to confused to half–panicked, to finally calling up Tice to find out what to do next. Hopefully, by the time they get their act together, we'll have found the dumpsite and gotten out of there undetected."

The "we" was me and Stanley Grebwicz, doubled up on the back of his Snowcat, working our way crosslots to the Hemford's woods from a little–used county road a half mile to the west.

"So maybe Pete's perfect for this," Bimbo conceded. "But you still didn't say why I gotta be there."

"Two reasons." Three if you count the fact I wanted to keep her on a short leash until the time came to hand everything over to the Sheriff's Department. "First, you're the only one of us who has a legitimate excuse to be in the house, in case the Koons get wind of this and try to throw you both out. Eddie rented the place for the whole month, right? Paid in full? So as his, uh, significant other, you have every right to occupy the house for a few days. And second, after the episode out here yesterday with Toma and the boys, I think it's safer we move you somewhere else. Just for another day or two," I assured her. "It was just Stavo's pride that made him take this last shot. I'm sure he'll be willing to negotiate on your terms, after what happened to Toma."

I confess, I'd rearranged the facts a bit as concerns Bimbo's rampaging husband, et cetera. I told her it was Stavo who had threatened me with a full body cast if I didn't tell where she was staying.

Bimbo pouted her pretty red lips. "It's pretty goddam lousy, is all I can say. My own father siccin' that son of a bitch Toma on me like that."

I sympathized. "It's getting so you can't trust anyone. Luckily Chester was able to handle things."

She smiled wickedly. "Manhandle, you mean."

I smiled back. Chester had briefed me on my arrival. Cowboy Toma wouldn't be roaming the range for awhile, not with a dislocated knee. The bopsy twins had gotten off with fat lips and shiners.

Now Pete was looking doubtful. "A couple of days, Hackshaw? I thought this was gonna be a one–night deal. We keep these Hemford rubes guessing while you get the evidence you need. Then everybody fades and you call in the cops."

"That's the heart of the plan, yes. But I was thinking, since we may need a place for Bimbo to stay anyway, and since finding where the chemicals were dumped won't necessarily prove Tice and the Hemfords killed your brother—"

"Why do I get the feeling I'm being conned?"

"Yeah," Bimbo agreed. "What's goin' on, Hackshaw?"

I knew this would be the trickiest part. I had hoped avenging Slow Eddie's death would be enough of a motivator, but I kept forgetting I was dealing with people whose number one rule was always look out for number one, romantic or familial ties notwithstanding. Think of it as pulling off a Br'er Rabbit. I had to get two veteran grifters to do what I wanted them to do by convincing them it was something they wanted to do anyway.

I reluctantly decided the best course was to resort to the truth—most of it, anyway—and trust that their professional instincts, their love of the game for its own sake, would carry the day.

"All right, here's the thing. I think we can use the setup out at the rental house, maybe combined with a cryptic phone call or two, to draw Webster Tice and the Hemfords to us. Force them into showing their hand, as it were. Then we confront them with what we know—mainly Tice, he's the money man—and we pretend to blackmail them, just like Eddie was planning to do in the first place."

"Pretend?" Bimbo asked.

"In order to trick a confession out of them, which we'll secretly record. That way we'll have proof to give the cops, and proof for Stavo, too, that Queen Mary's gypsy curse didn't have a thing to do with Eddie's death after all. It'll work, I'm sure of it, but it may take two or three nights out there to properly draw them in."

"No way I can stay three nights, Hackshaw," Pete said. "I've got a wedding to shoot Saturday."

"Just give it two nights, then. For Eddie."

"Aw, c'mon, don't lay that shit on me. I'm supposed to have a guilty conscience about not avenging a guy who didn't even have a conscience?"

I didn't answer; I just stared across the kitchen table at him until he ducked his head, cleared his throat, and said, "All right. Maybe I can do two nights."

"You know what I'm thinkin'?" Bimbo said. "It could be a pretty good sting you're puttin' together. Why we gotta just pretend to take the money? Why don't we see how much this Tice guy'd pay for real?"

"Because the whole idea is to nail these bastards for illegal dumping—and for murdering poor Eddie, of course. We're setting them up for the police."

"So why can't we set `em up for the money first, then after that you can blow `em in to the cops."

"Because unlike you, I won't be leaving town on the next available caravan. If the cops found out I'd actually taken money in a blackmail scheme, they'd give me a cell right next to Tice and the Hemfords."

"Hah!" She shook back her long, wavy black hair and crossed her arms. "Pete gets even for Eddie, okay. And you prob'ly get some big story for your newspaper. But what do I get outa riskin' my neck?"

"A powerful bargaining chip to use on Stavo. Look, you want him to pay back Toma's family, right, so you can get out of the marriage? And give you more control over family finances, let you put your kids in school—"

"Hey, how'd you know about my kids?"

"Your mother told me, that's how. Stavo's against it because he's afraid the young ones will drift away from gypsy ways if they get an education. But he has a more immediate fear; losing control over the whole vitsa if he can't put this mulo business behind him. That's where a taped confession from Tice and the others comes in. We'll make you a copy before handing the original over to the police, see? Then you go to Stavo and make a deal. You tell him you can prove to him and the kris that Queen Mary's curse had nothing to do with Eddie's death. All he has to do is agree to your demands."

She abruptly sat back. "Huh. That's not too bad. Only, how d'ya know these guys won't come after me and Pete with a shotgun, huh? I mean, if they already killed Eddie—"

"Because eliminating one unknown, out–of–town con man and dressing it up to look like an accident is one thing, but murdering three more people, including a well–known local newsman, is something else." At least, I fervently hoped it was. "That's why we need to suck in Tice early on; he may be ruthless, but he's not stupid. He'll try to cut a deal, you can bank on it. He may have second thoughts later, sure, and decide to take us out instead of making the payoff. But we're not going to show up for the payoff, because by then we'll have him on tape and we'll have turned everything over to the police."

"Y'know, setting up the bug might not be so easy as you think, Hackshaw," Pete warned. "If these rubes bite, they're gonna be nervous goin' in. Real nervous. You can bet they'll search us to see if we're wired, so that's out. You'll need to plant mikes around the room someplace, but they might check for those, too. And how you gonna hide the tape recorder?"

"I'm not even going to try," I said. "I'm going to leave it right out where everybody can see it."

* * *

Berk Savage sounds like a soap opera character, but looks like a roadie for The Grateful Dead; receding hairline, compensating pony tail, vegetarian's emaciation mixed with a hint of dissipation from headier times (pun intended). He was still in the suspect category among most Kirkvillians, less for his encrusted Woodstock appearance than simply because he's a newcomer. But the locals were slowly warming as word filtered out that the aging hippie with the fix–it shop on Main knows electronic gadgets the way an Eskimo knows snow. And he's reasonable, to boot.

He had the answering machine ready and waiting on the counter when I arrived.

"Thanks for the rush job," I told him, as I dug deep for fifty dollars and made it with ten to spare.

"Actually it was a kick, working up the modifications you wanted." He jerked his thumb toward the jumble of used gear that lined the back shelf. "Luckily I had another old Panasonic, almost the same model, I could cannibalize for parts. The really interesting thing was figuring out how to trigger the recording tape like you wanted."

"But it works, right?"

"Yeah, it works great. You'll need to record a message. I put in a new cassette like you asked, thirty minutes." He shifted the thing on the counter and showed me how to hook it up to a telephone, how to activate it, and so on. "Really, it's like any old analog recording machine, with one difference. When someone calls and hangs up without leaving a message, it just rewinds and waits for the next call, just like normal. But if someone calls and leaves a message, it records the message all right, but then the tape keeps running, with the speaker phone here acting as a live microphone, picking up and recording any conversation going on in the room."

"Excellent." I counted out the money. "I imagine you must be curious why I needed—"

"I gave up curious a long time ago, man." He scooped the bills and popped open the cash drawer on his register, glancing up. "If you want a receipt, Hackshaw, I'll have to charge you sales tax."

✤ ✤ ✤

I could've phoned Harold Morecock, but Elmwood Manor was only a stone's throw and, besides, Harold likes the personal touch.

Snow flurries had changed to fat flakes by then and a somber gray sky hovered above the manor, further emphasizing the gothic in its Gothic Revival styling. Dear old Edna the housekeeper led me on a barely ambulatory amble from the portico's double doors to the master's study. The spacious built–in bookshelves had long since become overrun with Harold's collections of paperback potboilers, bad movies on VHS, eight–track cassettes of insipid pop balladeers; the list goes on, but I don't have the strength.

He was bent over his fancy computer, his index fingers doing a two–step across the keyboard, his small, slight body resplendent in a blue Nehru jacket and bell–bottom jeans. Cable had proved a godsend for Harold; he'd no doubt been overdosing on "The Partridge Family" reruns again.

"Drat!" I think he learned his cursing from Marvel Comics. "Forgive my temper, Hackshaw, it's just that my mouse is malfunctioning."

"Gadzooks," I said.

"Yes, and I'm left trying to revise chapter one of my manuscript with combination keystroke commands, which I keep mixing up. Every time I try to boldface I end up underlining and when I try to underline I delete. I won't even go into what's happening with my spell–checker."

"I don't think I can help you there." At the *Advertiser*, we still consider White–Out high–tech.

He muttered a bit more, then stabbed a couple of big keys on the side of the board. The text on the screen disappeared, followed a nanosecond later by some sort of electronic aquarium; colorful fishies swimming across the otherwise blank monitor. "I was due a break anyway. People just have no idea how physically draining the creative process is. Anyway, it's good of you to drop by. Shall I ring for Edna to bring us some refreshments?"

"I'm afraid I don't have that kind of time."

"Ah, this is an official visit, then?"

"Half and half," I said. I'd wracked my brain on the way over, trying to think of a small favor I could do Harold so he'd feel obligated to do one for me. "For one thing, I think I've come up with another potential buzzword for your new business book. Cohort."

"Cohort? Like an associate?"

"No, like the subdivisions of a Roman legion. I've noticed it's being used a lot these days by demographers and market researchers and people like that, which means it's only a matter of time before the politicians and the business journals glom onto it and obscure the meaning even further."

"Well, it does have some resonance, I'll grant you. Of course, I'd need to come up with a viable application."

"I was thinking, instead of using chapters in the book, you could label them as cohorts. Lend it that suggestion of ancient conquerors."

"Hmmm." He pondered. "'Cohort One: Organizing The Troops'. Yes, I can see how it might give a certain cachet…"

"I can almost hear the thunder of a thousand marching sandals."

He seemed pleased with my input, silly and calculated as it was. But then that old Nemesis of Harold's, a shaky attention span, reared its ugly head.

"The only thing is, I've been half considering the possibility of changing focus to the early Indian civilizations of meso–America, specifically the Mayans. You know, how a stone–age peoples who didn't even have the wheel could have, two thousand years ago, conceived and constructed such elaborate cities of stone. I think it has a great deal to say for their leaders' abilities to motivate the workforce to such incredible levels of productivity."

"Yeah, I suppose human sacrifice is quite a motivator, all right."

"I was speaking of other ritual practices, Hackshaw." He was frowning at me, but brightened suddenly. "But you know, there may be a good metaphor to be exploited there. Human sacrifice and corporate downsizing."

"I'm no expert, Harold, but I think I'd stick with Alexander the Great."

"You may be right. Truth to tell, my mind isn't focused on creative endeavors. Now, here's an area where you *are* something of an expert—romantic entanglements. Tell me, what did you think of Penny Wise?"

"Ah, preoccupied with amour today? Well, she seems very nice. Perfectly suited for you, I'd say." Right down to her name. "I think she's definitely worth considering as the first and future Mrs. Harold Morecock."

"Let's not rush matters. You know how cautious a man in my position must be when it comes to the fairer sex."

"Of course." His dear departed mother of a mother had raised him to believe that no female could possibly love him for anything but his money. He'd taken it to heart, unfortunately, and had been a bachelor for all of his fifty–odd years.

Make that fifty odd years.

"On the other hand, Harold, there's a time for caution and a time for risk, as any smart investor knows. You're not getting any younger," I added pointedly.

He dismissed the topic with a wave. "I don't know why I even brought it up. Penny and I are still getting to know each other. What with my distractions with the new book project and my portfolio and all my other interests, we've only managed to go out a few times. For the most part, we just talk on the phone a lot."

I'll just bet. "Coincidentally, that brings me to the other reason for my visit, Harold. I'd like to borrow your girlfriend's services for a night or two."

CHAPTER 27

By seven o'clock, the day's ambivalent weather had made up its mind to turn nasty, as if Mother Nature in her cruel fashion had decided I didn't have enough to contend with.

"Hey! Not so damn close." Stanley Grebwicz shouted to be heard over the biting wind and the steady growl of the snowmobile. "Slide back a little, Hackshaw."

"You told me to hang on tight!"

"I didn't tell you to corn hole me, did I?"

Not for the first time, I asked myself why in God's name I was doing any of this. One tentative arm at a time, I loosened the bear hug I had on his midriff and eased back far enough to slip my gloved hands under the strap that girdled the seat between us.

If the building storm had any redeeming value, it was that its direction, coming predominantly out of the northeast, insured that the sound of the Snowcat's engine would carry away from the Hemford homestead itself. It also contained within its fury relatively little snow, what there was of it coming at us almost horizontally in hard, icy chips that nipped like small dogs at the exposed skin of my cheeks and jaw. That and a high moon meant visibility, unless you were attempting to peer directly into the wind, was reasonably good despite the storm.

Stanley leaned back to nudge me with his elbow and pointed to a large oak tree just inside the fence we were paralleling. I didn't need to catch the words to understand his meaning; nailed to the oak's trunk was yet another orange and black NO TRESPASSING sign.

"No wonder Hemford's been such a prick about letting us cross that shitty farm of his," Stanley had told me out at the Wayfarer Lounge the previous night, when I'd asked for his help. According to him, Earl Hemford was one of the few rural property owners in town who refused to allow snowmobilers or hunters or anyone else to so much as traverse their land. It was that slight, more than the thin prospect of recovering any of his mother's fifteen hundred dollars, that had prompted Stanley to offer his chauffeuring services.

The Snowcat dipped suddenly and just as suddenly bucked like a rodeo bronco, nearly throwing me off. The terrain was increasingly rugged and irregular as we moved from the open, snow–crusted hay fields and pastures into the western reaches of Hemford's woods. We'd had to stop at one point to snip an opening through a barbed wire fence and a second time to check our bearings and look for landmarks to guide us. After the first quarter mile, Stanley had spotted the yellow glow of the kitchenette light at the Bing Road rental house, far to our right. It sat up on the ridge, a few hundred yards to the south, appearing through the filter of flying snow like a second moon hovering on the horizon. I'll admit that, even had I been up to the job of trekking in alone and on foot, I'd have been disoriented and fumbling in ten minutes. It was only Stanley's navigation abilities, honed from years of experience night riding with the Gullywhumpers, that provided us with any reasonable expectation of locating the dumpsite hidden in all those acres of trees and scrub and, not incidentally, getting back out again in a hurry if need be.

He shouted something as we topped a hillock, but I couldn't hear through the wind and the visored helmet I was wearing. He slowed the machine to a stop, engine cycling down to a low purr, and switched off the headlight.

"Over there, see?" He pointed again, this time to the left, away from the fence line that continued its march until it disappeared in the darkness and the trees. "That's gotta be the track."

He was pointing to a gap through a stand of bare maples and ash. We realized from the outset that there had to be an access road of some kind leading into the woods from the open fields surrounding Hemford's house and barns; a track sufficient for a large truck to use in any season. We also figured the track probably began life as a tractor lane or a glorified cow path, providing direct access through the woods to the pastures on our side of the property back when the place had been a working dairy farm. Disuse and winter conditions would've obscured the route of the track this side of the woods, but the gap Stanley spotted was a clear give–away.

"I think we oughta take the machine in a ways farther," he said. "Keep the headlight off and the speed down for the noise."

"I thought the plan was to locate the track and walk the rest of the way."

"That's when we weren't sure what we'd be dealing with. But now we know we got the storm working for us and the woods and ridges keepin' us outa sight from the Hemford Road side."

"But we're apt to lose that advantage," I said, "the farther into the woods we go."

"If we lose decent cover, we'll leave the Snowcat and hike the rest of the way in. That way we got it closer by, in case we have to haul ass in a hurry." He shrugged. "It's six of one, half a dozen of the other, Hackshaw. Either we risk makin' a little noise goin' in or we risk havin' no transportation when we need it most."

I didn't give him an argument; he was probably right, and anyway, I didn't relish schlepping into the teeth of that wind any longer than necessary.

He throttled the engine up a few ticks and eased the machine over the lip of the rise, down the slope toward the gap in the trees. While we made a deliberate descent, my mind raced back and forth, examining pieces of the scheme, looking for weaknesses and dangers not thought of, finding no obvious flaws but worrying nonetheless about the many ifs and imponderables.

Essentially, I was operating under the premise that the best way to get someone to swallow a lie is to sugarcoat it with a few grains of truth. It's an approach that usually works just fine, but even a therapeutic lie can have side effects, and side effects are by nature unpredictable.

I give you one more tidbit from the Hackshaw archive of useless trivia and blatant column fillers:

You remember all the fantastic human interest stories that came out of the Soviet Union during the final, faltering Brezhnev years, about centenarians in the Ukraine and the Caucuses still living with their mothers? How the Kremlin, desperate for any good news, was holding up these enclaves of ancient geezers to prove how beneficial life in a socialist paradise can be? And how Western scientists began flying down to the Crimea by the planeload, laden with equipment and tripping over each other in their eagerness to understand the incredible longevity of these simple people?

Just what was their secret? the scientists wondered. Was it some sort of special yogurt cultures? The pure mountain air? A freak of the gene pool?

Uh–uh. It turns out the phenomenon was largely attributable to one factor: avoiding drafts.

You see, back around 1917 the Russian Czar, and then the Bolsheviks, were frantically building up armies by conscripting just about any able–bodied male under fifty they could lay hands on. But the folks down in the southern provinces weren't even ethnic Russians in the first place and had no use for either the Czar or Lenin's communist revolutionaries. So what did hundreds of these thirty–something peasants do when they got word of conscription gangs on the prowl? They grew their beards a bit shaggier, and rubbed fireash into their hair and their wind–creased faces, and worked stoops and shuffles into their gaits. And when the roaming bureaucrats came to town looking for cannon fodder, the locals lied like crazy, adding twenty, twenty–five, even thirty years to their true ages. And the bureaucrats, as bureaucrats will, dutifully recorded the names and claimed ages of these peasants and their wives before returning to Moscow to report that most of the eligible young men had apparently gone into hiding.

Now cycle ahead sixty years, with the Soviet authorities trying to put together a modern census for the country and poring through any old official records they can find. Lo and behold, the bean counters discover they've got all these scores of Methuselahs down in the hinterlands still turning over sod instead of lying under it. Naturally, they went down to investigate, and just as naturally, the old folks they questioned were too scared to admit they had misreported their ages decades earlier to avoid the Bolshevik's draft. By this time, they'd become experts at hoodwinking Moscow's apparatchiks, and besides, all the sudden attention was kind of nice. So eighty–five and ninety–year–old peasants smiled for the cameras and pretended to be a hundred and twelve, and the Kremlin crowed and the scientists probed and the world marveled.

You see my point. Even a beautiful lie can lead you to complications you never imagined.

Which might explain why, despite the vicious wind chill, I was sweating profusely inside the nylon snowsuit Stanley had borrowed for me from his friend the lawyer.

Meanwhile:

At first the track through the trees was a piece of cake, undulating down and up as gently as a kiddy ride at the fair. Stanley kept our speed slow and constant; the buzz of the engine mixed with the whistling wind and trailed off harmlessly in our wake while, around us, the woods thickened into a tangle of old hardwood growth and bushy conifers, low brush and winter–dead vines. Then we came to a sudden rise in the trail, no more than twenty feet from valley to peak, but steep enough that Stanley had to goose the gas to get us up the thing. We advanced in a roar and a rush, my helmeted head bouncing like a pinball, first backward, then forward, and lastly sideways as Stanley skidded us to a halt at the top.

He nudged and pointed again.

Out there, a quarter–mile away beyond the edge of the woods and the dormant fields, were several dark outlines and tiny rectangles of light that had to be the Hemford farmhouse and barns.

The storm gusted and swirled around us. "We'd better get off this high ground pronto," I said.

"Yeah." He reached for the throttle, then hesitated. "Hey, what's that? Straight down past those two big pines."

I couldn't decipher what I was seeing at first, but after a moment my eyes refocused and the shimmering shape glimpsed through a curtain of leafless trees took form.

"Some sort of pond?"

"Let's check it out."

The slope was more gradual on this side, the track angling to the left for a hundred feet or so before curving back to our right in a long arc. As soon as we lost the advantage of the ridge, we no longer could see the pond; not until the ranks of trees on either side of the track petered out onto low, open ground. And there it was.

It probably had once been a watering hole for the cows, a man–made rectangle eighty feet long and half as wide that had been bulldozed in the middle of a natural clearing. The shade of the woods would've drawn the cattle in during the heat of summer, providing a cool place where they could graze on wild grasses and drink at the pond.

Stanley swung the Snowcat around so that it would be facing back up the trail and cut the engine. I swung a leg over and climbed off the machine, feeling like a saddle–sore tenderfoot, and waited for Stanley to come alongside. He had a flashlight in hand when he did, and wordlessly led the way the last dozen yards to the edge of the frozen pond. Its surface was silvery gray in the moonlight, most of the snow having been carried away by the fierce winds. As we got closer, the ground around us proved to be rutted with the criss–crossings of dozens of tire tracks from a large, heavy vehicle. The tracks were molded into the red clay soil and as frozen stiff as the pond surface.

We flipped up the visors on our helmets.

"I guess we found the right place."

"Yeah." Stanley scoured the perimeter of the pond with his flash-light. "Looks like the whole place is rimmed with tire marks."

"Mmm." I gestured for him to follow with the light and picked my way down the slope at one of the narrow ends of the rectangle. When I got to the edge, I took from the pocket of my snowsuit a plastic baggy and the gardening shovel I'd borrowed from my tenant, Mrs. Johnson. Then I knelt and began to chisel away at the ice. I broke through easily, nearly losing my balance; the ice was thinner than I expected—thinner than it should've been for one of the coldest Jan-uaries on record.

"Whew!" Stanley was leaning over my shoulder, trying to hold the light still. "You catch that smell, man? That ain't swamp gas."

"No. Look at that." There was a thin film of brown water floating below the ice cap. I gingerly stuck the blade of the hand shovel into it and could feel something, like wet putty, just under the surface. When I pulled the blade back, it was coated with a sickly greenish sludge.

"Gotcha," I murmured.

"C'mon, Hackshaw, scoop some of that shit into the bag and let's get the fuck outa here. This place's givin' me the creeps."

It was unanimous. I half–filled the baggy and sealed it. Then, on reflection, I took out the second baggy I was carrying and double–bagged the mess before carefully slipping it into one of the suit's zip-pered pockets.

We were almost back to the snowmobile when off to our left came the snap of a dead branch.

Stanley dropped into a crouch. I was too startled to do much more than suck in a lungful of icy air and hold it while my wide eyes followed his searching beam.

When it found it's quarry, we both exhaled.

Our bogeyman was a pair of deer, a doe and its fawn, sheltering in the leeward side of a big spruce. They stood stock–still for a few seconds, mesmerized by the flashlight, their eyes seeming to glow like burning coals.

"Christ, look at the little one," Stanley said in a hoarse whisper. "It must be sick or somethin'."

The deer bolted at the sound of his voice, first mother and then child high–stepping away through the brittle brush. But not before I too saw the fawn's misshapen jaw and drooping mouth and lolling tongue.

"I don't think that's from disease," I said quietly. "It's a birth defect."

CHAPTER 28

My simmering anger was all that kept me warm, first on the bone–jarring ride back across the fields to Stanley's Chevy pickup and later on, as I parked my four–by–four behind Pete Williamson's battered little Plymouth and let myself into the rental house through the side door.

"It's just me," I called out as I stamped off my feet on the cramped mudroom's mat.

Pete and Bimbo were straight ahead at the opposite end of the kitchen, seated in the lawn chairs drawn up around the card table, coats draped off the backs of the chairs, smoking and sipping coffee. Looking as domestic as a pair of Siamese cats.

"Feels better in here now," I said as I approached. "I guess you found the thermostat all right."

We'd had no trouble getting inside earlier in the day, just after dark. The driveway had enough snow in it to be a problem for Pete's Horizon, but I'd gone in first with the Jeep, running it up and back a few times to flatten out the drifts. The key for the side door was right where it had been the last time, under the plant pot on the stoop. The place was chilly when we arrived—the Koons had kept the furnace set just high enough to keep the plumbing from freezing—but I'd left that detail for Pete to handle, sticking around only long enough to hook up the answering machine and give it a test before leaving for my rendezvous with Stanley Grebwicz.

"Yeah," Pete said. "We found it okay."

Something in his voice didn't sound kosher. Add in the fact Bimbo hadn't uttered a word yet and I knew we had trouble even before I heard the floor squeak and caught movement out of the corner of my right eye.

Earl Hemford stepped through the archway from the living room, an over–and–under shotgun leveled waist high. Behind him was a taller, scrawnier version of himself, but twenty years younger; his son, Early. Also clutching a long gun, in his case a rifle.

"I knew damn well you'd be in this, Hackshaw."

I wasn't sure how best to answer him, so I didn't. Instead, I worked off my gloves, sneaking a peek at my watch. Ten past eight. Twenty minutes to go. Unless…

"So," I said to Pete, "you folks have been discussing things for a while now?"

He caught my meaning and shook his head. "Just a few minutes. These boys showed up just after the top of the hour."

That was good; it meant the scenario I'd worked out was still valid.

"We were just gettin' acquainted when you pulled up." Earl smiled, sort of, and wagged the shotgun. "Come on over and join the party."

"Sure." I stepped from the shadows into the kitchenette area, brightly lit by the swag lamp dangling over the table—the better for the Hemfords to spot Pete doing his thing in the bay window, which they obviously had.

Right about then, Bimbo found her voice.

"Hey, mister," she said, pausing for a tug on her cigarette. "I thought we was gonna talk a deal."

"Shut up, bitch. We'll talk when I say we'll talk. Early, keep `em covered."

Junior raised his rifle higher and pinched his eyes tighter. Earl propped the shotgun in the corner and picked up the phone, paying no mind to the boxy answering machine that sat next to it. While he dialed, I tried not to check my watch again or to return the glances of my co–conspirators. After a few weighty seconds, he began talking into the receiver.

"Yeah, babe. You get ahold of him?" Hemford grunted. "Yeah, no sweat. Says he's the guy's brother. Yeah, I know. Guess who else just walked in. Uh–huh." A long pause. "Yeah, well, tell him I don't give a fuck what he wants or don't want, okay? Just get your asses over here now." He hung up and retrieved his artillery.

His son asked anxiously, "What we gonna do now, Pa?"

"Nothin'. We wait for Tice and your ma, is all."

"You know," I said, "there's no need for all this hardware, Earl. We're just looking to do a business deal, like the lady said."

"Save your bullshit till the others get here. Meanwhile, shut your mouth, Hackshaw. `Less you wanna give me a reason to shut it for you. I'd like that just fine."

When in doubt, obey the man holding the double–barreled shotgun. I shut my mouth.

Earl and Junior each found a wall to lean on, the boy letting the rifle barrel dangle while he played with the open zipper of his parka, picked his nose, pushed his ski cap farther up his forehead, shifted his weight from one foot to the other, all under the general heading of fidgeting. Hemford senior made one concession to the warm room, spreading open his tan field jacket, but otherwise kept completely still, the shotgun cradled, eyes at half mast but watchful, like a man in a duck blind waiting for a fly–over.

Meanwhile Pete and Bimbo sucked their cancer sticks and nursed cold coffees, neither one interested enough to get up and pour a warm–up from the coffeemaker they had set up on the kitchen counter. I had the feeling they'd both been in situations like this before. Not exactly like this, of course, but close enough. Players in a con that was reaching critical mass, waiting to see which way the pieces were going to fall; as planned, in which case they'd stick with the script, or apart at the seams, in which case it was every man for himself, women included.

It was evident, given the short time span and Hemford's phone call to his wife, that he hadn't given a lot of thought to the situation. He'd merely seen that Slow Eddie Williamson, or his spirit, or a look–alike, had taken up residence at the rental house again and so he'd come charging over here, the proverbial bull in a china shop. Now he was waiting for Delia and the money man to show up and tell him what to do next.

Well and good. It was the purpose of the con, to draw in all the principals and spring a new blackmail demand on them. The big question—the one that had my foot tapping nervously—was would the others get here soon enough to suit my purposes?

And the only answer I could think of was to wait and see. And maybe pray a little, too.

It seemed like an hour crawled by, but a glimpse of my watch said only fifteen minutes; it was now twenty–five past the hour. Everything was going according to plan, I assured myself—if you overlook the weaponry aimed at us.

The main problem was logistical. That phone sitting on the table was going to ring in five more minutes, and in order for the call to have optimum impact, all the bad guys needed to be on hand to hear it come in live. Because if anyone tried to play back the message…

From outside came the thump, thump of car doors slamming shut. Earl signaled Early, who hurried over to the mudroom and eased back the side door's cafe curtain.

"It's them, Pa."

Delia Hemford came in first, bundled up in a white and tan fake fur coat, followed by Webster Tice, shrink–wrapped inside a red–white–and–blue ski jacket, hands jammed into the pockets, flecks of snow stuck atop his thinning sandy hair. Tice looked almost as nervous as I felt. Delia looked pissed at the world, particularly the speck of it occupied by her husband.

"You hike back on home now," she told her gangly son. He started a protest, but she cut it off with a sharp word and a glare and sent him packing. Then she lit into Earl.

"Well, you just couldn't wait, could ya? Had to come chargin' over here like Rambo before anybody could figure out what the hell was even goin' on."

"What'm I supposed to think's goin' on, that prick Williamson was back over here hauntin' the place? What else could it be except another shakedown?" He hefted the shotgun in my general direction, which is all the aim he needed if his finger should happen to convulse suddenly. "Didn't I tell ya Hackshaw was mixed up in this? He figured out about the truck and then he went out and found Williamson's brother and they worked out some plan to try and spook us. Look at him." Meaning Pete. "He looks almost just like the other one."

"I got eyes." She proved it by running them up and down Pete, then me. "Well, Hackshaw. Looks like you should've brought your Louisville Slugger."

"I bet you say that to all the boys, Delia."

She accepted the jibe with a small smile—I heard Bimbo titter, too—but Earl reached over and slapped the back of my head.

"That's my *wife* you're talkin' to, asshole. And don't think I forgot about you tryin' to brain me with that bat."

"As I remember it, you brained yourself leaping into my bedroom wall."

He took another swipe, but I ducked away this time.

Delia sized up the room's final occupant. "So who's the bimbo?"

Bimbo's smile had thorns. "You mean who's the other bimbo, right, lady?"

Delia balled her fists and took a step forward, but Earl interceded. "Says she was Williamson's girlfriend. Forget about her, she's just the bait, like the brother. I told you all along it was Hackshaw we'd have to worry about, nosin' around the neighbors with all his questions—"

Tice decided it was time to take charge before Hemford gave away the whole store.

"If everyone would just calm down. Okay? Now, what's going on here, Hackshaw? What are you and these other people up to?"

"As if you didn't know." I thought about laying it all out bit by bit, how I'd tumbled to him and his lowdown, scummy dumping scheme. But there wasn't time for much exposition, so I cut right to the heart of things. "What we're `up to' is collecting on a payment you owed Pete's brother, Eddie. Call it a consulting fee, if you like. You pay us what we want and we won't be forced to consult with the county authorities regarding your company's unorthodox methods of toxic waste disposal."

"Unorthodox waste disposal? I have no idea what you're talking about."

I should have known. He wasn't even going to try to be clever about it, just flat out deny everything and phone the lawyers.

"Really? Then why'd you come running over here when Delia called you?"

He blinked at that. "Delia called to tell me Earl and her son had gotten into some sort of dispute with one of the neighbors. When an employee of mine asks for my help or advice, I always try to do whatever I can."

"Come on, you can do better than that. But why don't we just cut through all the bullshit and get down to what my friends and I know about your arrangement with Hemford and what it's going to cost you to make us forget it."

"If I were you, Hackshaw, I'd be very careful about making unsubstantiated accusations—"

That's when the telephone rang.

"Shit," Delia said. "Now who the hell could that be?"

I decided to play Br'er Rabbit again, stepping forward and reaching toward the phone. "Let's find out."

"No!" Tice said. "Leave it, Hackshaw."

I shrugged, happy to oblige.

The ringing stopped abruptly in the middle of the fourth ring. There was a pause of maybe ten seconds while the machine intercepted the call and informed the caller that no one was able to come to the phone. We couldn't hear that part—thank God, since it was my voice on the tape. Then came a click, and a husky, somewhat officious female voice filled the room.

"Mr. Smith, this is Lois Greevy at Monroe Environmental Services Lab. I'm sorry to be calling so late." A rueful chuckle here, nicely delivered. "Actually, I'm sorry to be *working* so late, but I'm trying to clear my desk for the end of the month. At any rate, I've tried reaching you several times during business hours and haven't managed to catch you in. The thing is, I have in hand the lab results from that sample you brought in a couple of weeks ago—it's quite a hodge-podge of nasty stuff, by the way—but you didn't leave an address where the report should be sent."

She suggested "Mr. Smith" call her with the information or stop by the office soon, reminded him that he owed a seventy dollar fee for the analysis, and hung up.

Perfection. Penny Wise had improvised a bit on the script I'd provided, but to good end. Anyone who didn't know better wouldn't suspect the caller was anything but a conscientious clerk trying to collect on a completed job order.

Unless they happened to notice that the red light that came on when the machine began to record· the message was still on, not blinking on and off as it normally would.

"Well." I stepped away from the table, taking all eyes with me. "Isn't that interesting."

"It doesn't prove a thing."

"And it doesn't ever have to," I pointed out. "That lab report can sit in Miss Greevy's in basket until it gets written off as a bad debt and tossed. Or—" I indicated Pete. "—the other Mr. Smith here can pick it up and send it along to the cops, the DEC, the EPA, and all the other pertinent initials. Along with directions on how to find Hemford's woods. And your leather fabricating plant."

Tice tried to stare daggers at me, but his eyes were too dulled from anxiety and resignation to pull it off. Maybe it was dawning on him that the lawyers were sure to cost him far more than I would.

Finally he said, "How much, Hackshaw?"

"Fifty thousand dollars."

"Fifty thousand!"

It came out in a ragged chorus, Tice on tenor, Hemford bass, and Delia soprano.

"Jesus," Earl muttered, "that fuck Williamson only asked for twenty-five."

"Shut up!" Delia snapped at him. "God, Earl, why don'tcha just write out a confession while you're at it."

It was going better than I could've hoped.

Tice sighed heavily, then set his jaw; portrait of a man resigned to his fate but still determined to negotiate the terms. "Look, I can't come up with fifty thousand—"

"Sure you can. I figure you would've spent almost that much to fix up that palatial monstrosity you call a house, and that was just a ruse to keep me busy anyway. This way you get the same end result, only Babs doesn't get her solarium addition."

"Be reasonable, Hackshaw." He glared over at Hemford. "All I can raise is twenty-five thousand."

"I'm being very reasonable. If Slow Eddie figured it was worth twenty-five thousand to keep quiet about your illegal dumping, I figure it's gotta be worth twice that much to keep quiet about illegal dumping *and* murder."

The word staggered him. "I didn't murder anybody! Christ, we'd agreed on the amount, I was putting the money together to make the pay–off—"

"And Eddie just happened to get killed in the meantime? Come on, Tice. You agreed to pay him off all right, but when he showed up for the money, you and your partner here knocked him out, stuffed him in his car and gassed him—"

"No! I swear, I had nothing to do with it!"

Heavy on the "I" part. Again he shot a look at Hemford, but this time Earl shot back.

"Don't you start with that shit again. I told you before it wasn't me."

"You didn't want me to make the pay–off in the first place." Tice switched back to me. "He offered to get rid of Williamson himself for ten thousand—"

"I never said nothin' about *killin'*. Me and Early were gonna beat the crap outa him, is all. Put the fear a God into him and chase his ass outa town. Tell `em, Delia."

"That's what they talked about doin'." She didn't sound all that sure, though.

"Anyway, I got proof we didn't do it," Earl said, the twin muzzles of the shotgun bobbing with each word like the bouncing ball on "Sing Along With Mitch". "Me and Early was home all night that Saturday when Williamson got snuffed, puttin' in a new head gasket and rebuildin' the carb on that old pickup a mine."

Pete spoke up from his seat at the table. "What kind of proof you call that? You think you can alibi each other and anybody'll believe it?"

"Yeah," Bimbo chimed in. "Jeez, mister, we know you guys did Eddie, so you might's well own up. Nobody's sayin' you didn't have your reasons—the business we're all in, these things happen sometimes, okay? But this here is business, too. You wanna bury poor Eddie's memory just like you guys buried all that chemical stuff out in the woods, you gotta make amends with us. Alls we want is for you to do right by Pete here, Eddie's only livin' relative, and me, Eddie's fiance', for our great personal loss—" I held onto a straight face somehow. "—and also make it worth Hackshaw's time to not do any newspaper stories." She ended with a flourish of bejeweled hands. "It's good business, is all. Like my father says, sometimes you just gotta pay the two dollars."

She was only trying to draw him out for the tape—I think—but Earl still wasn't biting.

"I didn't kill *nobody*," he insisted. "Me and Early was out in the barn till way past midnight. Delia can back me up on that."

"Hah!" Tice leaped in; without looking, as it turns out. "Delia wasn't even home herself half the..."

CHAPTER 29

By the time Tice realized his error, it was way too late. Earl Hemford was scrutinizing his face with grim intensity.

Then, too quietly, Earl said, "How'd you know she wasn't home?"

"Well, I—I remember seeing her in the village that Saturday night, that's all." Tice looked to Delia for help. "Coming out of the IGA, weren't you?"

"Um, well, let me think…"

"Think about what? You didn't bring home any damn groceries. You were supposed to be all the way over to your sister's place in Brockport—that's where you said you were gonna be."

"I *know*. I—know." Delia raked back a wisp of chiffon hair with those press-on switchblades of hers. "What I mean is, that's where I *was*. Over at Kitty's. I guess Web must've just—mistaken me for somebody else?"

"Yes," Tice said, nodding frantically. "I must've just—made a mistake."

Right. A second Dolly Parton clone browsing at the Kirkville IGA? Not even Earl Hemford was quite that stupid. But it did take him a few more beats to add up the score and carry the two.

He looked bug-eyed at Delia.

Then over at Tice.

Then Delia again.

And back to Tice, who by this time was backpedaling, head shaking in denial, one hand held up like a traffic cop, the other still plunged into his jacket pocket.

"Yeah," Hemford said finally, his voice like wet gravel. "You made a mistake, all right."

"It's not what you think, Earl, I swear."

"You dirty, sneakin' son of a *bitch*!"

Hemford launched himself on the last word, crossing the kitchen in two bounds, slamming the butt of the shotgun against Tice's chest and knocking him flat. Tice's left hand scrambled across the vinyl flooring, reaching toward one of the cabinet handles to help pull himself back up, but Hemford kicked it away and straddled him, his heavy duck boots planted on either side of Tice's torso, the shotgun at the ready and aimed straight down at Tice's ashen face.

"You been screwin' my wife, you bastard? Huh? You been *screwin'* my *wife*?" His back was to the rest of us, but it sounded like he was sobbing as he ranted. "Jesus, Delia, how could you go with this fuckin' weasel? I mean, how could you do it, you two–timin' bitch—*look at him*!"

Before you decide what a hero you'd have been in my shoes, understand that all this takes much more time to describe than it did to actually occur. It was no more than a couple blinks of the eye, really, from the moment Hemford lunged after Tice to the part where he was standing over him, crying and cursing and looking ready to blow his head off. And besides, have you ever been crowded into a tight space with a lunatic wielding a double–barreled shotgun? A lunatic who wasn't any more fond of you than he was of the poor sap lying on the floor? Let me tell you, it crystallizes your priorities in a hurry.

And even as it was happening, Delia was busy adding to the chaos. The rest of us might've been petrified into inaction, but not her.

"Would ya just calm down, baby, would ya please just listen to me?" Working her way toward him, almost tip–toeing, so afraid she'd set him off. "He doesn't mean anything to me, baby cakes, you know I'm a bad girl some times, is all, but I need my big Early–burly—"

The shot, when it came, wasn't even immediately identifiable as such, sounding more like a slap than a thunderclap. I think Delia and the others were just as confused.

But then Earl's shotgun clattered to the floor and he turned back toward us in an ungainly slow–motion pirouette, knees beginning to buckle, quaking hands reaching up toward his face. Eyes shiny with horror as his fingertips found the brilliant red river flowing from the hole just above his Adam's apple.

Earl, with a terrible gurgling sound, falling into Delia's outstretched arms, slipping through her grasp, sliding down, his dead weight pulling her to the floor, his head settling in her lap, the smear of blood down her fake fur rendering it ugly as fresh road kill.

You remember what I said before, how even an exquisitely crafted lie can have unintended consequences? Consider this an extreme example. Time and place went away for a moment and, through the tunnel vision that comes with shock and guilt, I saw just the two of us; bloody Earl curled on the floor like a crumpled piece of discarded white trash, and me staring down at his body and silently proclaiming, over and over, *It wasn't my fault.*

"It wasn't my fault." Tice this time, stealing my line and welcome to it. "He—he didn't give me any choice."

He was sitting up. There was a puncture through the right pocket of his jacket, bits of charred down showing through, and a palm–size pistol in his hand.

"Lord, lord, lord." Delia was rocking gently, her husband's head cradled in her lap, the blood no longer pumping from the wound in his neck. "He's gone. Gone."

"It was him or me!" Tice walked on his knees toward her. "You saw, Delia. I didn't want to. He didn't give me any choice!"

"Wasn't your fault," she murmured. "It was me. Lord, I never figured I'd care if...this big, mean son of a bitch..."

It was touching, in a Tennessee Williams–meets–Erskine Caldwell sort of way. Forgive me, but I'm more a Bambi man myself and I remembered the look of that poor, deformed fawn out in Hemford's poisoned woods. If I had to feel sorry for someone, it seemed a better choice than either Earl or myself.

Tice caught me inching away along the wall—a reflexive retreat; I scarcely realized I was doing it—and brought the gun up. "Stop, Hackshaw. Just—don't move."

"Okay. Fine."

"Just—let me think a minute."

"What's to think about?" Bimbo's dark eyes glittered in the lamplight. "All we all gotta do is get outa here. You keep your money, mister. Right, Pete? Hackshaw? We ain't gonna say nothin' about nothin' to nobody."

"Absolutely." Pete. Eager to get back to his peaceful world of F-stops and ethnic weddings. "All I ever really wanted was some payback for my brother and—" His gaze flitted over the body. "—I guess I got it."

Tice was back on his feet. "I know it's bad, Delia, but we can deal with this. We can *use* it."

She looked up at him.

"Think about it, Delia. Earl's gone, so what difference does it make to him? We can—arrange things, put all the blame on him. Nobody has to find out about the other stuff. You just have to say you were having an affair at this house with Eddie Williamson, see? And Earl found out about it and killed him."

"That won't work, Web."

"Yes, it will! He threatened to kill you, too, and when you called me for help, a family friend, your husband's employer, I agreed to meet with you. Only he found us out and accused *us* of being lovers, and he had the shotgun—"

"No." Shaking her head. "It can't be that way. They'd get Early, too. You told me yourself, if Earl killed Williamson and faked that accident, he had to have help. And who else but Early would he use?"

"Well—listen, the kid could volunteer to cooperate in exchange for immunity. He might not end up doing any time at all—"

"*No*, Web. Early says they didn't ever touch that man, I told you that."

"And I told you that's exactly what they'd say. You know they were lying."

"Forget it, Web. I already got my husband killed listenin' to your sweet talk, I'm not gonna risk my boy, too." Delia carefully lowered Earl's head to the grubby vinyl floor and got to her feet, the back of her hand swiping at the streaks of mascara under her eyes. "We can't let `em connect up Williamson's murder with Earl and that's that. We gotta come up with somethin' else."

Tice chewed at his lower lip a moment. "I got it! He beat you sometimes, right?" Like it was a godsend; Delia was still batting a thousand when it came to picking men. "So this doesn't have to connect to Eddie Williamson at all. We could clean up the mess, move the body someplace else—your place maybe, out in one of the barns. Then you tell the police Earl came after you with that shotgun, and you had to kill him."

"Oh, now *I* killed him? What's wrong with he caught you and me goin' at it—"

"*No*. Look, if my name comes into it, you know, *that way*, that's gonna make the police curious. They'll start digging deeper, and then who knows what they'll find out?"

Delia smirked. "Not to mention what Babs'll find out."

He threw up his arms. "Just let me think, all right? I'll come up with something."

"You better," she said. "Startin' with what we're gonna do about these three."

Pete, Bimbo and I had been doing our best to blend in with the cheesy yellow and green wallpaper, more than content to let the villains continue incriminating themselves for the message machine's running tape.

"You don't have to worry about us," I said, concentrating on Tice and his nervous little pistol. "Whatever you decide to tell the police is okay with us, right, kids?" The others nodded energetically. When Tice failed to react, I threw in, "We'll even back you up, if need be."

"Back me up?" Those perpetually watery eyes of Tice's, near to overflowing, washed over me. "What about the money? A minute ago you were blackmailing me for fifty thousand dollars, now you're offering to back up my story with the police? Just what the hell are you playing at?"

"Nothing. As far as the money, Web, well, sure, we saw an opportunity and we took a shot—no pun intended. But getting mixed up in a killing wasn't part of the plan."

"What about the Williamson killing? You all weren't too skittish to use that to your advantage, were you? You're up to something, Hackshaw. I don't know what it is, but until I can figure us a way out of this, you three aren't going any place."

He marched us around the small house at gunpoint, trying to find a secure place to stash us, finally settling on the basement. Its major attraction was that there was no way out except by the door off the mudroom, and the door had a heavy slide bolt mounted above the knob.

Which Tice slid shut behind us while we were still making our way down the steep, unfinished wooden stairs.

"Great," Pete whispered. "Now what, Hackshaw? That fuckin' nut up there's liable to burn this whole place down on top us."

"I don't think so."

"Hah! You don't think so." Bimbo. "The dipshit just killed that other dipshit right in front of us, what's he got to lose, him and that bleached bitch—"

"That was self–defense. And I don't think Tice, or Delia for that matter, had anything to do with killing Eddie. You heard what I heard, those two lovebirds were cozied up together someplace that Saturday night." I mulled it for a moment, trying to convince myself as much as anything. "It *had* to be Earl and his boy who did the killing. Maybe it's like Earl said, he was only planning to scare off Eddie, but things went too far."

"Yeah," Pete said, his breath coming out in little puffs in the chilly air, "and things just went too far again. Tice is panicked thinking about all he's got to lose, and the woman's not gonna let him give up her son to the cops. Why should they have to, when they've got three perfect patsies to pin everything on? That cop investigating Eddie's death already suspects you, Hackshaw, and me and Bimbo have records—"

"I still don't think either one of `em's got the stomach for a triple murder," I insisted. "On the other hand, there's no sense just standing around waiting."

There wasn't much down there. Four little transom–style windows far too small for anyone to climb through. The furnace and hot water heater grouped together on a raised concrete pad in one corner, a sump pump poking up from a hole in the floor in the other; an old stack of magazines and two empty cardboard boxes tucked away under the stairs, a length of clothesline strung from a couple of the floor joist…

I stared up at the clothesline for another moment, then had Pete, who was a few inches taller, reach up and untie it from the eye–hooks. There was about thirty feet of it in all, plenty for my purposes. I cautiously climbed back up the stairs, made a loop on the end of the rope, and slipped it over the door knob. Then I eased back down the stairs and tied the other end around the bottom tread, yanking hard to get out as much of the slack in the line as I could.

"There," I said, rising. "They're gonna lock us in, we'll lock them out."

I crossed over to the furnace and sat down on its concrete pad.. Bimbo followed suit, taking the other end of the pad and fishing out a cigarette. It was less my company than the warming blue and orange flame of the heating flange that had attracted her.

All the while, we could hear Tice and Delia pacing the floor above us, arguing, scheming, trying to decide what to do with the dead body in the kitchen and the three live ones below. Their words were sometimes crystal clear, other times muffled and indecipherable, like the signal from a distant radio station on a late–night car trip.

Pete Williamson was doing plenty of pacing of his own. Maybe it was the stretch he'd spent in prison that made our confinement particularly unnerving for him.

"You're pretty goddam cool, Hackshaw. How the hell can you just sit there while those two are up there trying to decide whether to kill us? You really think that stupid clothesline is going to keep `em from getting to us?"

"It'll slow `em down."

"Yeah? For how long?"

I pulled back my jacket sleeve to check my watch. As I did, the phone upstairs began to ring, and I allowed myself a small smile.

"Long enough, I think."

Tice and Delia let it ring; one, two, three; on the fourth ring, the machine cut in again. The caller, I knew, would hang up without leaving a message.

I exhaled. "I think we can all relax now. Help is on the way."

When I had reviewed the plan with Pete and Bimbo earlier, I had explained about the phone calls from Penny Wise. I'd arranged for Penny to call the rental house every half hour throughout the evening. If everything was okay, Pete would pick up and identify himself by name. If, however, Pete did not answer and the machine picked up the call, Penny would assume our bait had worked and the bad guys had shown up, in which case she was to deliver the phony message to "Mr. Smith."

As far as Pete and Bimbo had known, there were only two reasons for Penny's call: first, to help convince Tice and the others that the cat was truly out of the bag—they'd see the futility of denial, my reasoning went, and get down to the business of negotiating with us to keep quiet about the illegal dumping and the subsequent murder of Eddie Williamson. And second, by leaving a message, Penny activated the recording tape, which had been rigged by Berk Savage to pick up any ensuing conversation.

What I hadn't told my co–conspirators was that I'd given Penny a second set of instructions. After delivering her message, she was to call back again in half an hour. If Pete or I didn't pick up and identify ourselves by name, she was to call 911 and report a fire at the Bing Road house. I figured that a half hour was enough time for us to lay out our blackmail demand and get the Hemfords and Tice to incriminate themselves. They'd either be gone from the house by then, having reached an agreement with us on where and when the money would be exchanged, or they'd be holding us hostage while trying to figure out a cheaper and more permanent way to remove us as a threat. In the latter event, it seemed only prudent to have some way to call in the cavalry.

The reason I hadn't told Pete and Bimbo about it was because I didn't want them glancing at their watches and maybe trying too hard to push Tice and the Hemfords into talking; it was difficult enough to keep myself under control, and I was used to deadline pressures.

Now, as I came clean, Bimbo laughed softly. "Know what I think, Hackshaw?" She looked sidelong at me, angling her head a bit to see past a green tag that was hanging from the furnace's gas cock. "I think for a guy's supposed to be a straight arrow, you're pretty damn crooked."

"Coming from you, dearheart, I'll assume that's a compliment." A half–hearted retort, because I was only half–listening to her. Something had begun nagging at my brain; something to do with that dangling green tag. I reached out and turned it toward me. "Hmmm, now isn't that interesting. Do you believe in coincidence, Bimbo?"

Before she could answer, we all heard the sirens screaming in the night, coming fast. They heard it upstairs, too. The murmur of arguing voices was abruptly replaced by the scurry of feet to and fro, and to again. Then we heard the basement door bolt sliding back, followed by the angry rattle of the tied–off knob, punctuated by a pathetic, helpless wail from Webster Tice.

"Hackshaw! You lying, cheating, lowlife bastard!"

Turns out it was the evening's last good chuckle.

CHAPTER 30

"Cut him loose? You gotta be kidding."

"We've got no reason to hold him. On the contrary—"

"No reason? I've got him dead–bang on illegal entry, concealing evidence in a felony, obstruction, calling in a false fire report—"

"Mel. Keep your eye on the ball, okay? We've just been handed the keys to two homicides and a major toxic dumping case, and you want to prosecute our star witness on a laundry list of technicalities?" Captain Dick Schulz shook his head. "The D.A. won't hear of it and neither will I. Why, Hackshaw's liable to receive a citation from the DEC for exposing Tice's operation."

I dipped my head modestly. "Really, Captain, I was only doing the job my readers expect."

"Oh, shut up." Stoneman's glower swung to his boss. "Once again public relations takes precedence over enforcing the law, is that it?"

"You're letting your personal biases override your judgment, Investigator Stoneman," Schulz said, sternly for him. "He's given us his statement, and we know how to reach him if we need to. So cut him loose. Now."

With that, he did a one–eighty and marched out of the interrogation room. Stoneman stared at me across the table, silently seething. I waited him out, knowing anything I could say, even the slightest gesture or look, be it of scorn or sympathy, would only fan the flames.

He'd deluded himself into thinking he had me nailed last night at the Bing Road house, when he had burst in along with the Kirkville VFD. In fact he was damn near giddy at the prospect, crowing about how clever he'd been to keep up surveillance on me on his own time, so certain was he that I'd eventually incriminate myself. ("Step on your own dick," is how he actually phrased it.) It mattered not one whit to Stoneman that I was, as Captain Schulz had said, handing him a major case on a platter, complete with an audio tape of the conspirators discussing their crimes and a soil sample from the chemical stew in Hemford's pond.

I'd done my utmost to explain to the miserable goon how foolish and petty he'd look if he persisted in trying to link me criminally to Eddie Williamson's scheme and its aftermath. But it was like talking to a brick wall. Hatred is both deaf and dumb, and anyway, a bull keeps charging because that's all it knows to do.

Just when I thought he'd lapsed into profound catatonia, Stoneman exhaled, ran a hand across his stubbled chin, and rumbled, "Go, Hackshaw. Get out of my sight."

It was just past dawn when I took my leave of the kindergarten–cum–substation in South Chilton. The morning was clear but bitter cold, down in the single digits; the hard–packed snow on the path to the parking lot screeched with each footfall, like walking on Styrofoam pellets.

I paused a moment, gulping in the frigid air in hopes it would blow away my weariness. It would be too much to ask that it blow away my ambivalence as well.

Normally, I would've been eager to get to the office to see if my exclusive had made it into the *Advertiser* in reasonably good order. I had called Ruth from the substation around midnight to tell her what had happened and to have her pull the front page that Ron was just then setting up on his printer in favor of the piece I'd written earlier and stuck in my desk. I barely had enough time to dictate some additions and suggest some deletions before Stoneman cut off the call and dragged me back to the interrogation room for the second of what was to become multiple retellings of the events leading up to Earl Hemford's demise. I'd had to leave the major editing decisions to Ruth, in other words; my scoop was liable to end up reading like the highlights from the last Chilton Town Board meeting.

But it was too late to worry about it. Even with the delay caused by remaking page one, the paper should've by then been printed and bundled and on its happy way to front stoops throughout the tri–town area. Which was just as well, since I had other things on my mind. I hadn't wanted to disillusion Captain Schulz and the assistant D.A., so delighted were they to have Web Tice neatly packaged, not only for illegal dumping and possibly manslaughter for shooting Earl Hemford, but also as an accessory to murder in the Williamson case. But I'd had all night to think about things and I'd reached the conclusion that the authorities were going to have a very difficult time indeed getting a conviction on the latter charge.

The anemic bleat of a compact car's horn interrupted my ruminations. Pete Williamson was just then putting toward the exit with all the speed his funky little Horizon could muster, tossing me a farewell honk in the process. That was the one concession we'd negotiated out at the house; Stoneman didn't have enough room in his car for everyone, so he'd grudgingly allowed me and Pete to drive our own vehicles down to the substation. Accompanied, of course, by a pair of large and well–armed deputies.

I waved to Pete as I continued toward my Jeep, head tucked into the collar of my pea jacket and shoulders hunched. I was halfway across the lot before I noticed the square old Cadillac Deville idling on the far side of the Jeep.

As I approached, Stavo climbed ponderously from the back seat, followed by a paunchy old man wearing a brown fedora. Jimmy stayed put behind the wheel, the mouse under his eye failing to diminish his moronic grin. I was relieved to see that no one else was in the car.

I said, "Waiting for Bimbo?"

"Yeah, we been sittin' around here half the night. Her mama's inside with her, makin' sure all those fuckin' cops don't try to stick her with nothin'." He dragged on his cigar. "Gives me gas, hangin' around all those cops."

I automatically took a step back. "I was told they'll let her go as soon as she finishes giving her deposition."

That elicited a contemptuous growl from the old guy. He had wild gray eyebrows, hard black eyes, a nose like an overripe strawberry, and permanent frown lines deep as drainage ditches on either side of a thick–lipped mouth. Only the round gold earring differentiated him from a Sicilian capo.

"This is Uncle Tes," Stavo said. "He was baro before me. Now he speaks for the kris."

I nodded pleasantly at the bilious grump. "Nice to meet you."

He reciprocated with another growl, then barked some rapid–fire Romany at Stavo. Stavo took it in stoically, hands jammed into the pockets of his heavy wool overcoat. When the old man finished, Stavo walked me away a few feet and spoke in a tired, flat voice.

"Uncle Tes ain't happy. He says the kris don't wanna wait no more to settle this thing with the mulo." His droopy black mustache was developing tiny icicles. "My people, the ones who stayed, been gettin' killed over in Niagara Falls. No business. Tes says it's all my fault. First I let my own daughter run off with that piece of shit Williamson, then my wife puts a curse on the bastard, he goes and dies and ends up bringin' bad luck onto the whole Wanka vitsa. Now he says I been lettin' a gadjo string me along like I'm still wet behind the ears."

"He's trying to take leadership away from you."

"The old fart could do it, too." He looked at me with big puppy eyes, pit bull breed. "I told everybody I was gonna have this whole thing cleared up by now so's we could head to Florida without bringin' no mulo down there with us. You was gonna give me proof me and Mary didn't have nothin' to do with Williamson's dyin'—that's why I backed off and let you run. Now my Bimbo's stuck inside there with the cops, the rest of the vitsa's here in town, packed up and ready to head south with or without me, and I'm standin' around freezin' my ass off—and still I don't got the proof you promised."

"The D.A.'s not going to bother with Bimbo."

"Huh, that ain't what I mean, Hackshaw. It ain't *your* law I'm worried about."

I knew it wasn't. God knows why I should've felt any twinges of guilt about Stavo's plight. So maybe I'd conned him a little. Tit for tat; it's what he and his people did for a living. I should feel bad, just because he'd agreed to keep his minions from following me around and beating me up for a couple of days? If you ask me, these damn gypsies have more gall than a Senate ethics committee.

When you include the fact that all this hand wringing about curses and mulos was ridiculous anyway, I had every reason to simply hop in my Jeep and leave.

On the other hand, I had a bud of an idea that could turn the whole matter into what the Washington spinmeisters call a win–win situation.

I said, "The rest of your people are here in town?"

"Yeah. What's left of 'em."

"Good. That's good."

"Huh!" He snorted. "What's so good about it?"

"Look, I need to make a couple of phone calls first, but if you'll agree to back me up—only for a few more hours—I think I may be able to put Slow Eddie's ghost to rest once and for all."

At a quarter to eight, the comfortably middle–class residents of Rolling Meadows Estates were still in the process of mounting the usual weekday exurb exodus. A Chil–Kirk school bus was wending its way through the tract, picking up kiddies in bunches while assorted dads and moms saw them off, their sedans and minivans and station wagons idling in driveways, defrosting for the expressway commute into metro Rochester.

Naturally all activity stopped and all eyebrows rose as our caravan slowly passed in review; my Jeep, followed by Stavo's Caddie towing his thirty–foot camper, and Jimmy in the Lincoln pulling a slightly smaller trailer, and behind him three more aged Detroit gas guzzlers similarly laden.

It was about the worst thing I could think to do, from Bud and Marion Koon's perspective; embarrass them in front of the neighbors.

Koon was standing in the open doorway of his garage, flanked by the rear ends of a Volvo sedan and a Ford subcompact. Wearing that silly Russian hat and a camel coat, holding a briefcase in his right hand, his mouth agape.

My Jeep and the Deville turned in, filling both sides of the double driveway. Jimmy and the others pulled up out on the street.

"Hackshaw? What is this? Who are these—people?"

I was out from behind the wheel and moving over to help Queen Mary launch herself from the back seat of the caddie.

"These people," I told Koon, "are your audience. I told them you were going to sing, and they insisted on coming along to hear."

"Sing? What in the hell—?"

"A bitter–sweet ballad about the dying moments of Slow Eddie Williamson," I said, "sung to the tune of 'Hang Down Your Head, Tom Dooley.'"

The missus appeared in the doorway at the back of the garage, hugging herself. "Bud?"

"In a minute, Marion. I don't know what you're trying to prove with this circus, Hackshaw, but it isn't funny."

"Sure it is. A comedy of errors, in fact."

I held Mary steady on the slick blacktop until Stavo could add his ballast. Bimbo exited the car next, followed by dear Uncle Tes. Jimmy and his brother and nearly a dozen more members of the Wanka clan were climbing out of their vehicles and moving up the drive en masse, some of them toting guitars and tambourines. (My suggestion; I thought it would add authenticity.)

"Look, Hackshaw, I'm not in the mood for your games. Besides the fact I'm already late for work, we were up half the night dealing with the police, thanks to you and your friends."

"Oh, so you already know about Hemford? And the chemical dumping, et cetera?"

"Of course, we already know. You think the police wouldn't call us after finding a bloody shootout at one of our properties? We had to go over and secure the place after they got through turning it upside down." He aimed his index finger at me. "Now, I'm warning you, if you and this mob don't clear out of here, *I'll* call the police."

"Go ahead. While we're waiting, Stavo's people can break out the hibachis and make camp." I shrugged. "I was hoping to work this out just between us, but if you'd rather go on the record, that's fine. One way or the other, Koon, I'm going to have a discussion with *somebody* about what happened to Eddie Williamson out at your Bing Road rental."

Mrs. Koon, still huddled in the kitchen doorway, visibly trembled on hearing that last comment. "Oh, my god."

"Calm *down*, Marion." He should talk; he looked like he was about to divest himself of his breakfast. "You don't—I don't know what it is you're driving at, Hackshaw."

"Really. Well, why don't we move our frozen assets inside and I'll explain it to you."

He hesitated just long enough to let us both know I'd won; the opening gambit, anyway. Then: "All of you?" Probably thinking about the wear and tear on the carpets.

"A representative group," I said. "The others can stay with the caravan, okay, Stavo?"

Stavo grunted assent and Mary added, "Is your play, Hackshaw."

CHAPTER 31

❦

We followed Koon single–file through the garage and into the pristine kitchen; me, Stavo, Mary, Uncle Tes, who looked everything over as if he suspected the whole place might be marimay, and Bimbo, who looked everything over as if to decide how much of it would fit in her purse.

Meanwhile the Koons stood stiffly side–by–side, not quite touching, strained as the couple in Wood's *American Gothic*, sans pitch fork. They didn't loosen up much after I made the introductions, but Bud at least removed the stupid hat and Marion at least remembered her manners.

"Well, whatever this is about, I suppose we should sit," she said. "Um, would anyone like coffee?"

I'm the only one who took up her offer, afterward settling onto a stool at the breakfast bar. The others accommodated themselves on the adjoining family room's sofa and chairs, Bimbo slipping off her coat to reveal an ankle–length floral skirt, several generations worth of hammered silver jewelry, and an off–the–shoulders peasant blouse that enveloped her bosom like a hammock. (Despite everything, you can't not notice these things; beauty commands.)

Our hosts remained standing throughout.

"Okay, here's the thing," I told them. "For reasons I won't bother going into, the Wankas need to hear the particulars surrounding

Eddie Williamson's death. Now, I know that you two know what happened to him—"

"You don't know any such thing." Koon. "You're just trying to make more trouble so you can sell newspapers. As it is, I suppose you'll write some inflated piece about what those Hemford people were up to out there, blowing up a few spilled chemicals to sound like another Chernobyl."

"As a matter of fact I already have, only without the hyperbole." For the most part. "That's what this whole thing was about, wasn't it? Trying to keep the public from finding out what you and your wife already knew; that the land adjoining yours was contaminated with toxic chemicals."

He sputtered out another weak denial, but I kept up the offensive.

"Here's the way it figures," I said. "You like to brag about your business acumen, Koon, and when you found out you were renting to a sharp–talking investment adviser, you couldn't help tooting your own horn. So you told `Mr. Smith' about all your rental properties, your stock portfolio, and—here's where you put your foot in it—your plans to develop the excess land that came with the Bing Road house into a mini–tract of new homes. A couple weeks later, after Eddie tumbled to what was going on out in Hemford's woods, he remembered your grandiose plans and then *he* got ideas of his own. How to kill two birds with one stone, so to speak."

I let the implication hang while I sipped my coffee. Koon was impassive, but I definitely had Marion twitching.

"Williamson was planning to hit up Webster Tice for twenty–five thousand to keep quiet about the toxic dumping. Not a bad payday, but our Eddie was greedy. So, why not add a little sweetener from the landlord, right? After all, if word got out, chances are your development scheme would go down, what with the risk of all those nasty chemicals leaching over into your soil, and you'd be out a big profit. How much did he ask for, Koon, ten thousand? Maybe fifteen?"

"This is sheer fantasy, Hackshaw."

"Uh–uh. I don't have that good an imagination. But I do have a pretty good head for remembering small tidbits of information, little known facts. For example, remember a couple of years ago, when old Carson Jenkins was supposed to have died in a fall from his barn loft? Only it turned out he was killed first and later thrown from the loft?"

"Don't tell me you're going to try to connect us to that incident, too."

"No, no. I mention it because it was while covering Jenkins's death that I learned about bruises—how living flesh will bruise easily, but dead flesh mostly won't. Now, it didn't occur to me early on." Unless early that morning counts. "But thinking back on Eddie Williamson's faked auto accident, I got curious about the condition of the body. So I woke up Doc Gordon about an hour ago and had him review the autopsy findings for me. Know what? Other than the severed neck and lacerations from his face slamming through the windshield of his Mercury, Eddie's body showed no bruises or contusions at all."

"So?" Koon's frown deepened. "That makes sense, doesn't it? If Williamson was already dead when he was put into the car, you just said, a dead body won't bruise."

"Yeah, but what about *before* he died? Look, the working theory, the one the cops are right now trying to sort out, is that Earl Hemford and his son overpowered Eddie and then probably shoved him inside his own car and fed a hose from the exhaust pipe through a crack in the window, thereby killing him with carbon monoxide emissions. But Eddie wouldn't have gotten in that car willingly—he would've fought back. Yet his body showed no signs of a struggle. And Doc says the skull showed no trauma, either, other than the lacerations from the broken windshield, so Eddie wasn't knocked out first."

"Well," Marion Koon said timidly, glancing at her husband, "maybe he was forced into the car at gunpoint. He had no opportunity to fight back."

"In that case, he would've fought the car itself, trying to get out, frantically punching and kicking at the doors and side windows as soon as he realized what was going on. It's human nature. That would've damaged both him and the car—and neither showed any signs. But," I added, "The part about forcing him at gunpoint makes sense, Marion. In fact, I'll bet that's how you two got him down into the basement over at Bing Road, wasn't it?"

Her eyes were wet; her mouth opened, but no words came out. Her husband tried to cover.

"Bruises, no bruises—what's next, Hackshaw? Dogs that didn't bark?"

"I also called Jack Trautwig this morning." A Kirkville heating and air conditioning contractor; that tell–tale green inspection tag on the furnace out at Bing Road? It was his. The Koons turned a similar shade at the mention of his name. "Tell me if I'm warm. After Eddie braced you with his blackmail demand, you two drove over to the house, this would've been sometime Saturday, probably early afternoon. Maybe you thought a gun would scare him off, Koon, but it didn't work. Eddie called your bluff. You didn't know what to do next, so you decided to lock him in the basement while you tried to sort things out. You left, then came back a few hours later—and found him lying dead beside the furnace. He'd curled up there to try and ward off the basement's chill. What he didn't know was that the furnace had a problem, the flue was partially blocked by an old nest of some kind. Trautwig said it might've been a squirrel. Eddie was especially vulnerable to carbon monoxide poisoning because he was a heavy smoker. He didn't put up a struggle because he didn't know he was in danger. He just went to sleep."

Marion was flat–out sobbing now.

"I'm sure you two weren't aware of the blockage, any more than he was. It was simply an unattended maintenance problem, the kind of thing that gets overlooked all the time." I couldn't resist the urge to editorialize. "Particularly in rental properties when the landlords never raise their sights higher than their bottom line. Anyway, after you found him, you came up with the idea of staging a car accident over at the Park Road drop–off. You wanted evidence, Koon? I've already got Jack Trautwig's statement that you called him on the following Monday to have him look at 'a possible leak' in the furnace."

"Oh, god, Bud—"

"Let me handle this, Marion."

The look on Koon's face reminded me of Webster Tice the night before; resigned but still prepared to haggle.

"What did you mean before," he asked me, "about hoping to keep things off the record?"

"That's the deal. You tell us, in your own words, what happened to Eddie Williamson in exchange for my promise that I won't go to the police or publish anything."

"Your promise?" He sneered. "We're supposed to put our trust in your word of honor?"

"Would you like me to swear on a copy of *The Wall Street Journal*?" It seemed only fair; I'd sworn *at* a few copies. "It's a take it or leave it proposition. I'm willing to let this matter end right here, but I want two things from you; an honest accounting of what happened and, shall we say, a modest restitution payment."

"Ah–hah!" Everyone's eyebrows rose, Koon's the highest. "Now we get down to brass tacks. This is just another goddam shakedown."

He actually seemed to find the idea comforting. Greed and opportunism were motivators he could relate to. The Wankas, too, if the sudden gleam in their collective eye was any indicator. Too bad I had to disappoint them.

"Restitution in the amount of twenty–five hundred dollars," I said. "To pay back Arlene Grebwicz and Rolly Keller the money they lost in Slow Eddie's riverboat scam."

"We didn't have anything to do with that!"

"I know, but they deserve to get their money back. And *you* deserve to get stuck with the bill, Koon. Partial payment for being greedy and selfish and an all–around pain in the ass. We'll let Providence and your conscience dun you for the rest."

"It's outrageous! I won't pay it."

"Yes—we will." Marion's voice vibrated like a tuning fork. "This thing's been tearing at me, Bud, you know that. And yet you stand here and—and negotiate? As if you're jewing down a car salesman?"

I snuck an I–told–you–so glance at Stavo, but the irony of Marion's slur didn't register with him.

She turned to me. "The whole thing's my fault. I'm the one who locked Edgar Williamson in the basement." She let out a long, ragged breath. "That Saturday, I went by the Bing Road house on the pretext of seeing if our new tenant was settling in all right."

"A pretext?"

"A method we use to keep tabs on our properties, making it seem as if we just dropped in to say hello. Bud likes to call them snap inspections. In fact, he was in the city that day, doing the same thing at a pair of duplexes we own on the north side."

What a fun couple.

"At any rate, he—Mr. Smith, as I knew him—came to the door and I more or less invited myself in. When I saw the place was nearly empty, I became suspicious and demanded to know what was going on. That's when Williamson's mask came off, almost like a Jekyll and Hyde transformation. He told me what he'd found out about the toxic dumping, just as you guessed, Hackshaw. I didn't believe him at first, but he kept giving more and more details about a polluted pond out in the woods and making a connection to that manufacturing plant in the village—he seemed to know what he was talking about. So anyway, he demanded money to keep quiet about it, ten thousand dollars. I was outraged. Furious." Her voice dropped and she suddenly became intensely interested in the tops of her house slippers. "Some of our properties are in rough neighborhoods, so I've gotten in the habit of carrying a small gun in my handbag when I collect rents. I didn't even realize I'd taken it out, and once I had it out, I didn't know what to do next. Finally I decided to lock Williamson in the basement, then go home and wait for Bud to get back. He'd know how to handle things."

I looked at her glum husband.

"You know the rest, Hackshaw. When she told me what happened, we drove back out to Bing Road and found him lying next to the furnace. I figured it had to be from carbon monoxide, didn't know what else it could be. So, we talked and fretted about it and, later that night, I came up with the idea of staging a car accident. We went back out to the house, got rid of some things that might've been incriminating—"

"Like Eddie's binoculars," I said, "and all the fake materials relating to his phony riverboat gambling con."

"Yes. We just scooped everything he'd left on the table into a garbage bag and dumped it. Then we hauled the body up and out to his car and—that's it." He shrugged. "I only did it to protect Marion."

It was obvious from his wife's expression that even she didn't buy that excuse.

"Come on, Koon," I said. "You did it so you wouldn't have to explain to the police why Marion had locked Eddie down there in the first place, because then everybody would know about the toxic cesspool out in the woods and you'd lose out on the chance to develop your property."

"You really think you'd have done anything different, Hackshaw? Assuming you had anything of value to protect in the first place."

"Bud," Marion said wearily. "Would you just shut up."

❦ ❦ ❦

Later, out on the driveway, Bimbo threw her arms around me and planted her lush red lips on mine.

"That's for helpin' me get Toma outa my life."

"My pleasure." I grinned at her. Then I remembered whom I was dealing with and I checked my pockets, just to reassure myself that my wallet and the checks for Arlene and Rolly were still there.

Bimbo pretended not to notice. "Papa's gonna help me pay back the bastard's family, only we ain't gonna give `em the whole fourteen thousand, not after I spent six years—"

"Fourteen? I thought you told me twenty thousand?"

"I meant like adjusted for the inflation."

Queen Mary gave me a hug, too, and Stavo offered his hand, along with a mild reproach.

"You know, Hackshaw, the way you played those two gadjo, you coulda took `em for double what you got," he said. "Triple, if you let Mama here take a hand. Then the both of us coulda made somethin' on this deal, huh?"

"Oh, I think you'll at least break even, Stavo." I pointed toward the caravan parked along the street, specifically the second car from the end. Hooked to it was Eddie Williamson's little Nomad camping trailer.

"Huh," Stavo grunted. "The no–good shit owes me that much."

"And we did get the confession you wanted," I said. "I hope it's good enough to put all this mulo business to rest once and for all."

Stavo looked to Uncle Tes. The clan elder pursed his lips and stuck out his jaw and spent several seconds in Solomonic contemplation. Finally he nodded curtly, and there was an audible sigh from Stavo and Mary. Then the old man added a caveat.

"But to be on the safe side," he said, "we still gonna need them three live chickens."

Don't ask; I sure as hell didn't.

Epilogue

As scarce as the truth is, the supply has always been in excess of the demand.

I wish I could take credit, but according to *Bartlett's* that pithy aphorism was penned more than a hundred years ago by a cracker-barrel wit who called himself Josh Billings. (A pseudonym, of course; the man was a cynic, not a fool.)

Anyway, wiser words, et cetera. In fact, I'm thinking of adopting it as my personal motto.

Not that I'm bitter.

As I expected, the county decided not to bring a murder charge against either Webster Tice or the Hemfords for the death of Slow Eddie Williamson. There was simply no evidence against them, for the obvious reason. But that doesn't mean they escaped entirely unscathed from the maw of our judicial system. Almost, but not entirely.

The details remained somewhat murky, but it appeared that Tice had started using the Hemford place as a cheap alternative dumping ground about six years earlier, which was around the time the legitimate disposal company CLF had been using doubled its rates. Also around the time Tice built his house, taking on a mortgage that was nearly as big and ugly.

Equally murky were the behind–the–scenes legal machinations between the prosecutor's office and Tice's attorney, but in the end—you guessed it—a plea bargain was struck. In exchange for avoiding any charges for fatally discharging a firearm into Earl Hemford's neck, Tice copped to a mixed bag of misdemeanor and felony counts that all revolved around illegal disposal of toxic substances and endangering the public welfare. It boiled down to a year in the county lock–up—which means he was out in five months—and fines totaling twenty thousand dollars, not counting whatever he ended up shelling out to his lawyers.

Speaking of lawyers, the civil side of things is still being batted around like a shuttlecock at a DAR picnic. Various county, state and federal agencies declared Hemford's woods a hazardous waste site and ever since have been trying to decide who should handle the cleanup. Meanwhile, Webster Tice's uncle interrupted his Boca Raton retirement to retake control of CLF, Inc. His first official act was to fire his nephew; his second official act was to inform all the government agencies that his company is incorporated and that a corporation is not responsible for the irresponsible acts of one of its officers. And, besides, if the government insisted on forcing CLF to pay for more than a token portion of the reclamation costs, Old Man Tice claimed he'd be forced to close his doors and put the company into bankruptcy. He played the jobs card, in other words, a time–honored dodge among industrialists. Just to prove he was serious, he laid off a third of his workers at the outset, blaming it on foreign competition, overzealous regulators and unfair media coverage.

More on that later.

As for Delia, she decided to throw herself on the mercy of the court about two seconds after she learned that the presiding judge was a heterosexual male. Her basic defense was that she was just an old–fashioned, lemon haired, 38–D cup girl who always did whatever the big strong men in her life told her to do. And recently widowed, to boot. Not surprisingly, the judge's compassion was sufficiently aroused to let her off lightly; one hundred hours of community service, which she worked off handing out orange juice at the county Red Cross's perpetual blood drives.

Early Hemford, by the way, wasn't even charged for helping his old man and Tice dump thousands of gallons of toxics into the local ground water. In exchange for his promise to never, ever do anything bad again, young Early received a semi–stern lecture from an assistant district attorney and was sent on his way. And, I have to admit, maybe the system did the right thing in his case. Within a week, Early had a steady job at an auto body shop over in Brockport and seems to have been leading a clean, quiet existence ever since. Of course, the neighbors said much the same thing about John Wayne Gacey, Jeffrey Dahmer, et al, so I suppose only time will tell.

As with most family dramas, the real estate crowd did almost as well as the legal profession. To begin with, Babs Tice dumped both her husband and the house he built for her, and the latter proved far more difficult to unload. It was eventually taken off the market by a cult of religious loonies who, I'm told, are using it as a commune, where they're now raising organic vegetables and counting off the weeks until the end of the world. I can't blame them; if I had to live in that place, I'd be gloomy, too.

Then there was the Koons. They gradually sold off all their rental properties, including the Bing Road house. I have no idea what they did with their profits, but I suspect they followed Harold Morecock's maxim of not investing in anything that eats or requires maintenance, with special emphasis on the latter. I have a feeling their marriage went through a major restructuring, too. Marion, the last time I saw her, had let her hair grow long and her natural gray come through, and somehow appeared younger for it. Or maybe it was just the hint of a smile she threw my way while Bud was busy pretending not to notice me at all.

As for the missing money—the more than five thousand dollars that Slow Eddie took in from his riverboat and rental house scams—I've given it a lot of thought and my guess is Bimbo had it all the time.

Con men have some rules of survival, one of which is to keep your cash handy, but not so handy it ends up in the wrong hands if the cops or a gang of angry townsfolk break down the door. It's the same principle that caused Slow Eddie to live in the trailer out at remote Hamlin Beach Park, rather than at the rental house. It stands to reason that if he knew enough to keep himself safe from the risks, he'd do the same for his bankroll; he would've kept all but walking–around money at the trailer with Bimbo.

Remember, the reason she gave me for not taking off right after she found out Eddie was dead is because she was broke, and it made sense to believe her. At the time. But now we know she had a more powerful reason for sticking around; her children. I figure her plan all along had been to keep out of Stavo's clutches until he was desperate enough to take her back on her own terms, which is exactly what happened. The five grand was her ace in the hole, a sort of reverse dowry to help cover the cost of paying back Toma's family.

I suppose I should be ticked at her, but that would be like holding a grudge against a house cat for scratching up the sofa leg; it's the nature of the beast. And Arlene Grebwicz and Rolly and the others got their money back, so all's well that ends well.

Unless you count me.

Depending on who you talk to, I either quit the *Advertiser* or was fired.

The final brouhaha between Ruth and me started on that very Thursday, when I finally got around to reading a copy of the paper. Somehow, in her deadline haste and her neurotic fear of libel suits, my sister managed to edit my tenacious exclusive down to nine lousy column inches of ho–hum. Any duller and "Masterpiece Theatre" would've bought up the film rights.

I went ballistic, to put it politely. And Ruth came right back at me, claiming that my story lacked sufficient attribution, was too speculative and slanted, and blah, blah, blah. Picky, picky, I say; given the time constraints and the mental strain of trying to sort out who did what and why, I figure I was lucky to spell all the names right.

It all came to a boil a week later, when the layoffs started at CLF and many of the newly–unemployed blamed the *Advertiser* and its intrepid editor–in–chief for stirring up trouble in the first place.

Kill the messenger, naturally.

Anyway, words were said—things even two basically loving siblings find difficult to forget—and there was nothing left but for yours truly to walk out the door and seek other employment. Full–time house restoration comes immediately to mind, although there's not much of that to be had in the depths of an upstate winter, so maybe I'll just starve for a while.

Did I mention I'm not bitter?

Don't believe everything you read.

Final wise words: It's not what you know, or even who you know; it's who you tell.

And you can quote me on that.

About the Author

Stephen F. Wilcox, a former newspaper reporter, lives with his wife and son in a small, idyllic Erie Canal village near Rochester, New York. To learn more, visit his online newspaper, *The Wilcox Gazette*, at **stephenfwilcox.com.**

0-595-21509-2